STUCK IN PARADISE WITH YOU

LAURA CARTER

Boldwood

First published in Great Britain in 2024 by Boldwood Books Ltd.

Copyright © Laura Carter, 2024

Cover Design by Rachel Lawston

Cover Images: Rachel Lawston

A CIP catalogue record for this book is available from the British Library.

Paperback ISBN 978-1-78513-579-8

Large Print ISBN 978-1-78513-580-4

Hardback ISBN 978-1-78513-578-1

Ebook ISBN 978-1-78513-581-1

Kindle ISBN 978-1-78513-582-8

Audio CD ISBN 978-1-78513-573-6

MP3 CD ISBN 978-1-78513-574-3

Digital audio download ISBN 978-1-78513-575-0

This book is printed on certified sustainable paper. Boldwood Books is dedicated to putting sustainability at the heart of our business. For more information please visit https://www. boldwoodbooks.com/about-us/sustainability/

Boldwood Books Ltd, 23 Bowerdean Street, London, SW6 3TN

www.boldwoodbooks.com

For Sam. There's no one else I'd rather weather a storm with.

PROLOGUE
SEPTEMBER 2017

Carrie,

If you've got this far, you're reading my letter. Thank you for not returning straight to sender, and please don't throw this in the trash before you've heard me out.

You've blocked my emails, you've disappeared from social media and won't reply to my messages. My calls ring out. So this is my last resort: an old-fashioned, written letter. The final one.

I'm back in New York. The baby isn't mine.

When the firm found out about you and me, the partners all but gave me an ultimatum:

either I went, or they plateaued you. So I resigned.

I had no idea what I was supposed to do. There you were. Beautiful, arresting, smart and funny. The woman I'd become undeniably besotted with. But Anya was pregnant, I thought with my child. I had to try to do the right thing by her and the baby.

I moved to Chicago to be with them. You might remember me telling you that Anya had gone back home to Seattle after we separated. It was strained and awkward. We fought and griped at each other continually, as if all the reasons we split in the first place were heightened by the pregnancy.

Anya had the baby two weeks ago. He's cute and fragile, but he isn't mine. It transpires she'd been seeing someone before we separated, and it turns out they were still at it behind my back the entire time I was in Chicago.

It's a kick in the gut, I won't lie, but I can honestly tell you it doesn't hurt as much as the thought of you never speaking to me again.

If you don't reply, I promise I won't try again; I'll leave you to move on with your life. But please know that I can't. I don't think I ever will, because I'll never find someone who has the effect on me that you do.

We can be together now, Carrie; there's nothing left to stand in our way.

I love you.

Luke

1

CARRIE

'Oh, my little pup, I've missed you so much.'

Stepping into my Manhattan loft apartment, I bend to scoop up my pug, Eddie, whom I co-doggy-parent with my neighbor and best friend Callum.

'You are such a cute, ickle fur ball,' I say, scratching Eddie's ears as he licks my cheek.

Behind Eddie, Callum closes the door to my apartment as he comes inside and says, 'Thanks, honey. I've missed you, too, but less of the fur ball talk.'

Rolling my eyes, I reach out with my dog-free arm and pull Callum into a hug. 'Hey, you. How've you both been while I've been in Delaware?'

'One of us has been messing all over the floor

and even smudged crap into my brand-new rug,' Callum says, now with his head in my refrigerator and taking out a can of club soda.

'And what about the dog?' I tease.

'Ha. Ha. Very funny. You know, puppy training would be much easier if Eddie had two parents around.'

I set the dog on the lounge floor and he runs toward his empty food and water bowls beneath my kitchen counter. Callum pours some of his soda into Eddie's water bowl.

I watch as the dog drinks then opens his mouth like a yawning hippo, and I wait for him to either belch or explode from the carbon dioxide bubbles. Thankfully, neither happens, so I decide not to comment on another of Callum's puppy-parenting flaws, for now.

'I know,' I say apologetically, removing my rain jacket and hanging it over the extended arm of the luggage I just wheeled in from the airport. 'I'm sorry. How about Chinese takeout this evening, on me?'

It's Sunday evening. Callum and I usually stay in with takeout on Sunday evenings, and the beauty of living next door to each other – in addition to being able to share doggy-care – is that we can eat food and watch movies in our pajamas, then walk ten yards to bed.

He leans back against the work surface. 'I would but I have a date tonight.'

'A date? But you broke up with Tom two days ago.' Not that I should be surprised. Callum describes himself as a serial monogamist. He practices monogamy but in a different relationship every six to eight weeks. 'Plus, it's Sunday. Pajama day.'

'Don't judge, sister,' he says, pointing a finger in my direction as I bring myself to sit on a kitchen stool. 'I would have been on a date with Ben last night but I was on daycare duties and I haven't got my head around the idea of canoodling in front of the pooch yet.'

'Gross.' I pick up Eddie from where our short-haired four-month-old is now sniffing my toes, which are sore from being squished into pointed work heels all day and traipsing through airports. 'Poor Eddie doesn't need to see Daddy's gyrating butt, do you?'

Eddie barks. Case in point.

'You should take a leaf out of my book,' Callum tells me. 'How long has it been for you? Like, for*ever*.'

'Not for*ever*, and I've been busy. Which is actually the reason I asked you to come straight over.' I wince. 'I have to go away again on a red-eye tomorrow morning. Only for five days – I should be back on Friday in time for you to have your Friday night out.'

Callum sighs. 'Carrie...'

'I know, I know. I'm really sorry. It's not like I want to go but I don't have a choice. The Tax partner, Eric, got sick and I've been basically told by Rachel, the head of the entire New York office, that I have to go to the Caribbean. The client likes face-to-face meetings, apparently, and he's a *huge* client.'

'The Caribbean? Again? Who'd have thought an offshore tax specialist could have so much fun?'

I smile. 'It won't be fun. It will be hideous, I promise. Dull, dry, boring. I'd much rather be here with you and Eddie. But you know how har—'

'—hard you've worked to change the narrative of your career. You're on the cusp of partnership and at thirty-one, that's a big deal. You need to be a yes girl for a short while longer. Yada, yada, yada.'

Though he's feigning a yawn and looking to the wood beams above him, I step off my stool and kiss him on the cheek. 'Thank you. I will make it up to you.' His flannel shirt smells a little like cigarettes and a lot like wet dog, but I decide not to tell him.

'You know you will.' He reaches into the jar of dog treats I keep beside my coffee maker and offers one to Eddie, which is snaffled and carried off to the rug in the lounge area. 'Seriously, though, babes, there has to be more to life for you than running yourself into the ground for work.'

I draw in a breath, not because Callum's words catch me off-guard – they don't, I've heard them before – but because there isn't much more. With the exceptions of my mom out in the suburbs, my dad down in Florida, Callum and Eddie, work is everything to me, and that's just the way it is. Rather than explain this for the zillionth time, I search for our pug, who's now spitting crumbs of biscuit onto my upholstered footstool.

I made a mistake early in my work life. One that could have cost me my career and one that has forced me to prove myself at every possible juncture as someone who doesn't sleep her way to the top. I've slogged so hard and for so long, I don't know what I'd do without my job.

'So, where in the Caribbean this time?' Callum asks, thankfully moving on to happier things.

I hop down from my stool and fill the water unit on the coffee machine to hide my delight. 'A private island called Charithonia.'

'Charithonia? Isn't that Joe Hettich's island?'

'Is it?' I ask with fake nonchalance.

He nudges into my side. 'You know it is!'

Laughter escapes me. Only a month ago, we were talking about how rock goddess Molly Martin married her third husband on the billionaire philanthropist's island.

'First class flights, too.' On account of Joe Hettich owning the airline. 'And five days fully catered in his private resort.'

'I've changed my mind; this is a great idea, and I think you need a chaperone.'

I turn to stand next to him, both of us resting back against the countertop, looking across my lounge-cum-diner-cum-kitchen space, and I lean my head onto his shoulder as we watch Eddie tearing up a stuffed toy. 'See, there is more to life.'

Callum kisses my temple. 'You know that's not what I mean. When I've smoked and drank myself into early cardiac failure, I'd like you to have more than just Eddie for company.'

2

CARRIE

Despite the ungodly hour of the morning and Callum's *very* late night – with a man whose tight ass is apparently still sleeping in his bed – my best friend and Eddie are standing on the sidewalk outside our West Village building. The swanky chauffeur-driven car I'm being whisked off to JFK in is another perk of working for Joe Hettich.

As a senior tax advisor at my accountancy firm, I've met with extremely wealthy and well-respected people. Famous people, too. Yet the prospect of flying to Charithonia Island to meet Mr Hettich is intimidating.

Eighteen months ago, I switched accountancy

firms from the firm I had worked for since the very first day of my career, and the same firm that I realized would *never* make me partner, despite seven long years of trying to correct their prejudices. I moved to a firm that took me on with a promise of partnership by the end of quarter three – this month – assuming I play my cards right.

Hence why I am in serious need of a nap en route to the airport. I double check I have my e-boarding cards and my passport, hope again that I've packed appropriate luggage for a Caribbean resort in early September, but one at which I'll be engaged as a professional, and lean my head against the cool window for a few long blinks.

'Would you like me to draw up the divider, Ms Briggs?' the driver asks. He's all fancily clad in a black suit, shirt and tie.

'That would be lovely, thank you.'

By the time I open my eyes, we're slowing to a stop outside my airport terminal. The driver opens my door before I even have a chance to unfasten my seatbelt and I step out of the car to a trolley that's already being loaded with my luggage.

I'm whisked through the airport and security and taken to a first-class lounge, where I'm placed on a high seat at a champagne bar and poured a flute of Krug bubbles. All the while, referred to only as Ms Briggs.

I know this isn't what Callum meant when he said there must be more to life than travelling from place to place and working long hours. He wants me to have a someone, to let someone in.

But right now, this all feels pretty great to me.

Far, far safer than heartbreak.

* * *

I'm one of the first passengers on the plane and, like my fellow, unbelievably fancy class flyers, I'm given a tour of our reserved areas of the aircraft. My seat fully reclines into a flat bed and I'm assured the four-course meal I will be served is fine dining. I'm shown to two social areas – a hangout and a bar – and provided with complimentary loungewear to change into and save my own white pinstripe, high-waisted shorts and matching jacket from the perils of travel.

I wouldn't ordinarily fly in white but deciding on an outfit that works for the heat of the Caribbean and looks business professional was no easy feat.

On the rare occasion I take a vacation, I get out of the USA, away from it all. If Callum and I take a sunshine holiday, the packing is easy. Even easier if I book myself an adventure break somewhere like Fiji or New Zealand.

With my cabin baggage stowed, I take a seat at the bar. While the remainder of the passengers are boarded, I eat caviar and enjoy my glass of fizz. The whole experience is remarkable. Very much how the other half live. So far, this last-minute trip isn't too much of an imposition.

'Cabin crew, cross check and seats for takeoff,' the captain announces.

I take my own seat inside my personal cubicle and flick through the entertainment offering, settling on a country music album, despite my inclination to enjoy a movie, because I really ought to research a little about Joe Hettich and his empire.

From my leather laptop carrier (a treat to self from last year's bonus), I take the wad of documents my secretary emergency couriered to my apartment about Mr Hettich's businesses. But first, I open my laptop, sign in to Wi-Fi, and head to my client's website.

As I scroll to the bottom of the main page and click *About Us*, my country music is switched to the airline's safety briefing, and the corresponding video appears on my inflight screen.

Only, I can't focus on the video that is awash with celebrity cameos because another face draws my attention much more.

On my laptop screen is a photographed image of the relatively recently appointed CFO of Hettich's empire. And it feels as if his topaz-blue eyes are staring into mine.

Luke.

I look back at his picture, my heartrate skyrocketing, my insides leaping like a thousand frogs are bouncing around in there.

And if he's the CFO, then the person I'm set to have business meetings with this week is also—

I unbuckle my seat belt and call for an air stewardess as I haphazardly stuff my belongings back into my cabin luggage.

'Excuse me! Excuse me, I need to get off this plane!'

A young, blonde stewardess rushes my way. 'Ms Briggs, you need to take your seat for takeoff.'

'I'm sorry, I can't. I need to get off the plane.' I lock my laptop case, ready to go. Ready to run from a collision with a ghost from my past. My biggest ever mistake.

She places a gentle yet firm hand on my forearm. 'Ms Briggs, we're already moving. I'm going to need you to take your seat.'

When I glance through the small oval window, I see we're taxiing.

Holy Mother of All Things Fucked.

3

LUKE

My luggage has been taken to my pod and I've been handed a rum punch at one of Hettich's poolside bars. I've been coming out here to see Joe three or four times a year for the last four years, since the inception of his private resort, yet it still wows me every visit.

Charithonia island – named after his wife's favorite butterfly, which is native to the Caribbean, same as her – is a small island nestled among the British Virgin Islands. It's exclusive to Joe, his family's main residence offshore, ten guest pods each with its own infinity pool and hot tub, and a small cluster of housing which is home to a highly efficient army of staff. When they aren't here, Joe and his wife, Ella, split their time between London and New York residences.

Kicking my feet up onto a footstool, I take a swig of the kind of rum punch you can only get under the sunshine of this stunning part of the world. It's been a baptism of fire taking over the role of CFO for the Hettich group. A dream role, in many respects, and one I never would have imagined reaching eight years ago, when I was gunning to become the youngest ever partner of my accountancy firm, but one that comes with a proportionate amount of stress for the title.

Leaning my head back, the sun warming my face and bringing spots to my eyes even behind my shades, those stresses feel happily far away for a minute or two.

'Chalmers!' Joe's voice is loud, always a holler, and comes from somewhere behind me.

Joe and I met at Princeton a disgustingly long time ago – he was studying for a second degree and me my first. He was best man at my wedding – if only I'd listened when he offered to cover for me if I wanted to make a run for it the night before, then I wouldn't have winded up a divorcee before I was even thirty. In our eighteen years of friendship, Joe has gone from running a small business from his college bedroom to having a global empire. We are worlds apart. While I was getting divorced and fundamentally stalling my career, he was building airplanes, investing in innovative technology, and becoming a world-renowned philanthropist.

But he's the kind of man who knows exactly where he came from – a rundown town in West Yorkshire, England – and who his real friends are.

And boy has he paid me back for years of friendship. In a way I never would have asked for, by making me his CFO, but I'm extremely grateful. Work is kind of my solace, my distraction, my other half and family.

I stand as Joe bounds down stone steps from his palatial home to the large infinity pool and welcomes me with his big arms and stiff chest, near winding me as he thumps my back. His tasseled sombrero falls off his tightly curled hair, staying attached to him by a band under his chin.

'You made it. Good to see you, matey,' he says.

It's only Monday and... 'You saw me on Friday in the office,' I tell him.

'This is true. But there's nothing like seeing you at home. What are we drinking, old boy? Rum punch?' He signals to Monique, a member of his kitchen staff who is surreptitiously hovering in the distance, gesticulating that he'd like a drink. 'Pretty please with a cherry on top!' he calls to her. Then turning back to me, he asks, 'The brewing storm didn't put you off, then?'

I raise my brows as we come to sit again on opposite sides of the table, though both facing the view of the crystal-clear waters below from our elevated location on the hilly island. There isn't a sign of a storm in the sky as far as we can see across the Atlantic.

'The news is saying it could turn into a hurricane over the next couple of days,' I tell him.

'Pfft. They always say that. Drama-lamas. I've spent many a hurricane season out here and they always fizzle out or go off course eventually. Nothing to worry about.'

Looking to the horizon, I'm inclined to agree.

Once Monique has served Joe a drink, which he slurps with satisfaction through a straw, he says 'So...' in the way every conversation no one wants to have begins. 'The word in the office is that you're single, again, matey. What happened to Lauren – or Laura or Layla?'

'Lou. And we just ran our course. No story.'

As I speak, Ella, Joe's wife, appears, floating down the steps toward us in a floor-sweeping, turquoise kimono and holding what looks like another three rum punches.

'When are you going to settle down, Luke Chalmers?' she asks. 'From the kitchen,' she adds, setting down our drinks on the table and coming to sit on Joe's lap, her arm draped around his neck. These guys have built a business together, had four kids together, and never lost their youthful romance. It's special, admirable and enviable.

'Settling doesn't come off for everyone,' I tell her.

'Not if you stick to a two-months-and-you're-out rule,' she says, chomping a glazed cherry from the top of her drink.

'I don't have a rule.'

'Mmmhmm. Name one woman since your divorce that you've been with for more than two months.'

She's got me there. Though there was one time. One relationship. One person. After my wife and I separated. It might only have lasted six weeks but under different circumstances, she might have been the—

The sound of one of Joe's speed boats – and then its appearance on the Caribbean Sea from behind the rock face of the island – stops me from completing the thought: she might have been *the one*.

Good thing, too. I don't need to go back there; I don't need to have thoughts about—

Rising from my chair to get a closer look, I think I'm seeing things, a figment of my imagination. It must be the heat, or the alcohol, making my mind play tricks on me. I for sure hope so. Otherwise, the woman I am staring down at as the speedboat pulls into the beach beneath us is...

'Carrie?' I spin around to look at Joe. 'What the fuck is Carrie doing here?'

'Carrie? Who do you mean?' he says, his voice many decibels louder than it ought to be.

Who do I mean? Only the woman I was madly, utterly, undeniably, heartbreakingly crushed by seven years go.

'Don't mess with me, Joe. Is that Carrie Briggs down there?' I can feel something I don't like coursing through me. *Panic? Anger? Something else?* I feel jittery, my hands shaking, all the parts of me beneath my ribcage see-sawing. It must be anger.

Joe holds up his palms. 'Yes, it is. I'm sorry to blindside you but I needed you to come and deal with this tax stuff and I wasn't convinced you would if—'

'With *Carrie*?' My voice is verging on screechy. 'Where the hell is Eric?'

The partner at the accountancy firm we usually deal with. Safe Eric. Pompous Eric who kisses Joe's ass but who I absolutely have never lusted after.

'He's sick, couldn't make it. I'm told Carrie is the next best thing at the firm and she agreed to come last minute.'

Ella rises from Joe's lap. I don't miss her scowling at him, however brief it is, before she comes to my side and looks down at the woman getting off the boat and walking barefoot, shoes in hand, along the wood-decked pathway off the sand and up the steps to the resort.

'It's been a long time, Luke. There's nothing still there between you two, is there?' Ella asks, not meeting my eyes, which is good because I don't have to meet hers in return.

Instead, I can seethe or flip out in whatever manner I like as I watch my one ex, who used to make my heartrate soar the way it is right now, climb the stone steps in a smart white suit.

Looking a lot more womanly than the junior associate I fell for years ago.

'Nothing,' I manage. 'Nothing there at all.'

Yet my head is screaming at me, *I need to get off this island. Now.*

She was one brief moment in time. But a cataclysmic one, nonetheless.

My feet are already backing me away from the rock's edge. I'm already fleeing.

Until I back into Joe's big frame, who's now standing behind me. His cactus-print shirt might as well be real because it couldn't cause me any more discomfort than I already feel.

'I need you, Luke. This is a job for my CFO.'

Shit. Shit. Shit. Shit. Shit.

One person on this island ruined my career once. Another, whose big, burly weight is behind me now, made it. I owe him.

I think I nod – *I'll stay*. But I have no idea if my synapses are firing. I'm paralyzed by something, an emotion, and I don't know what it is, but it feels awfully close to *fear*.

I shift my position to face Joe and Ella. 'I need to... ah...' *What do I need?* 'Go... for a run.' That will fix this. Burn off whatever I'm feeling. Shake off seeing Carrie again for the first time in seven years. If I can't fix it, I can at least try to process the absolute predicament I am stuck in.

Joe eyes me, his brows low and knitted together. He knows the story of Carrie and me. He also knows me well enough to see my mind spiraling behind my controlled façade, even though I hope he can't.

'You're going for a run after one of Monique's rum punches?' Ella asks. 'Are you mad?'

'No better time for it,' I say, hoping she doesn't catch the tremor in my voice.

'Before you do...' Joe pulls an envelope from the back pocket of his lime-green shorts. 'An invitation to dinner tonight. Troy's finest Caribbean dishes and matched wines.'

I take the offering from him. 'I'm already there.'

'Great, because you've also left a very similar invitation for Carrie in her pod. CFO to tax advisor. We'll see you both at eight. I like to get to know my advisors before they tell me things I don't want to hear.'

'Dinner.' I gawk. 'With Carrie.' *Fuck.* 'That saying about giving with one hand and taking away with the other springs to mind,' I mutter, not quietly enough.

'The Lord giveth and the Lord taketh away, my friend,' Joe tells me, striding back to the table and gulping down his cocktail.

'Did you just refer to yourself as God?' I ask, my cardiorespiratory system calming now that I'm on safer ground, bantering with my friend.

Joe holds out his arms as if to say, *Take a look around you.* 'This is *my* island.'

Ella rolls her eyes playfully and I chortle. 'What a dickhead.'

But my lightness is fleeting because sixty yards away from us, Carrie has made it to the top of the beach steps, where she rotates on the spot, taking in the view from the highest point of the island.

I dart behind the nearest palm tree, knocking over a silver wine bucket in a stand as I go, and lean my shoulders back against the firm trunk as I try not to hyperventilate.

I'm going for that run.

4

CARRIE

Wow. Just *wow*.

Eric must be gutted he has stomach flu. No pun intended.

I've climbed the stone steps to Mr Hettich's private resort, roasting under the heat of the afternoon sun. But nothing, not even the ever-present and lingering knowledge that Luke Chalmers is somewhere on this island, can destroy the view for me.

I turn three-sixty degrees on the spot at the top of the hillside while Mr Hettich's staff come by me carrying my luggage.

Two large dogs – English pointers, I think – have followed us up from the beach, tails wagging.

The resort is centered around what I presume is

the main house and residence of my client. Around it, I count ten individual holiday cottages, each with a pool and hot tub on its veranda. The main house is three tiered, like a beautiful white wedding cake – each layer round. The top floor has a white peaked roof, as opposed to figurines of a bride and groom, but it stands above a middle tier that has a pillared terrace set with multiple dining tables, then below that, steps lead down to a large infinity pool with a swim-up bar, sun loungers and tables with expensive-looking parasols.

This truly is how the other half live. Or, more like how the wealthiest 1 per cent of the population live.

Beyond the accommodation is lush greenery that covers most of the teardrop-shaped land, except for one area of what looks like much more modest accommodation, down the hillside. Presumably, the area that looks more like the kind of holiday accommodation I would fund myself, the staff digs. *Incredible.*

The land trails around its northern side into smooth, white-sand beaches, which dissolve into crystal-clear waters. Even from this high-up vantage point, I can see rocks beneath the flat surface. Fifteen or twenty yards into the water, a few boats – dinghies and speedboats – are anchored. Conversely, the southern side of the island seems to drop from rocks to water. There's a boat house and dock on that side, too, and I can see the tip of a mast pole. I can only imagine the size of the boat it belongs to.

There's not even a wispy cloud in the bluest of skies and the only sound I hear is the tweeting of birds. Until a clatter steals my attention, like something metal being dropped to the tiles around the main pool. I could swear there's a flash of person moving behind a palm tree when I look but when I blink, it's gone.

Before I locate the source of the sound, Jenny, one of the crew who drove me by boat from Tortola to Charithonia, asks, 'Ms Briggs— Sorry, Carrie. Can I show you to your pod?'

'I... Ah... I'm...' *Mind* blown. 'Yes, that would be super, thank you.'

She smiles in a way that's sweet, obliging and knowing all at once. 'This way.'

As sweet as she may be, with her words, she has unkindly brought me back from dreamland. I remember now why I was so eager to get off the airplane on the tarmac at JFK. To give up a first-class seat and all of *this*.

I search the landscape as we move, looking for Luke.

Could I be so lucky to have *two* men who should have been meeting this week come down with gastroenteritis?

Luke Chalmers would deserve worse. Much worse. I'm thinking about what that might look like – German measles, dengue, elephantiasis – as Jenny opens the door to my pod.

To describe my bedroom for the next four nights as a pod truly does it a disservice.

In the center of the round room is a circle-shaped bed that could sleep an entire family. Despite its shape, the crisp white bedding is tucked under the mattress without a crease. Some things defy logic. This entire trip being one such thing.

A bow has been tied across the diameter of the bed using gold silk, as if it's a gift. I wonder if anyone would notice me sneaking it home with me as luggage?

Set perfectly in the middle of my would-be loot is a glimmering gold envelope, which I absolutely will open, but not before I've checked out the ensuite, which has a tub I could literally swim in, a flat-screen television that's extended from the ceiling, and a glass door through to an outside shower.

This is *nuts*. Categorically nuts.

'Is everything okay for you, Carrie?' Jenny asks.

'*Okay?* Ha. For sure, thank you.'

Jenny must be twenty-three or four, maybe younger, yet she doesn't seem fazed by the setting in the slightest.

I'll bet this is a seasonal job. Looking after guests who'll tip extremely well and playing around with Mr Hettich's boats and toys in her spare time. Maybe frolicking with the other crew – one of whom, Henry, was young, tanned and buff beneath his fitted black polo and butt-hugging Bermuda shorts. I wasn't intending to look but some things demand attention.

'Great, then I'll leave you to it. There are towels in the wardrobe and welcome drinks and snacks have just arrived on the veranda. If you need anything at all, there are numbers for the bar, the main kitchen and the water crew by the phone on the bedside table. Oh, and don't forget to open the invitation on your bed.'

I thank Jenny, not knowing whether I'm supposed to tip her or not, and then make a snap decision to tip all the staff when I leave.

After waving her off, I take a rum punch, which comes with a delightful pinch of nutmeg on top, from the table on my personal veranda. Sipping the smooth but hard liquor, I relieve my hot feet of my toe-pinching, leather flats and take the gold envelope from the bed, setting down my glass to find out what awaits me.

Dear Carrie,
We would be delighted if you would join us for dinner at 8 p.m. on the main terrace.
Beach-smart dress code.
Yours,
Luke Chalmers
(And the Hettich family)

Stomach flu was wishful thinking.
Is this a joke?
Luke. Luke? Inviting me?? To dinner???
I sit down onto the edge of the bed before I fall down. As I stare at the card in my hand, I remember the first note Luke ever left me.

I'd been his associate for more than a year, the two of us sharing an office. He was on the cusp of making partner at the accountancy firm we worked for then.

It had been months of crush, wanton and lust on my part but he'd had a wife. I knew things hadn't been great between them for a long time and six weeks before he wrote the note, they'd separated.

In those six weeks, it seemed like everything I felt for him was amplified. There was a lingering tension in our office from the moment we both entered until the lights went out at night.

I wanted him so badly, I could barely concentrate on my work.

I could feel it ramping up for him too. The grazes and accidental touches, the looks that were held a moment too long.

Then one morning, I returned to the office from a meeting to find a handwritten note folded under the keyboard on my desk.

Room 210, The Old Court Hotel, 12 p.m.
Luke x

I felt a rush, a thrill, unlike anything I'd ever felt before when I held that piece of paper. But today's note should have come with a trigger warning, or at least an apology.

I turn the card over in my hand to make sure there are no hidden words on the other side.

Nothing.

Instinctively, I pick up my phone and message Callum:

I can't do this.

He fires back:

You can do this. He doesn't have a
hold over you anymore. Don't
throw away your career on him,
again. Pull up those big girl
panties! I love you, Cx

Almost simultaneously, my boss, the big boss, Eric's boss, the head of the New York office who told me I was coming on this trip, sends me a message:

Good Luck. Hettich is eccentric
but great. Enjoy the views! Rachel.

Oh God, I actually have to go through with this.

5

LUKE

I'm pacing the tiled floor in my pod, air con blasting because I'm hot, though the fact my linen shirt is sticking to my skin is nothing to do with the temperature outside.

It is everything to do with seeing Carrie again.

Not just fleetingly seeing her. Not bumping into her as we both get out of a cab, alight the subway or head into a Midtown bar after work.

This is *dinner*. Sitting across the table from her. Hours of excruciating small talk, pretense. A multitude of unspoken questions about the past.

I haven't seen her for seven years. She's part of the very worst time in my life. My career in tatters, a divorce imminent, family life obliterated, and the woman I was utterly infatuated with blocking me, not returning my emails, returning to sender six handwritten letters I mailed to her, with all but the first unopened. Making abundantly clear that when everything else was dealt with, there could *still* never be a chance for us.

She's my nemesis. And though I'm loathe to admit it, no matter how much Ella presses me, my Achille's heel.

There's a tap on my door. It's only seven-thirty, so I know before I answer that Joe will be waiting for me, and that he's here to ask... 'Chalmers, a pre-drink?'

I stare at him, similarly dressed in cream chinos and a linen shirt – though to his eccentric Hawaiian print, I'm wearing pale blue, and to his turtle-inspired bucket hat, I'm wearing none. The upshot is, his outfit is significantly more relaxed than mine.

Have I overdone this? Have I subconsciously over-dressed to appear fine?

I am fine, a soprano version of my inner voice sings.

I am so not fine, normal-pitched me retorts.

'I can't do this, Hettich.'

'It's only a sundowner, old boy.'

'The sun set an hour ago, and you know what I mean. *This*. Dinner. Meetings. *Carrie*.'

He steps inside and closes the door behind him, eyeing me, hands in pockets as if his next words will be emphatic. 'You could run. It would be cowardly and, honestly, career ending because, one, there comes a point in life when you have to face your past, and two, I don't understand all this tax and accounting kerfuffle, which is why I employed *you* and gave you a hellish signing-on bonus to deal with it for me.'

The bonus was nice but, '*Cowardly?* More like letting sleeping dogs lie. Not dredging up the past.'

He holds up his hands – *Take or leave my warning.*

'You can run or you can accept the challenge. Finally deal with the reason you're a lonely and increasingly old man.'

'Hey!'

'Did you have those flecks of grey last time you saw her?'

My hand automatically goes to my product-styled hair. 'No, but that's probably because she caused half of them,' I mutter.

He gestures to the door with a pointed thumb. 'Let's get a cocktail and calm those geriatric nerves.'

'You're four years older than me!'

'Therefore, four years wiser. It's time to man up, Chalmers, not least because I ordered a crate of Pusser's rum and it arrived this morning.'

Ordinarily, Joe's favorite cocktail – a Painkiller made with Pusser's rum – would be a great idea, but as it happens, I already feel numb. Turning out the lights, I reluctantly head to the terrace, following the flapping flippers of Joe's outrageous hat.

* * *

Two Painkillers have helped. Standing on the terrace with Joe, watching sail boats drifting across the ocean, Ella's playlist of chilled re-recordings of chart-topping hits playing in the background, tea lights twisted round and dancing on the palm trees, I feel more myself.

Joe and I are talking about going sailing on Wednesday, maybe taking out a couple of jet skis.

'They're upgraded since your last trip. The guys tell me they're faster than anything else they've ridden.'

By 'guys', he means his staff, who really have a pleasant lifestyle out here. True, they make them-selves available for Joe's every whim, but they get free accommodation and a free pass to all the island's amenities, including use of the main resort when Joe and his family and friends aren't around.

'Hey, you two. My sister said I'd find you out here.' I turn to see Alisha, Ella's sister, coming our way, a cocktail in hand, her long dress twisting around her ankles. Today's look is long plaits of hair coiled on top of her head, signature large gold hoops tapping her neck as she moves.

'Alisha, it's been a while,' I tell her, folding her into an embrace. She has on her usual lathering of lemon moisturizer, which smells nice but is mostly to fend off mosquitoes, which are rife this time of year, whether or not the island has been fogged.

'Certainly too long,' she says. Though born in the British Virgin Islands, Alisha now lives on St Martin and has a slightly different rhythm to her accent than her sister. 'How *are* you, Luke-y? Still footloose and fancy free, bedding anyone who'll have you and buying my nieces and nephews bigger gifts than I'll ever afford just so they like you best?'

I laugh so hard, my head drops back. It's a release I've needed.

'It's not about the price, Alisha, it's about how cool they are. You know that.'

She shakes her head, pointing a long red fingernail at me. 'You play fair. Remember blood is thicker than water.'

'That sounds like a threat,' I tease.

'Boy, you know it is. But it's good to see you.'

'You, too.'

'Ella and the kids are nearly ready; they'll be out in a minute,' she says. 'The kids wanted to dress up. Noah is Buzz Lightyear, Toby is Rusty from *Cars*, Char is Peppa Pig, and my awful sister has dressed the bubba as a minion.'

'I'm glad I was out here with a Painkiller,' Joe says. 'They'll be high on life and drama.'

'Oh yes,' Alisha says, giggling. 'There have been a few crossed words.' She gestures toward a table that's been set for eleven people behind us. 'Who else is joining us, Joe?'

He finishes his drink and signals in the direction of the bar and Monique for another. 'Us three, Ella and the entire cast of Disney Plus, Jenny and Henry because they'll be helping to crew *Ella II* if we take her out on Wednesday.'

I've always liked this about Joe – he involves his staff. He doesn't treat them like second-rate citizens and that's how it should be done, in my view. I'll never be wealthy enough to need round-the-clock help on my own private island, but my fictitious staff would be well looked after too.

Still, his kindness toward his staff is wiped out by the tormenting glint in his eyes as he looks my way and adds... 'And hopefully, my tax advisor, if she accepts Luke's invitation.'

If looks could kill, this week would have just become a *Knives Out* sort of week. Who murdered Joe Hettich? *Me*. With my mind.

'Am I missing something?' Alisha asks, switching her focus between Joe and me.

I subconsciously check my watch, feeling increasingly fidgety.

'Now's not the time to catch on,' Joe says.

'Because there's nothing to catch,' I tell them.

I should have known she'd be perfectly punctual. She always was.

Carrie appears, walking along the pathway etched into the top of the rock face, heading our way.

She's wearing a lilac pleated skirt that finishes just below her knee, nipped in at her waist by a belt. I remember the feel of her waist in my hands, exactly where her white blouse tucks in.

I watch her every step as she moves closer toward us, reaching the terrace and heading our way. I can't take my eyes off her, like a bug to fluorescent light.

She's summer smart – presumably her invitation had the same dress code stated on it as mine – but she's much smarter, chicer, more girl-out-of-the-city than the rest of us.

Not girl, I amend as she comes closer, her perfume reaching me on the barely there breeze. She's not the girl I fell for; she's a woman.

Her long auburn hair falls in waves around her shoulders. My fingers twitch at the thought of how I used to run them through her soft curls. Her white blouse is open enough at the neck for me to see slender collarbones that I've kissed before. Her lips are painted a subtle shade of pink – invitingly so. And her features seem to hold more stories; they seem wiser.

I wonder if this version of Carrie would have been smart enough never to have gotten involved with me. Smart enough to have saved me from a whole load of heartache.

Speaking of which, that organ is currently thumping against my ribcage like a pneumatic drill.

Carrie makes straight for Joe but there's a split second of hesitation, in which I know she clocks me in her peripheral vision.

'Mr Hettich, it's an absolute pleasure,' she says, sounding unwaveringly confident, as if her world hasn't just been knocked off its axis, as mine has.

'Carrie, lovely to finally meet you,' my so-called buddy says, hitting right off the bat with a reminder that we share a past. A heated, explosive, life-altering past. 'Thank you for joining us for dinner. I like to get to know who I'm working with before we get down to business.'

Joe would have gone in for a hug – that's his style, whether he's in work mode or not – but Carrie thrusts out her hand and shakes forcefully, succinctly. 'I'm thrilled to be here. Your island is stunning.'

'Thank you, my wife will be delighted to hear it. She designed everything on it. Ella will be here in a minute or two.'

'I can't wait to meet her, Mr Hettich.' She's poised but stiff with it, increasingly so. Still not looking anywhere other than at Joe or out to sea.

'It's Joe or Hettich, I'll respond to either, but no need for the mister.'

She smiles and I see the familiar shape of her face, the rise of her cheekbones, the softening of her emerald-green eyes. She's magnetic, still. Impossible to resist.

Just like driving by a car crash on the I-95 and rubbernecking.

'Joe,' she says, nodding once.

'Let me introduce you to Alisha,' Joe says. 'And you already know my CFO, Luke.'

Now, I feel her intentionally avoiding me, her cheeks flushing, her eyes laser-focused on Alisha, as she says tightly, 'Really nice to meet you,' and shakes her hand.

I think I've stopped breathing. Not to be melodramatic or anything but I might genuinely be experiencing the initial stages of a cardiac arrest as I wait for what I know is coming.

To anyone else, the way Carrie's chest stutters with her next inhalation might go unnoticed, but I remember everything about her body and the way it reacts. I see it. I see her.

Yet I'm still unprepared for the moment our eyes lock on to each other's. Still taken aback by hearing my name leave her soft, full, fucking annoyingly kissable lips.

'Luke.'

She holds out a hand and I forget I'm holding a drink in mine as I thrust my Painkiller at her, splashing it over her outfit and somehow losing my grip of everything, as the glass shatters on the decking, the drink soaking my pants in the process.

'Shit, sorry. I— Can somebody help?' I ask.

Am I going to drop something every goddamn time I see her?

Monique appears from out of nowhere with a rag for the white tiles and another for Carrie's clothes.

Fuck. If I was nervous before...

I see her jaw roll before she tells me, 'Don't worry about it. Clothes can be dry-cleaned.'

In her firm tone, I hear her meaning. Stains can be erased from clothes. Our history can't be overcome so easily.

Her scathing look hits me like a proverbial slap across the face. It's a look that reminds me that *she* blocked *me*. That *she* didn't return my calls, my endless emails, my texts, my letters that were returned unread. She left no room for a second chance; she didn't leave the door open for us to stay in touch, be friends. Even if platonically, I'd have taken it.

I feel my eyes narrow. All the pain. All the hurt.

No. She doesn't have the right to be pissed at me.

She's damn right history can't be erased.

I *loathe* this woman.

6

CARRIE

Seeing Luke in the flesh after all the years is the way I imagine a small nut would feel if it were to be cracked by a sledgehammer. My shell feels broken, my insides bared and smashed to pieces.

The last time I saw him, he was rushing into a meeting, faltering in his stride momentarily when he saw me in the corridor. Though we were a secret at work because he was about to be made a partner and I was his junior associate, we shared a knowing smile. An expression that held a heated promise.

Yet, hours later, as I lay dressed in red lingerie that I'd bought for Luke's birthday, waiting for him on the bed of *our* hotel room, he was plotting a return to his pregnant wife.

I need to hold it together.

No matter that the half-moon creases at the sides of his mouth when he smiles seem deeper, sweeter now. That the stubble lining his strong jaw is the same length I used to feel when I held his face in my palms, though flecked with grey that makes him appear knowledgeable, more experienced. That the lines at the edges of his eyes make him seem softer, more welcoming. Or that the body I used to know so well seems unchanged where his shirt hugs his torso. Broader perhaps but still firm, still desirable.

Despite all of that. Setting aside the way he has instantly turned my insides to mush. Ignoring the voice in my head screaming that I detest him for what he did to me. I need to remember that I'm here in my capacity as a professional. An advisor to his business.

I straighten my now damp and cocktail-stained clothes and clear my throat. 'Thank you for the dinner invitation,' I tell him, hating myself for being civilized as much as I hate him for using me and casting me aside when the novelty and excitement of us had worn off.

'That always was your problem,' he says, his voice low and ill-tempered, for my ears only, as Joe and Alisha talk amongst themselves.

'My problem?' I snipe, unintentionally exposing my emotions.

'Putting two and two together and jumping to the wrong conclusions. Not sitting back in the problem for long enough to wait for the solution to come along. I didn't invite you; Hettich did.'

'Ah, a metaphor. What are you, a lyricist now? Ever the chameleon.'

'Take it as you will.'

A waitress appears, wearing a crisp white shirt with *Charithonia* embroidered onto the pocket in gold thread, holding a tray of nibbles. Luke takes an olive on a stick, sucking it into his mouth with a *pop* and a smirk.

I do the same.

He wants to play nasty? I'll play.

'Well, I'm lucky I had an excellent mentor as a junior associate, Luke. You taught me an awful lot about the kind of advisor I need to be, and the kind of person I absolutely don't.'

With that burn, I turn my back on him and step toward Hettich, but as I do, I'm almost bowled off my feet by a running child, surging toward Luke with outstretched airplane arms and dressed as Buzz Lightyear.

'To infinity and beyond!'

The boy, maybe seven or eight, crashes into Luke, who sweeps him up into the air like he weighs the same as a feather and raises him above his head, spinning on the spot so that Buzz is flying. Then he drops him seamlessly onto his hip, as if he's held this boy countless times before.

'How you doing, buddy?' Luke asks. Any trace of hostility is gone, replaced by something much warmer, fatherly.

'Is dinner ready yet?' the boy asks Luke. And to me, he says, 'Hi, I'm Noah. I'm seven. Who are you?'

He's adorable, if a tad brusque. 'I'm Carrie. Nice to meet you, Noah.'

'Is dinner ready?'

Luke chuckles in a way that catches me off-guard. The sound of it, the sight of it, makes something low in my abdomen vibrate like jelly on a moving train. I always liked his laugh. Before I discovered he's a total lying dickhead.

'Dinner isn't ready yet but let's find you a snack, huh?' Luke says, keeping hold of the boy. 'Just don't tell your mom or I'll be in trouble.'

Noah holds a finger to Luke's lips and says, 'Our secret.'

Only as they walk away in search of the snacks

that have been set out on two tall bar tables nearby do I calculate. Noah is seven. *Seven*.

He doesn't look especially like Luke but he doesn't *not* look like him either. They clearly have a strong bond.

Noah is the baby. *The* baby.

Don't tell your mom.

Please tell me *Mom* isn't here.

I'm thrown so completely, heart palpitating-ly, sweat glands leaking-ly, that I hardly register the other three children, all dressed up, who come to join us for dinner. Nor the arrival of Ella, Joe's wife, or the two crew who picked me up from Tortola earlier and who will be taking us sailing apparently on Wednesday.

The only thing I do manage to process is that I need to come up with some kind of lie to get out of being trapped on a boat in the middle of the ocean with Luke and his *family*.

I cackle at the me of a few hours ago who thought this nightmare couldn't get any worse. It just got a hell of a lot worse.

Surely, there's a point in this terrifying dream that's equivalent to me tripping over a curb or falling from a cliff and I get to wake up with a start and realize this was all in my imagination.

I should be so lucky.

I'm somehow forced to sit opposite Luke at the long table. On one side of him is Noah and on the other, Alisha.

Alisha. Alisha. The pair of them flirt and touch openly, clearly a couple. But neither one of them is wearing a wedding ring – not that I've been focusing too much on finding this out – and I can't remember Luke's wife's name but I don't think it was Alisha.

I was an *A*, though. Alisha. Alicia. Alice. Anna.

Anya! I'm sure it was Anya.

So Noah is Luke's son but Alisha isn't his wife. Or, at least, the estranged wife I thought Luke had separated from but was actually just taking a break from. A break he used to screw me, make me fall disastrously head-over-heels for him, then run away from me to another state, where his wife was waiting to take him back. *Could Noah even be Luke and Alisha's son?*

If so, Luke dumped me to go back to his wife, then traded her in for another model too. And almost immediately, if my calculations are correct. Who knows, maybe I wasn't his only play toy?

Sounds like Luke.

Now who's sleeping their way to the top?

After seven years of unravelling that narrative

about me in the office because of him, I can't believe I'm seeing Luke do it now.

Why am I here?

Why didn't Luke cancel when he knew Eric was sick? Why did he bring me here to flaunt his family in front of me?

To show me what I've missed out on?

Except I didn't give it up by choice.

I never had any say in how things ended between us.

I look out to sea, feigning admiring the view through blurred vision, until the pressure behind my eyes subsides and I start to think more clearly.

It's a few days; I just have to get through it.

Besides Callum and our pug, my career is my life. I won't let Luke kibosh it. Not again.

'Have you seen the news about the storm, Joe?'

The question comes from Jenny, the woman who zipped me over here by speed boat and who's sitting to my far left. She's throwing the question to the opposite end of the table, my far right, where Hettich is sitting, being served first a plate of food fresh off the grill.

I'm grateful for the diversions of both the heavenly aromas of butter and garlic and Jenny's question.

'If you believe the news, Jenny, I'll be the first man to land on Venus,' Hettich replies.

'Mars, honey,' Ella says, strapping their youngest child – the minion – whose highchair is between me and Ella, into a full cloak-style bib and handing her a corn on the cob. 'Women are from Venus.'

Miraculously, I laugh along with the rest of the table.

I don't know why but my eyes flick to Luke and before he darts his focus away, I see that his attention is trained on me, which brings any good humor I was feeling to an abrupt halt.

'What does the news say, Jenny?' Hettich asks.

'They've upgraded the storm to a category one hurricane. They're calling it Isabel. They think she'll be a category four by the time she reaches the Leeward Islands on Thursday evening or the early hours of Friday.'

Hettich shakes his head. 'She'll never hit. They never do.'

'I wouldn't be so sure, boss.' Henry, the other guy who picked me up with Jenny, chips in.

They're both wearing matching Charithonia uniforms – now smart black shirts, also with *Charithonia* in gold thread on the pockets, and black slacks. Where Jenny has clearly washed and blow-dried her long flowing locks, Henry looks much the same as earlier today – sun-kissed skin and hair stiffened by saltwater and wind – though now his polarized shades are sitting in his hair. He's handsome, very. They'd make an especially attractive couple, actually.

Maybe I should warn them that workplace romances are an utter catastrophe.

'They think she could be a direct hit,' Henry adds.

Jenny hums in agreement, clearing her mouth of bread before speaking. 'There are two more storms brewing and you know what the weather guys are like, excited at the prospect of apocalypse, but they say if the three collide, this could be the largest hurricane to ever make landfall from the Atlantic.'

What? I'm listening. *Should I be worried?* I glance around the table but with the exception of Luke, no one else seems perturbed. I let my shoulders fall the ten inches they just rose. Or maybe they've been up there since I arrived on this island.

'Those guys need ratings,' Hettich says, waving his empty fork dismissively. 'There'll be hundreds of YouTube and TikTok videos simulating a superstorm online already. When I feel Isabel's wind in my hair, that's when I'll believe it. You watch, it'll miss the Caribbean altogether and hit somewhere like Florida.'

Florida? My dad and stepmom live in Florida.

I reach for a glass of water from the table to soothe my tight throat.

Then a voice I could pick out of a rowdy room says quietly, 'That won't happen, don't worry.'

When I look up, Luke has turned his attention to Noah, asking him if he needs help cutting up his burger, but I know his words were aimed at me. *He remembers.*

Not that one memory of where my dad lives undoes his many failures, but it was a kind thing for him to say.

I'm thankful when my mixed grill of lobster, huge prawns and steak is placed in front of me. I can get lost in this, pretend that I'm not watching the way Luke flirts with Alisha and takes care of Noah through my third eye as I eat.

The child who is dressed as Peppa Pig and sitting next to Alisha, without any cause, it seems, flicks a forkful of mac-pie – which Henry assures everyone at the table is the best in the Caribbean – at the minion sandwiched between Ella and me.

'Moooooooooom!' the minion yells as Alisha

takes the offending fork from Peppa and chastises her the way moms do.

Huh. I think I might be sussing out who belongs to whom around the table now. Buzz Lightyear and Peppa Pig, AKA Noah and Char, belong to Alisha and Luke. The minion, Sanza, and, I think, Rusty from *Cars*, Toby, who's sitting opposite Jenny and next to Henry, are Ella and Joe's two children.

We've got ourselves a little am-dram kindergarten.

'Say sorry to Sanza,' Alisha tells Char, who scowls at Sanza the minion, then, for her mom's benefit, grins sickly-sweetly and chirps, 'Soooooooory.'

'Do you accept her apology, Sanza?' Ella asks.

Sanza giggles in response.

Bizarrely, it reminds me how much I pined for a sibling or cousins when I was younger. When my parents separated, I was eighteen and conflicted. They needed to separate, they made each other miserable, but I wanted my family to stay as a unit even if it was a dysfunctional one because it was all I'd known. It was a lonely time. I always thought a sister, a brother, a cousin to share in the misery else help me ignore it, would have been nice.

'Your kids are cute,' I say, looking at Alisha but

side-eying Luke, not wanting to pay him any compliment, even if it is in reference to his children.

Alisha looks startled, pointing at Peppa Pig. 'Char?'

'And Noah,' I say, narrowly escaping meeting Luke's eyes as I glance to Noah next to him.

Alisha laughs. 'Oh, they aren't mine, honey.'

Everyone chuckles, so I go along with it, all the while feeling like someone has lit a fire in my cheeks.

'Sorry,' I say. 'I guess I thought.'

I'm mindlessly gesturing between Alisha and Luke, and, *oh God,* I bet he's thinking *that I care.*

I don't. I don't care whether he has kids or not. I just... thought he did.

'Not his either,' Alisha says. 'Neither of us have our own kids. They're both my sister's. She and Joe will have themselves a football team soon. Char is short for Charithonia, after the island.'

'Ohhhhhh,' I say, feeling like such an idiot.

'Luke is a good father figure, though,' Alisha adds, thankfully taking the focus off me. 'He's godfather to all these mites.'

'We are absolutely four and done,' Ella says. 'There'll be no football team.'

I smile, as if I don't feel the height of awkwardness. I've even managed to make Luke look embarrassed for me, if his twiddling with the base of his wine glass is anything to go by. Luke *never* used to embarrass. Not when people complimented him, not when he made an error, not when he made an incorrect assumption, and not when he whispered dirty talk against my neck.

My next inhale is unsteady. *I don't know Luke at all.* Not anymore.

While Ella and Alisha animatedly discuss the merits and harsh realities of children, I'm drawn like a magnet to the last face on earth I want to be sitting opposite.

I find Luke staring back at me. Smug. 'Problems and solutions, Carrie.'

Solution *this*. It may be immature flipping someone the bird under the dinner table but it really does feel good. So good, I'm able to plant a grin the size of a Cheshire cat's on my face as I do it.

'So you aren't sleeping your way *to* the top, then? You're just sleeping around *at* the top.'

His eyes narrow, his jaw stiffens, then he shakes his head, unspeaking, like I'm being too petulant to indulge me with a response. That's possibly true but I pick up my glass of wine and sip it with a supercilious smirk that could rival the one he was wearing just moments ago.

'What about you, Carrie? Do you have any kids?' Ella asks.

Phssssst. My wine sprays from my mouth.

'Sorry.' Then I choke, making an even bigger scene. 'Went down the wrong way,' I croak. In the process, obliterating my one-upmanship.

I hate Luke. *Hate* him.

When I'm composed, I tell Ella, 'I do, actually.' And I relish every split second of realization dawning on Luke.

You're not the only person who moved on, asswipe.

I let my words hang in the densely humid air just long enough to ensure they've registered, but I would never, *could* never, use children as pawns in a game. I spent my teenage years being exactly that between my parents.

So I tell them, 'He's about eight inches tall and weighs nine pounds. He has a feisty bark and a squishy nose. His name is Eddie.'

'You're a puppy momma?' Jenny asks giddily.

I nod. 'I co-doggy-parent an adorable pug.'

If I'm not mistaken, two peculiar things happen simultaneously. First, Luke's body seems to deflate with my words, as if he cares. That, I'm sure, is a figment of my imagination – not that I care. I don't.

Secondly, Ella and Joe share a most peculiar and unreadable look, but if I were wearing it, it would feel like... relief?

The upshot is, the table falls into silence. *What have I said?*

* * *

Thank goodness for Henry, Jenny and the random musings of the four children, who seem to provide the only safe and untargeted conversation of the long and tedious hour at the table.

It's only 9 p.m. and I'm exhausted by the back and forth between schmoozing my client and revisiting one of the bleakest periods of my life.

So when Ella declares she's going to put the kids to bed and Alisha offers to help, I consider my options.

A: more drinks with Joe, Henry, Jenny and, for my greatest sins, Luke, where we're now sitting on patio furniture at the pool bar and I'm hyper-aware of bugs landing on me, despite the citronella burning around us.

Or B: I feign a yawn.

'Gosh, I'm sorry. I think I should probably turn in too.'

'Won't you have a nightcap?' Joe asks.

I ought to. For any other client, I would dig deep and find the energy. But when 50 per cent of my client is Luke Chalmers...

'I would but I don't think I'll be much company,' I say, which is true. I don't want to be on this island, let alone sitting under the scrutiny of a man I got so, *so* wrong once upon a time. 'Jet lag is the worst,' I add, standing to make clear I won't backtrack.

'There's one hour's time difference between eastern time and Atlantic standard time,' Luke says, one eyebrow raised.

Dick.

I feel my nostrils flare as I glower at him, then turn to Joe and switch on my tax advisor smile. 'Oh, you know what I mean. Travel weariness.'

Everyone stands to give me an overly familiar hug goodnight – *a Caribbean thing? A private island thing?* Certainly an invasion of personal space thing.

Luke stays in his seat, looking out to a black sea, twinkling as it rocks back and forth under the light of the waxing moon. Only when Joe unsubtly jerks his head in my direction does Luke stand.

He comes close to me and I feel my entire body

stiffen at the scent of him I used to know. Fresh cologne and... masculinity. My mouth suddenly feels like I'm stranded in the desert without water.

He leans into me and in any other circumstances, if this wasn't work, I'd pull back.

In any other circumstances, this wouldn't be happening.

I don't know what to do.

We end up shoulder grazing and clumsily patting each other on the back.

'Are you going to Facetime your pug?' he mutters in my ear.

Scowling, I step back. 'Wouldn't you like to know what I get up to at night?'

Ha.

There's something like fire between us as we stare each other out, neither one of us willing to break first.

Then Alisha reappears and we both turn to her together. 'Joe, they want Dad.'

'Duty calls,' Joe says as he stands. 'Rum and Coke for me.'

I use the distraction to slip out into the night.

On my way back to my pod, I shoot a message to Callum:

> That may have been the most
> miserable dinner I have ever been
> to x

Slipping my phone back into my purse, it hits me. Whatever *it* is. My chest is tightening, my eyes are stinging, and I'm biting my lip in a bid not to cry.

As if my best friend has read my mind, I get a reply:

> No tears, pretty lady. He doesn't
> deserve them. I love you Cx

His words snap me out of whatever it was I was caught in for a moment.

> Tears. Paha. I'm a tough gal x

From Callum:

> To everyone who doesn't know
> you as well as I do. Sleep well,
> princess. Call me if you need
> me Cx

It's not until I'm lying on my bed staring at the

ceiling fan that Alisha's words over dinner hit me –
Neither of us have our own kids.

Luke doesn't have a child? But he left me for his
pregnant ex. *Didn't he?*

7

LUKE

It's Tuesday morning: a working day. I'm starting the day with a beach workout, putting off the million and one things awaiting me in my inbox and calendar, the most glaring of them all being going through the tax implications of Hettich's entire network of businesses with Carrie.

Carrie, who co-parents a pug. Odd way to phrase the fact that she's living with someone and she loves them enough to share a dog with them. She doesn't wear a wedding ring, but a dog suggests a long-term relationship, right?

Not that I give a damn one way or the other. I'm just... curious, I guess. She's someone I used to know.

Someone I had a relationship with. *Isn't everyone intrigued to a greater or lesser extent by what their exes are up to?*

Though I think about my ex-wife, Anya, and I genuinely couldn't give two hoots as to what she's doing in life anymore.

In any event, the Carrie who showed up to dinner last night might have worn the same perfume I used to love. It's not the perfume alone; it's the way it smells on her, the way it penetrates my mind and my skin, gets into my arteries and wraps itself around my hemoglobin, assaulting all of my organs with each inhalation. And she may have the same striking eyes and unrivalled smile—

As my bare feet tread through the hard sand at the shoreline, where the tide is heading out from the island, I have a vivid memory of the way she used to smile when we were in bed together. In the minutes, sometimes hours, we'd lie together after we'd made love, I used to crave her even more than in the heat of the moments before. She'd lie on my chest, gazing up at me with an expression that was so warm, it used to make me dizzy. Like I was weightless and spinning through the stars in space, where the fact we were colleagues and I was her superior didn't matter.

There was only ever one person in control when it was just the two of us, and it wasn't me.

I stop running; I've been running up and down the same five hundred yards of beach for nearly an hour. The sun has fully risen in that time.

We used to talk about places like this, taking trips together, Carrie and I. But our relationship never got that far. It was doomed from day one. Though Anya and I were separated, my marital status was still officially wed, and on the same day Anya told me by text message that she was pregnant, Carrie and I were spotted by a colleague, kissing outside my apartment before heading off in different directions to walk to the office separately.

It's ironic that I'm finally in paradise with her, by turquoise water, salt air filling my lungs and glorious sunshine beating down on me. The same paradise we used to talk about as my fingertips ran lazy trails up and down her naked spine, hers drawing circles on my chest, yet she's not the same woman at all.

The woman who sat opposite me at the dinner table last night was catty and snide. Cold and cutting. Even the smiles she gave were fake; I know because I know the way she looks when she's genuinely happy. The way her eyes crease at the edges as if she's aged prematurely.

That's what she was seven years ago. She was light and peace. She worked like a Trojan but she left the stress at the office. Her playfulness was infectious and light years from the months – or longer – of fractious darkness I'd left behind with Anya.

I suppose that's why it was so easy to fall for Carrie. And fall I did. Hard, fast, deeply. For a young woman I used to know.

But the woman I'm going to spend most of today with... I don't recognize her at all.

Hot and sweaty from my run, I take out my headphones, pull my shirt over my head and set them, together with my phone, down on the sand. I head into the ocean and plunge beneath the surface, feeling the dense saltwater wash over my skin, washing away the irritation that stopped me from sleeping well last night and the ill temper I woke with at 5 a.m.

Four days.

I can survive anything for four days. I've climbed Kilimanjaro, trekked the Amazon. I've completed an Ironman, for Christ's sake. This won't be the hardest test of my endurance.

On Friday, we'll fly away from this island and maybe it will be another seven years before I see her again.

Bring back boring, safe, middle-aged Eric, who has never brought out the worst, most juvenile behavior in me.

Sitting on the sandy bottom of the sea, I exhale the final bubbles of air from my lungs. *Nor has Eric, or anyone, ever brought out the best the way Carrie did.*

I surface with a gasp and flick excess water from my hair as I rub the sea off my face.

When I open my eyes, my cleansing comes to an abrupt end. Carrie the Witch is descending the white steps that are cut into the rock face at the far side of the beach. She's wearing a sunhat and a summer cover-up, but I recognize her gait, how she holds herself, and the long red hair that flows across her shoulders and bounces with her steps. Long red hair that I've wrapped around my hand and tugged away to expose her neck to my mouth as our bodies have driven each other wild.

And damn my body right now for betraying me. For wanting that back, if only for one time. For the way it's making my shorts feel too tight as I watch her set down a bag next to a pair of sun loungers, which is overhung by a thatched beach umbrella.

Maybe if she lies back and closes her eyes, I can sneak out of the ocean, up to the back of the beach and behind her to the steps without being noticed.

Avoiding any question as to whether I should make conversation that neither of us wants.

But now she's unbuttoning her long white shirt in a way that makes something inside me twinge, low down in my torso – *she used to wear my white shirts*. God, I *loved* how she looked in my white shirts. The way they'd smell like her when I re-dressed in them. Her intoxication stayed with me longer than the buzz from any alcohol could.

I look away, at something, anything, the mundane rocks and the water gently lapping at their bases. I think of... paragliding, surfing, yachting, my grandmother, Hettich. Yet still, I'm pulled to her like aluminum to a magnet as the shirt slips from her shoulders, down her arms, leaving her in a bikini.

It feels wrong to see what she doesn't want me to. Though I've seen her completely naked, that was always invited. She wanted me to see her then.

Currently, she doesn't even know I'm here, that I'm too engrossed to look away.

And this isn't the Carrie of years ago.

Though even at this distance, her body that was invitingly shapely in all the right places still is. Perhaps more so. Maybe her hips are wider, her shoulders broader, her butt—

Jesus!

She turns and I hear her yelp when she spots me, right before I crash myself under the water, about as surreptitious as the Chrysler Building at night.

8

CARRIE

'My fault?' Luke asks incredulously, pointing to himself and his very naked, very wet torso that I am doing my very best not to gawp at.

We're standing on the water's edge where, incensed by his outright invasion of my privacy, I stormed down from my lounger to confront him.

'You— *you* took off your clothes in front of *me*!' he demands.

'I'm at the beach! I had no idea that you were waiting in the ocean like some kind of salt water, reptile-y predator-y *alligator* waiting to snap, snap, snap me up!' I'm shrieking. Hurting even my own ears with the hysterical decibels I'm hitting. My arms are flailing to match the sound.

He scoffs, which pisses me off even more than him uninvitedly watching me get near naked in my swimwear.

'I was already on the beach, and you had a damn good vantage point coming down those stairs. How do I know you didn't see me and intentionally strip down into a skimpy bikini to flaunt yourself?'

Only now do I realize that I am *still* wearing said bikini. *Only* wearing said bikini. I thought I'd be down here early enough to avoid my clients and soak up the scenery. Pretend like this is the holiday I've been needing for*ever*, if only for an hour.

'Do you honestly think I would strip down for you on *purpose*? After everything you did?'

'*I* did?'

Yes! Can he even question who was in the wrong between us? *He* used *me*. Had a bit of fun while his relationship was in tatters and then left me when he was ready to pick it back up.

I'd not wanted to believe my mom – the only person who knew about Luke and me back then – when she'd said I shouldn't meddle with husbands and wives, that I'd end up heartbroken.

She was right.

I can't deal with this. Especially after a shockingly sleepless night and pre-caffeination.

But it looks like I won't have to for much longer because Luke stomps, as much as any man can stomp in soft sand, up the beach, flicking his top over his muscly shoulder. More so even than it used to be, I notice accidentally and fleetingly, not really looking properly.

'You weren't even supposed to be here, Carrie.'

No, I wasn't, but... 'I didn't come here knowing that *you* would be here. If I did, I would have run, not walked, away from any opportunity. Because you're not worth it, Luke.'

He turns back sharply to face me and I think maybe I went too far. That was bitter and nasty, and I'm not sure it's entirely truthful.

Luke points at me, *actually* points at me. 'How many times did I tell you to research your clients before walking into the lion's den?'

I scowl, hopefully showing as much repugnance as Miranda Priestly would demonstrate looking at a PA wearing last season's Prada. 'How did I *ever* fall for you?'

My own words make me swallow deeply with shame. *What is he turning me into?*

He shakes his head and turns his back on me again, this time walking slower, holding his shirt loosely down by his side. He calls back, without shifting his focus from the steps in front of him, 'Let's make sure we get through all the business we need to today, then we can go back to living our lives without ever crossing paths.'

'Happily!' I shout, wishing I could storm away too, except I have nowhere to go.

'For the record,' he shouts, drawing my attention to see him facing me again, now walking backwards as he nears the bottom of the wood staircase, 'alligators prefer freshwater. You meant crocodile.'

'Luke, I can honestly say, there's not a thing in the world I want to learn from you.'

But dammit, if I'm going to run with an insult, I'd like to at least get it right.

* * *

'I hate him, Callum. Truly, truly, unquestionably, unwaveringly, despise him.'

I'm doing laps of my circular pod, wrapped in a towel after showering off the beach, my phone set to speaker on the bed.

I thought a couple of strong coffees and the fancy-pants breakfast with flowers carved from fruit that I was served to my veranda would have taken the edge off the nuclear fission Luke caused in me this morning, but all I did was eat my fructose over-dose with needless ferocity.

Now, I have two work outfit options for this meeting hanging on the front of the wardrobe doors and I can't decide which to wear. I don't want to wear either, and that's making me even more angry.

I didn't pack for a one-on-one meeting with Luke Chalmers. I packed for... I don't know who... Just another client.

'What am I going to do?' I ask my best friend, slumping down onto the edge of the bed, rubbing my temples with my fingertips.

'First, you're going to take a deep breath, gorgeous. Come on, with me. In... and out... Feel better?'

'Mmm.' *Not really, though I'm grateful for Callum's effort.*

'Next, you're going to put on whatever fabulous workwear you've packed because you always look right on point for work – sophisticated, authoritative and hot. Then, you're going to look at yourself in the mirror and say, "Screw him". You're not dressing for him; you're dressing for yourself.'

'I can do that.' I stand with an infinitesimal amount more vigor.

With Callum still chatting down the line about a

guy he matched with on a dating app yesterday, I select a cream skirt and a sleeveless blouse, which ideally would have a roll-neck instead of a slightly too low V.

Once I'm dressed, I look at my reflection in the mirror and say, 'Screw you, Luke Chalmers. I'm dressing for myself.'

'See. One step at a time, babes.'

I nod at myself. 'What's next?'

Callum chuckles. 'Next, you go to your meeting, get your shit done, and come home to Eddie and me.'

With his words – and the thought of my comfiest clothes, a takeout, my own sofa and my favorite people – my body finally relaxes.

'Can't wait,' I tell myself, twisting my hair into a French roll and letting the shorter front ends fall loose.

* * *

Only when I'm ready for my meeting and carrying my laptop and relevant papers out of my pod does it occur to me that I don't actually know where on the island the meeting room is.

Lucky for me, Henry is waiting outside my door.

'Yikes!' I yelp, startled by his presence and wondering how long he's been outside, whether he heard my meltdown on the phone with Callum.

'Sorry, Carrie, I didn't mean to surprise you. Joe sent me to bring you to your meeting.'

He's dressed in his Charithonia uniform again – the daytime version with beige shorts and black polo – and wearing that dazzling smile he has that makes his white teeth seem bright against his sun-goldened skin.

'I appreciate it,' I say, pulling the door shut and, reluctantly, because I don't want to seem like a damsel in distress, allowing him to relieve me of my laptop.

'You look nice,' he tells me casually, as if he's very comfortable dishing out compliments.

I'm not so comfortable accepting them, so I ask, 'Where are we headed?'

Henry gestures along the pebbled walkway in the direction of the main house. 'There's a purpose-built office and meeting rooms behind the main house, next to the gym. Have you seen the gym yet? It's fully stocked.'

I'm certain he's familiar with the gym. He isn't muscly in that way a slightly older man can be but he's toned, for sure.

'No. Though I did have a short sea swim this morning.'

'The sea is sublime on a day like today.' *Sublime?* Not that he isn't right; it's just an odd choice of word. Then again, it suits his British accent. A bit Jude Law trying to impress on a first date. *Funny.*

'It was lovely.' Or it could have been, if the entire experience hadn't been ruined by Luke's presence. If my mind hadn't been boiling over with raging fury like a reluctantly pressure-cooked vegetable in a soup.

'The calm before the storm,' he says, raising one eyebrow.

For a moment, I think, *What have you heard?* Then I remember the conversation last night over dinner, about an *actual* storm.

'Do you think so? Should I be worried?'

He leans his head to one side. 'Yes. No.'

We walk past what looks like a small concrete utilities hut or pump house or similar with metal slatted doors, then reach a glass-walled building with a garden as a roof that makes the structure look like a little glass pop-up in an otherwise undisturbed nature conservation.

Henry holds open the front door for me to step inside and we walk along a tiled corridor, my nude heels ticking against the surface like a clock, taunting me with a countdown to a meeting I really don't want to go to. *Tick tock, tick tock.*

'I studied meteorology at university,' Henry tells me. 'I'm taking a break here, of sorts, earning some money to pay off my student debts and applying for weather jobs.'

We pass two fully kitted out office spaces, either side of the corridor, each with a desk three times the size of mine back in New York. On top of each of them are two large white computer screens and behind them, swanky cream leather chairs.

'But I don't need a post-grad to tell you that this is going to be a disastrous hurricane. It's all over the news now. Two of the three storms we were talking about at dinner last night have merged and it's a near mathematical certainty that the third will join.'

My feet have stopped moving. This is bad.

'Don't worry, though, we'll be safe, even if Isabel hits. Joe had this place built to withstand a cat five hurricane.'

Still not feeling terribly warm and fuzzy here.

'Under the main house, there's a bunker made of reinforced steel and concrete. It's the Hettich panic room. We'll ride her out down there.' He speaks with those curved lips and shiny white teeth showing again, like we're talking about a new rollercoaster at Disney Land.

Is he being flippant? 'This sounds horrific, Henry.'

'Cool, too, though, right? I mean, it'll be quite a story, seeing and surviving a cat five.'

While I'm proverbially scooping up my jaw from the floor, Henry continues forward, until he stops at another glass door, knocks twice and holds it open for me. 'It's this one,' he says, as if our life-threatening weather conversation didn't just happen.

'Ah, right.' Finally, my feet take instruction from my brain again, hurrying along to the door.

Inside, Joe Hettich is stretching by a wall of windows to the outdoors, wearing bright-pink sweatbands around his forehead and wrists, a lime-green running vest, and Lycra shorts. He pulls one foot behind him, up to his butt, and with his free hand, presses his index finger to his nose – *for balance?*

If I wasn't completely thrown by my conversation with Henry, I'm definitely bamboozled by Hettich's show.

I sense Luke's presence, see him like a shadow in my blind spot, but I don't acknowledge him.

'Thanks, H,' Joe tells Henry, who leaves, closing the door behind him. *Leaving* me. *Here.* With *these* two. 'Hey, Carrie. How did you sleep? Was everything okay for you?' He swaps legs to stretch his quads on the other side and I finally risk a quick glance at Luke, who is smirking. A smirk that feels less arrogant, more knowing, as if we're sharing an unspoken conversation. Like we used to. It's an expression that has the effect of liquifying me, like it used to.

Is this normal behavior? I ask with my eyes, hoping he can't see the tiny vibrations I'm feeling in my abdomen.

Happily, though, the distraction has momentarily made me forget that I don't want to be in the same room as Luke, and I respond to Joe. 'I slept well, thank you.'

It's an outright lie. I slept terribly – strange bed, yards from the man who shattered my heart, discombobulated from seeing him again, wishing I had turned down this trip and stayed home with Eddie, no matter what it might cost my career.

'The bed is extremely comfortable.'

Joe nods, as if he already knew the answer to the question. Then he stands on two feet again, reaches one arm up, plants his opposite hand on his hip, and starts tipping like a teapot, over and over, stretching his side.

'Luke tells me you took advantage of the beach this morning.'

'He did? Did he tell you he took advantage of the view, too?' I silently growl at Luke, *That's right, I know you were checking me out and you have no right speaking about me like you have anything to do with me, not in the slightest, not remotely, not at all.*

If I'm not mistaken, the skin of Luke's neck is deliciously taut and unusually flushed.

'There's nothing sweeter in life than an early morning sea swim in the Caribbean ocean,' Joe continues as if I hadn't responded to his question. 'The loves of my life aside, of course.' He starts jogging on the spot, knees high, and tells me breathlessly, 'It's relationships that make life. I feel qualified to say that.' He stills. 'When you've tasted the level of success and income I've had over the years, you learn that those things are nice, but connections to other humans, animals and life, that's why we're put on this planet.'

'Aren't you trying to put together a space program and move to Mars?' Luke asks. Despite myself, the question tickles me.

Give him his due, Joe's amused too. 'To make more connections, matey. Come on. Those were some heartfelt words I just spouted, let me have them.'

Some odd kind of exchange is happening between the men, but like Ella said last night and Luke just reminded me, men are from Mars, so...

I set my papers down on the large, shiny white oval desk and take my laptop out of its carrier, where Henry kindly left it on the table.

I'm busying myself with setting up, taking my fancy pen from my designer laptop case – both of which are things Callum bought me as special-occasion gifts. But I don't miss Luke rising from his seat and muttering, through gritted teeth, what sounds like, 'Is this your idea of playing it cool?'

In response – I see in my peripheral vision – Joe pats Luke on the arm and says, 'You'll thank me one day, friend.'

Then Luke moves to one end of the room and, casting my eyes in his direction, I see he's pouring coffees from a French press – *yes, please!* – while Joe hops (literally) to the exit.

'I trust you two will do good business, so I'll leave you to it.' Then he pulls the door closed behind him. Poking his head back through the narrow gap at the last moment, he adds, 'Don't kill each other.'

I gawp at the shut door. 'You told him?' I snap at Luke when I'm sure Joe is out of earshot.

He shrugs, breezy. All kinds of stupid effing breezy.

'He's my client, Luke, not a fucking therapist.'

He scoffs and I'd love to know what undertone he has now, but I'm too pissed to ask. 'Relax, almost-partner,' he says, sitting and sliding one of the coffees along to the seat perpendicular to his. 'I'm your client now and you've screwed me before, numerous times.'

Screwed? That word makes my stomach twist. Of course we were just *screwing* to him. That's why it was so easy for him to walk away.

He drags his fingers through his thick hair, which is already mussed up, as if he let it dry naturally after his dip in the ocean earlier.

'Joe's one of my oldest friends, Carrie. It's not like I've been making water-cooler gossip. He already knew about us.'

'There is no *us*,' I correct him, coming to sit in front of the coffee and adjusting my laptop position.

He sighs, maybe feeling an ounce of the exasperation I am. 'Fine. Our past, then. And, come on, didn't you tell anyone when we were together?'

'No!'

His vexation seems to be fleetingly – like, blink and you'd miss it – replaced by something else. *Hurt? Surprise?* But it's gone before I can decide. Maybe I imagined it.

'I told my mom,' I say, feeling a teensy amount bad about shouting.

'Your mom? Of all people, you told your mom?'

Yes, because I thought one day, you might at least meet her.

His shock speaks volumes.

'I did. And I should have listened to her because she told me not to get involved between a man and his wife.'

'We were separated,' he bites.

I ignore him because evidently, they weren't as separated as I thought. 'She said it would only end one way.'

I pick up my coffee, ready to end this conversation, and when I taste it, I realize he remembers how I like it – just a splash of milk and one sweetener.

'What way was that? With you blocking me and ignoring me for seven years?'

I did block him. Not that I knew he knew that. As for ignoring him – that would have required him trying to contact me, rather than moving states without even saying goodbye.

'No,' I tell him. 'With me getting hurt.'

Literally as soon as the words leave my mouth, I regret them. I feel rather than see his gaze trained on me and I daren't look up from my coffee. I daren't because with the word *hurt*, memories of those exact feelings have crashed over me like a wave and I don't want him to see.

I don't ever want him to know how much of a mess he left me in. How he has ruined me for all relationships since because I've never, not once, felt the kind of highs I felt when I was with him.

He rises from his seat, hands in pockets, and goes to the windows, looking out across the resort and to the vastness of the ocean.

9

LUKE

'Carrie, I think we need to make a pact. No personal talk, just business.'

I'm at my limit. *Damn Eric and his freaking gastroenteritis.* What I wouldn't give now for his offensively bellowing laugh and the way his lips make a wet clacking sound when he eats any kind of liquid food, especially breakfast cereal in milk.

I'm staring out of the window as I speak, wondering how in the world this woman is back in my life, us locked in a room together, trapped in a space so heavy with ill-will, it feels like a weight around my shoulders, bringing me down.

This is supposed to be the place I come to get happy. It's always been the place I can get away from life in New York, where I'm around the best friend who has seen me through the highs of winning college hockey games and the lows of deaths, break-ups, career slumps and taxes.

I guess Carrie ticks a few of those low boxes.

She told her mom? I can't remedy that with her cutting me out of her life the way she did. Telling your mom about your guy is serious. But she ghosted me, as if I was just someone she picked up on a dating app, went out with once, then tossed aside.

We might have been together for weeks but we knew each other for much longer. She might have been hurt by the way things ended and I get that, I was too, but I couldn't have stowed away my feelings as easily as she did. That's how I know definitively that she was never invested the way I was. It was one sided and it fucking killed me. It's *been* killing me for seven years.

There. I admit it. Are you happy, universe? Because I'm *happy*. At least I was just fine before yesterday.

'No personal talk, just business,' she says.

I turn from the window to see her chest rise and her shoulders roll back on her next breath.

It looks as if the tax advisor on the cusp of partnership has just showed up.

Excellent. Safe ground. No past, no bikinis, no... nothing.

'There've been recent changes to the tax laws in the Cayman Islands and Bermuda,' Carrie says, sipping her coffee and shuffling papers around the desk, as if we didn't just have as much of a heart-to-heart as we are likely to have *ever* from this day and forward.

Dismissive. She knows that game so well.

She turns in her seat until she's glaring at me. When I don't move, still trying to get any kind of a read on her but failing, she holds out her hands – *Are we doing this?*

I clear my throat. *Game face.* 'Changes we care about?'

She nods, twisting back in her seat to face the desk and her preparation. 'Absolutely. It's given me some ideas for how we could restructure the entire web of Hettich companies.'

'Let's hear it.'

'Could you come sit down, please? You're making me— You're straining my neck.' She speaks without looking at me, so I know I'm not straining her neck, but maybe I am making her nervous. Maybe the junior tutoring the senior is new and uncomfortable for her. Or maybe her dealing with the CFO of the

Hettich group is a big deal. Or maybe... maybe she's as disoriented by this whole unexpected experience as I am.

'Fine,' I say, shrugging. I don't want to sit. I have a weird energy that's making my legs twitchy. But I sit opposite her, trying to appear casual, while my hands are pressed to my thighs, stopping my legs from bouncing under the table.

For two hours, we – with mostly Carrie doing the talking – get lost in a hypothetical new-look Hettich empire. I test her and challenge her, asking questions at every feasible juncture and, damn her, she knows every answer, across all our jurisdictions. Or, at least, she's confident enough to make me believe she does.

At one point, I even start lapping the table, hands in pockets, umming and ahhing, neither confirming nor denying that I agree with her assessment, trying to throw her off. Yes, it's childish, but it doesn't work anyway.

I can tell from the way she side-eyes me as I wander the room that I'm irritating her, yet it doesn't mess with her mojo.

She's on fire. She's fucking brilliant at her job.

And it's as bittersweet as a candied lemon. On the one hand, I'm proud of her. My junior, whom I taught and supported, flourishing as a senior advisor. On the other hand, I'm annoyed that she's great. The woman who burned me. The woman for whom I killed my chances of partnership without thanks or even acknowledgment.

'I have another question,' I tell her. 'Some of our directors want to relocate and have a preference not to be flying back and forth to the Caribbean for board meetings. Does this new legislation have anything to say about that?'

She nods, sipping from the second coffee I've made her. Then she pulls up the relevant legislation on her laptop screen and points to it, right as my latest turn of the room brings me behind her chair. 'See this provision...'

I lean across her to read the words for myself, my hands braced either side of her on the tabletop. I haven't meant it to feel intimate, yet, as I read from her screen, the scent of her perfume mixed with something that's distinctly Carrie works its way into my bloodstream and travels straight to my hippocampus, and I'm thrust back to the first night we kissed.

We were in our office. New York City's skyline was dazzling through the window against the outside darkness, undisturbed by the dim lights inside.

It had been a long day and night, pulling the kind of hours that are unsustainable, for a significant client of mine.

Carrie asked me to review something she was drafting. I stepped from behind my desk and leaned across hers, just as I have done now. And just as she's doing now, her nearness, her scent, it infiltrated me, diverted my mind from what I was supposed to be doing.

As I looked to her, she glanced up to me, our faces inches apart, as they are now. Then we edged closer. First her, I think. Then me. A subconscious call and response. A reflexive move by my body that had thought about it for months. Until I was staring down at her soft pink lips, watching them slowly part, hearing her next shallow breath. Then I was kissing her. Slowly, tentatively. Nervously. Knowing it was wrong, unethical, but unwilling or unable to stop it.

Now, we're locked in a gaze, my heart hammering, making me feel like I've drunk ten coffees for breakfast, and I wonder if she's sharing the same memory as I am. Whether I'm having anything close to the effect on her that she's having on me.

Wondering whether she'll creep closer, if she'll

make the next move, and if she does, whether I'll stop it.

This is bad. This is dangerous. I'm being knocked senseless by her again, except this time, I already know how it ends.

'So, you're telling me I can't have all my directors sitting in the USA and claim the company is Cayman tax resident?' I croak, unsure whether my sentence is even coherent.

It's enough to break her hold over me, though. Her expression shifts from whatever it was, or what I imagined it was, to something cooler, safer.

'Not unless you want the next time you see me again to be seven years from your incarceration for tax evasion.'

I think she's deadly serious, until one side of her lips flutters, almost a spasm, then she smirks and I can't help but laugh. She follows my lead, until we're howling. Her holding her waist in her seat and me doubled over. There's no doubt that at some point, it becomes more about venting steam from a pressure cooker than the joke being funny.

Because whilst my imprisonment might be hilarious to her, to me, it's a lot less amusing.

'Ah, sorry to interrupt.'

Carrie's cheeks burn red at the sight of Alisha in the open doorway.

Our moment of liberation from the past is brought to an abrupt halt by Alisha's words, and it feels like we've been caught in the act... again.

We haven't, of course; we're just two people who can't stand each other, laughing about memories that haunt us, or something to that effect. I sober instantly but the burst of adrenaline I just got brought with it a reminder of excitement, salacious nights and stolen moments. Like an addict who's tasted their most haunting vice for the first time in a long time.

'You're not interrupting at all,' Carrie says, pushing out her chair and standing, almost to attention. 'I was actually thinking about stretching my legs for a few minutes, so I'll leave you guys to it.'

Just like that, she's gone, swept off on the Caribbean breeze. I watch the way her body moves, remembering it so well.

Quit it, Luke. Just goddamn stop with the flashbacks, the memories, the terrorizing yourself.

'Was I interrupting?' Alisha asks, stepping further into the room. She's dressed as if she's just come up from the beach – a sheer kimono over a bathing suit.

I shake my head. 'Not at all. She made a joke. Believe it or not.' I rub my freshly shaved chin. Carrie used to be funny. Hilarious, actually, but I've seen no sign of that humor in the last couple of days. Until that one wise crack. *Smart ass.*

'Mmmhmm.' Alisha folds her arms across her chest. 'Well, I just came on Noah's behalf to ask if you'll play soccer with him once your meeting is done. He wanted to come up here himself but I didn't think you'd thank me for allowing it, so this is the compromise. I only came in myself because it didn't look like much business was being done.' She raises one eyebrow.

'You've misread the room, trust me. Carrie and I are in a strictly business relationship these days.'

'Riiiiiight. You know she thinks you and I are together, don't you?'

Yes. And I have no intention of correcting her. 'I haven't noticed.'

'Yes, you have. It was plain as day at dinner last night.' She wags a brightly painted fingernail at me. 'Let me tell you, Chalmers, I won't be used as a rag-doll in whatever game of emotional intelligence this is.'

We're facing each other from opposite sides of the table. 'I can't help if Carrie jumps to conclusions,' I say. Then for my own benefit, I mutter, 'She's always been the same.'

Alisha plants her hands on her hips, looking as fierce as only she can. 'You need to tell her the truth.'

'Why do I?'

'Because you're not five years old and this isn't the school playground. If you don't correct her, I will.'

I reach for a tissue from a box on the desk and wave it in the air. I know Alisha well enough to know she doesn't bullshit, so I surrender. 'Can you give me today? Let me get through this meeting. I'll tell her tomorrow.' Because I fully intend to tell Joe I'm leaving the island *tonight*.

Alisha's bristles seem to soften. 'Why do you want her to think we're together? Are you trying to make her jealous? Are you trying to win her back?'

'Jealous? Back? Hell, no. You couldn't be further from the truth. In any event, she's seeing someone, shares a life and a dog with someone.'

She's moved on.

I'm pacing my side of the table, wound like a mechanical toy ready for release. When I find the words I'm searching for, I stop and once again face Alisha.

'Look, it's just safer this way. It's an insurmountable barrier, me being in a relationship, her being in a relationship. We've talked about it before; neither one of us would ever cheat.'

'If you hate each other, why do you need barriers between you?' Alisha asks a fair question.

'It's something that means we don't even have to get into what happened between us. You're a safe space.'

She comes to perch on the edge of the table. 'What exactly did happen between the two of you?'

I don't think I'm going to tell her, not the detail. But I find myself moving to the window, staring out to where I see Carrie wandering the terrace and talking into her phone, and words start tumbling out of me. How it all started between late nights and office flirting. The hotel rooms and the six weeks we dated in secret, having a crash course in getting to know each other because it was always just the two of us, hiding away in one of our apartments, eating, drinking, talking, making love, bathing together, dancing together, falling asleep in each other's arms.

'Then I got a message from Anya one day – a text message, would you believe? – and it said, "I'm pregnant", with an ultrasound picture. That was it.'

'I never knew that,' Alisha says.

I don't turn to look at her because I don't think I

want to see her expression, whether she's appalled that I was seeing someone so soon after Anya and I ended, whether she pities me because I fell for a girl like I'd never even fallen for the woman I married, then she was taken away by something that completely blindsided me.

'It threw me, completely. I didn't know what I was supposed to do and I couldn't process all my mixed emotions, let alone share them with Carrie. It was a mess I needed to get my head around.' I shake my head, dragging a hand through my hair. 'But I had no time because that same day, someone from work saw Carrie and me together and snitched to the partners. So I was called into an office and told either Carrie would be moved into a department she didn't want to be in, or I would have to leave the firm.'

I finally shift to see Alisha and find her attention fixed on me. 'That's...'

'I was on the cusp of partnership, so they wanted me to stay and Carrie would have ended up managed out, but I felt responsible for the mess. I was older, her mentor, I should have known better. I *did* know better but I just couldn't— Anyway, Anya had moved back to Chicago, to be near her parents, or so I thought, and I assumed she'd want to try to make a go of things for the sake of the baby.' I shake my head. 'It was an awful idea but I was all over the place and trying to do the right thing.'

'So what did you do?'

I shrug. 'I quit work and told them to keep Carrie but not tell her that I left so she could stay. I didn't want her to feel guilty or try anything stupid like quitting so they'd take me back.'

Only now, relaying it, I wonder if maybe I should have let them tell her because at least then she'd have known that I did it for her. Then again, it wouldn't have mattered. She was over us. Ready to pretend like we never happened.

I don't realize I've balled my hands into fists until my knuckles are hurting under the pressure. 'I went to Chicago, to do what I thought was decent. I tried to stay in touch with Carrie and explain everything but she ghosted me. Ignored every attempt I made because, I guess she'd just never bought in to us.' *Not the way I had.*

I grip the back of my neck, rubbing against the building pressure I feel. The heaviness of the time, the memory, the pain.

'Then fast-forward six months to a paternity test and, what do you know? The baby wasn't mine.' I shift along the wall of windows to continue watching

Carrie on the terrace, probably speaking to her significant other. 'We could have got back together but she made sure there'd never be a chance for us.'

I had no wife, no family, no job, no home and worst of all, no Carrie.

'You hurt her,' Alisha says emphatically.

I narrow my eyes on her. 'I messed up trying to do what I thought was right. But she shut us down completely.'

'I wasn't there, Luke, so I won't tell you what happened, but have you tried to sit in her point of view for a while?'

'She cut me out of her life, Alisha,' I snap unintendedly.

She reaches for a tissue and waves it as I did, in peace. I feel bad but I can't help how much of a trigger Carrie is for me.

'I'll leave you to it,' Alisha says, heading out. 'See you on the beach?'

I nod, too wound up for words.

By the door, she pauses to tell me, 'For the record, no woman refers to a man she loves as a co-doggy parent. I'm sure there's one less thing standing between you and Carrie than you think.'

10

CARRIE

The ocean is calm, a stark contrast to the way I'm feeling.

What just happened between Luke and me? That *look*... it was like... Never mind what it was like. What it *wasn't* was a *thing*.

Which doesn't at all explain why I'm feeling way hotter than the sticky Charithonia heat, which is a cool eighty-six degrees and about 99.9 per cent humidity. I fan myself, tugging the material of my blouse at the chest.

It isn't working, so I take out my phone and call Callum.

No answer. *Damn it.*

I glance back across my shoulder to the meeting

pod, making sure neither Luke nor his girlfriend have eyes on me. They don't, so I allow myself the indulgence of letting my hair down and tugging on the roots like a masseuse does during an Indian head massage, hoping it will yank some straight thinking into me.

Because the thing is, it's like everything I used to feel for Luke was there, in that one look, right there, for a heartbeat.

Like the way I felt relieved that he was giving training to a group of new associates the first time I met him, so I had an excuse for not being able to tear my focus from him. There was something about his voice that was smooth and confident, yet gravelly and manly all at once.

In the months that followed, when we were working in the same office, I'd pretend to be working on my own computer screen as I listened in to his calls with clients, not absorbing the substance of his words but just the way he conducted himself.

And later still, a year after we met, when I'd lie back on the sofa in his apartment, my legs across his thighs, his fingers gently, nonchalantly, massaging my ankles as he asked about my day, about my dreams and aspirations, about my upbringing. Just the two of us, hiding away from real life. I'd have divulged anything he wanted to know, the kind of top-priority state secrets people kill for, if I'd known any, because all I really wanted was for his words to wrap around me, for the light rough of his skin to move around my jaw, down my neck.

So now, standing on this terrace in paradise, like Eve who once ate the forbidden fruit, I'm scared. No, terrified, waiting for karma to bite again. I can't be here, physically, metaphorically. I can't be sent back to where he left me seven years ago. In pieces.

Bracing myself on the balcony of the terrace, I try a deep inhalation and exhalation. And again. And again.

When it doesn't work, I try to call the only other person who knows about Luke and me. Who *knew* about Luke and me when we were actually together.

I call my mom.

'Carrie! Where are you, what are you doing, and why?'

That's how Mom always answers the phone to me. It's not an interrogation, as much as a habit, lovingly meant.

'Well... I'm standing outside of a meeting room, having stepped out for air from my client, Luke Chalmers.'

'Okaaaaay.' She's distracted, doing something in

the background, shuffling things or picking them up. It sounds like her cell is wedged between her ear and her shoulder. 'Should I know who Luke Chalm — Luke? *Luke* Luke?'

'You remember him then?'

'Remember him? He broke my daughter's heart and ran off into the wind to let someone else put it back together again. Of course I *remember* him.'

I glance back to the meeting room, where I can see Luke is sitting on the tabletop, talking to Alisha, who is standing close by, listening intently. I wonder what they're talking about. I wonder how it looked when she walked in and we were laughing together.

I don't know that we were laughing *together* more than generally finding an outlet for some real pent-up pasts.

'Don't sugarcoat it, Mom, will you?' I ask, unable to stop watching the scene of domesticity in front of me. Hating the fact that I'm jealous of it.

Mom whispers something in the background. I think she might be in a coffee shop and ordering.

'Is now a bad time?' I ask.

'No, and don't you dare drop a bombshell and disappear like you usually do. There's a reason you called me, Carrie, and generally we know the answers to our questions before we ask them.'

'Please don't Psychology major me, Mom.' Mom is a part-time lecturer at NYU.

'I'm not Psychology-ing anything. But I *am* going to get a coffee to go and we *are* going to talk this out.'

I sigh but I think I'm relieved. Mom can generally stop me from spiraling and that's precisely what I need right now.

She moves through a hive of louder chatter, then it's quieter again and she asks, 'Why are you working with him again?'

'Urgh. Circumstances. He's the chief financial officer of one of the firm's clients and the client relationship partner is sick. Given I'm a big yes girl at the moment, I agreed to step in and didn't realize I'd be working with Luke until it was too late.'

'Excuse me, is anyone sitting here?' Mom exits stage left. 'Lovely, thank you. I'm Lily, nice to meet you.'

'Mom?'

'I'm here, honey.' And re-enters stage right. 'I have a seat next to a nice gentleman on a park bench and I'm all yours for the next... nineteen minutes until my next lecture.'

'Well, it shouldn't take that long. I've told you what's going on,' I say, rubbing my fingers over the shiny terrace rail. 'I don't even know why I called, really. I'm just— It's just that— Garghhhhh.'

'It's obviously a good thing that this is a one-off. You just need to power through, honey. Be your conscientious, professional self for the meeting, get the job done, don't engage with him in any matter that isn't business chatter and you walk away with your head held high. That man deserves nothing more.'

I nod, I think reassuring myself because Mom certainly can't see or hear it. 'You're right. I can do this.'

'For sure you can, honey. You're stronger than you think. You've got this.'

'Enough with the affirmations, Mom.'

'Sorry, darling. Habit.'

I sigh, not really meaning to but defaulting to being a daughter, Mom's little girl, anyone I need to be and want to be because I can be myself. 'He isn't married anymore. Not to the woman he was, anyway,' I tell her. 'He doesn't have any kids, either. Not that either thing matters. And he is seeing someone; he has a girlfriend.'

'Carrie.' Mom's tone is warning. 'You shouldn't care one way or the other. You need to let nasty sleeping mongrels lie.'

I might laugh if I didn't feel so flat. 'I don't care.'

He has a girlfriend and even if he didn't, I could never forget and certainly couldn't forgive what he did to me.

Yes, I ghosted him, I moved home, I changed as much about myself as I could. The only thing I kept was my job and that was the beginning of a battle of having to prove myself indefinitely. But it was all because of him *running*, using me and leaving me.

He went back to his wife and moved state. He never stuck around so we could get through the backlash of being outed at work together. A text message, that was all I got. A text message to tell me his wife was pregnant and he was going back to her.

Couldn't we have legitimized our relationship if there had been longevity in it?

That's the point, isn't it? We *could* have stuck it out, fought to have something. If I'd been asked back then, maybe I would have quit my job if it meant we could be together.

But he didn't give me a choice. He didn't give us a chance. He was so quick and desperate to go back to his wife.

'It's just...' I say. 'He loved her enough to go back and she was having his child. So why no wife now? Why no child?'

Now Mom sighs. 'I don't know, Carrie. Maybe he

left them both. Is that the kind of man you want to be with?'

She means a man like my dad. Though ironically, he did stick around until I went to college. He stayed for too long and I was brought up around arguments and slamming doors for the whole of my teenage years. These days, Mom pretty much resents that men exist as a species.

'But he seems so good with kids.'

With Noah and Toby, even Char and Sanza. I truly thought he was a father.

I also thought I was internalizing that nugget, but Mom responds as if I said it aloud.

'Honey, has it occurred to you that maybe there never was a child? That he had his fun with you and wanted the excuse to go back to his wife or just end things with you?'

'Ah… I… It hadn't, no. Not until you just said it.'

Make up a baby? He wouldn't have. Couldn't have.

Could he? He was always so honest. 'I'll tell you anything you want to know, Carrie; all you have to do is ask,' he once said to me as we lay propped on pillows, facing each other in bed. I remember wanting to ask him, Do you still love her, your wife? But the words never left my mouth.

If I had a time machine, would I go back and ask the question? Would I want to know the answer? Or would I want those six weeks we spent together to be as they were: blissfully ignorant of what was on the horizon?

'You can't trust a man like that and I should know.' She's referring to Dad, again – her own Achilles' heel. Dad strayed in the later years they were married and though only small amounts of detail have been drip-fed through heart-to-hearts and generally when Mom needs to find a bad example of a man, I know that he met someone else – at work, as it happens – and after months of adultery, Mom considers that the catalyst for the end of their marriage.

Me? I think it was cowardly and wrong, but I'd witnessed everything else that had led up to that point over the years preceding, coming like a heavy-laden freight train, agonizingly slowly down the tracks. Still, Dad's affair shocked me because that part I hadn't seen coming. That part, I would never have guessed from the man I loved so much.

'I know. I know, Mom. I do. I don't think Luke would have had a lie as big as a fake pregnancy in him, but he certainly pulled the wool over my eyes, so... maybe.'

Maybe all the romantic nights, the pillow talks, the stolen touches, the hip grazes and shoulder skims in meeting rooms and communal office spaces, all the glances that held heat and promise, were part of a big, ugly hoax.

I wish I had my shades with me because my eyes are stinging as I search the expanse of Caribbean Sea to find some strength. I can't be back here, in this dark place.

'Let's talk about this in person,' Mom says, as if she's a voice inside my head. 'I'm coming into the city tomorrow. Can we do lunch?'

'Erm, actually, no because I'm not in New York, I'm in the Caribbean, on Joe Hettich's private island.'

'Joe Hettich! *The* Joe Hettich?'

Remarkably, I chuckle at her reaction.

'The very same. Luke is his CFO.'

'Would it be terribly unprofessional to get a signed copy of his biography for— Wait, honey, do you know there's a superstorm coming to the Caribbean? Haven't you been watching the news?' Her pitch rises to the extent that I have to flick the volume down on the side of my phone.

'I do know but I've been assured it won't hit the island. Apparently, this is a regular spoof in hurricane season out here.' As I'm talking, I see Joe – no longer clad in bright sweat bands but now wrapped in an equally offensive sarong, hairy pecs everywhere – bounding up the steps toward the main house. 'Mom, I've got to go. You've been a huge help. I'm very clear on what I need to do. Thank you and I love you.'

'Joe!' I call before I've even hung up the phone. I wave to grab his attention, as if my shout into the serenity of paradise wasn't startling enough. 'Do you have a second?'

'Ahoy, matey!' Joe calls in a pirate voice. He slows his run and takes a few steps in my direction, though still far enough away from where I'm standing on the terrace that I need to speak loudly.

'Things are going really well with, ah, Luke.' His name feels like dirt in my mouth after my call with my mom. More so even than it has for the last two days, if that's possible.

'Glad to 'ear it, matey.' Gosh, this man is a lot. 'It'll make for more fun tomorrow. The seas will be calm and we'll set sail at two bells forenoon.'

What the actual fuck?

'Pardon?'

'I think it means 9 a.m. but me pirate speak is rusty. Nothing a drop of rum in me tum won't fix. Arghhhh.'

'Right, ha.' I genuinely try to laugh, to be civil, but this guy is so nuts, I don't know if I manage. 'Actually, about tomorrow. Or tonight, even—'

'Whoops, I'll be late for the masseuse. Let's pick this up later.' He starts galloping, *galloping* away toward the main house. Do pirates... *gallop*?

'Joe, it's just that I'd really like to...' He's out of sight. 'Leave this goddamn island,' I mutter to myself.

11

LUKE

'I had some calls to make,' Carrie says when she comes back into the meeting room, where I'm now alone and sitting back in my seat next to hers. 'Shall we get back to it?'

I feel my eyes narrow on her. Something's happened. There's a shift in her mood from the woman who was laughing half an hour ago, though probably just back to the ice-queen version of her that I thought for a moment might be thawing under the Caribbean sun.

'I ordered us lunch,' I say, internally smug because I add, 'Sushi but no sashimi salmon, only tuna. No egg and extra ginger.'

As fleeting as the break in her façade is, I notice

it. *Yeah, I remember that too.* She hates the texture of raw salmon. She likes eggs but hates omelets with sushi. And though we debated it every time we ordered in sushi to my place or for supper on late nights working in the office, she uses pickled ginger as a side to her meal, rather than a palate cleanser.

'I'll take mine to go once we're finished here.' She takes her seat and starts fidgeting with things on the desk, shuffling pages this way and that. 'I'd rather plough on and get this done.'

I roll my jaw tightly. 'Thank you, Luke, for being so thoughtful. I *am* hungry and I appreciate your efforts.' My words drip in sarcasm like syrup from a pancake as I twist my pen through my fingers, back and forth.

She glowers at the pen until the force of her silent insistence makes me still. 'You didn't make the sushi, Luke; you made a request.'

A thoughtful request. 'Let me ask you something, Carrie. When did you last let your hair down?'

Finally, she looks up from the pen I've pressed to the desk and tells me, 'My hair is down.'

Literally speaking, she's got me there. Figuratively, I'd bet she wouldn't know relaxed if it bit her on the ass.

She wouldn't recognize the girl who sat astride

me on my sofa and set down a challenge to see which of us could eat the most wasabi paste before crying tears of menacing green heat.

* * *

'Luke!' Noah shouts when he sees me heading down the steps to the beach where he and his siblings are playing. The dogs stand from where they were lying in cool sand where they've dug divots. Jessie bounds toward me and Woody stands his ground, barking at me, though his wagging tail is betraying him – he likes me.

'Hey, girl.' I bend to scratch Jessie's ears, just the way she likes it.

'Luke, Aunty Alisha said you'll play football with me,' Noah says. He means soccer, but Joe is a Brit who loves his football and outright refuses to call it by its name, no matter how many times he's confused the heck out of me.

I really can't be bothered. I feel physically and mentally drained after being locked in a room with Maleficent all day.

I was so tempted to eat her lunch out of spite, but I managed to get a handle on myself long enough for her to ask for it to be refrigerated and brought to her pod later.

But I need to set it all aside, shake it off, because I don't get to hang out with my godson as much as I'd like. So, I ruffle his thick mane of dark hair, just like I did Jessie's ears, and tell him, 'Absolutely, buddy, that's why I'm here.'

Ella and Alisha are digging holes with the two girls and I end up drawing out a soccer pitch by dragging my feet through the sand. As I'm doing so, Henry and Jenny (water crew), Glen (gardener), Roy (handyman) and Dionne (housemaid) appear with Joe, already roped into the game with Noah, Toby and me, so we have one team of four and one of five.

It occurs to me for a nanosecond that maybe we should have invited Carrie down to the beach with us. Not that I knew everyone would be here, but since we are, I don't want her to feel like an outsider. If nothing else, she could have evened out the numbers.

She used to play lacrosse in college and was always pretty handy in corporate sports events at our firm. Though, who knows if she'd play these days. It'd be hard to run around with a metal stanchion up one's ass.

Almost reflexively, I locate her pod on the hill,

any shred of compassion I fleetingly felt gone. She was horrible today. I don't want to use the B word, but she was acting like a gigantic B word.

'She's having some food, then she's getting a massage,' Joe tells me, trying and failing miserably at doing keepy-uppies with the soccer ball.

'Who?' I ask, stroking my neck as I feign nonchalance.

'The woman you're pining after,' Joe says, now trying to flick the ball from the sand with his feet and ultimately kicking sand over Ella and his youngest, receiving a verbal battering from his wife in response. No one puts Joe in his box quite so well as Ella. She's whip-smart and razor tongued.

Once everything has calmed, I tell him, 'There is *no* pining happening from anyone, to anyone, by anyone. Carrie's my distant past and very much not my present or future.'

'Riiiiiight, yeah.' He picks up the ball and starts jogging with high knees to the center of our small pitch. 'Funny how you know who I'm talking about.'

I follow him and snatch the ball from his arms, handing it to Noah, who's waiting on the center spot opposite Henry for kick off.

'It doesn't take a rocket scientist, Joe.' I'm rattled

because I'm rattled and it's plain as day that I'm rattled.

Maybe *I* need a massage.

'How come she's having a massage?' I ask, receiving the ball from Henry and passing it with the side of my foot on to Noah, whist Toby tries to intercept but instead falls in a heap on the sand, jumps up, brushes himself off, and keeps on running. He has Joe's unrelenting energy.

Jenny has taken the ball from Henry and passes it to Joe, who dribbles toward me. I soften my knees, ready to tackle him.

'Because she wants to leave and Greta was still around after my massage earlier, so I persuaded Carrie to have a treatment, relax and think on it. I can't get the jet down from New York until tomorrow anyway, and there isn't a commercial flight sooner.'

He kicks the ball, hoping to find Roy, but I stick out a foot and take it back, dribbling until I can kick it through the air toward Dionne, who uses her hands to catch it and bring it down to her feet.

'Daddy! Dee touched it with her fingers!' Toby shouts.

'Don't worry about it, buddy. You get a free pass now to touch it with your fingers too. Use it to your advantage,' Joe tells his son. Then to me, he says,

'She blamed wanting to leave on the storm but I'm pretty sure the only storm in her teacup is you, big fella.'

The ball comes to me from Glen and I steady it beneath one foot, unable to play and think at the same time. 'So she's leaving tomorrow now? Instead of Friday?'

I don't know why I feel blindsided by this but I do. It's a good thing. A great thing. All my issues with her can depart on the plane she leaves on. Fly away and disappear into the clouds, just like she did last time.

'You bothered?' Joe asks.

'Paha. No.' I sound as petulant as Toby. 'It's not that I'm bothered. It's just... she was supposed to be here until Friday, that's all. Something might come up, from our meeting today. I might think of something, a question, and it's always easier to bat these things out face-to-face.'

'Aha, yeah.'

As I glower at Joe, Toby sneaks up behind me and kicks the ball from under my foot, but Noah steals it from him and is running with it toward our goal line. Jenny darts forward to play keeper.

'Well, I haven't put the wheels in motion to get the jet, yet.'

Great, now I look like I want him to keep her here.

'Yeah, well, you should. Good riddance. Get Eric back.'

I like Eric. Balding head, hairy neck poking out of the top of his crinkled shirts, pretentious yet dull man with whom I have no past and in whom I have no romantic interest.

Noah scores and everyone on the beach cheers, regardless of whose side we're on. He runs by me and I offer him a fist pump.

We take the ball back to the center and kick off again. Toby wins the kick-off but his time with the ball is short-lived because Noah tackles him and kicks the ball to Henry, who passes to me. I pass back to Noah, who runs around Joe, leaving him tangled in his own feet and falling on the floor.

I hotfoot it to the other end of our pitch, out on the sideline nearest the sea, the hillside and resort in my view. I shout for the ball, arms in the air. Noah passes to Henry.

Then I'm stunned to stationary, rooted to the spot, arms frozen in the air, by the sight of a tall red-haired woman, with curves everywhere a man could wish for. She steps out of her infinity pool and onto the decking of her pod, overlooking the beach and our game, wearing only an emerald-green bikini, her long wet locks flowing down her naked shoulders.

Bam.

'What the fuck?' I'm struck flush in the face by the soccer ball. My legs buckle beneath me and I'm left in a heap on the floor, holding my nose.

'Watch your language!' Ella shouts, not at all concerned that I might have broken my nose.

I can hear Noah and Toby laughing as I groan and roll onto my back, opening my eyes to see Henry hovering over me. 'Sugar, sorry, Luke. You asked for the ball.'

'Is it broken?' I ask, daring to peel my hand away from my nose. Thankfully, my shades have remained intact, though their digging into my nose hasn't helped.

'Men,' Jenny says, now also leaning over me, hands on hips. 'It's a soccer ball, not a shot put. You're fine.'

I feel myself scowling. Maybe she's right, my nose is unlikely to be broken, but my pride... I can only bear to look through one eye up to Carrie's pod. She's no longer there and I really hope she didn't see.

It's not like I was ogling. I was just... distracted. Any normal human being would see movement overhead and take in his surroundings. It's... astuteness.

'Don't worry,' Joe says, offering me a hand to help me up. 'She only laughed for a minute.'

Ignoring his hand, I let my arms fold across my face as I moan. 'Hettich, I need to get off this island.'

'Not you too. How many massages is this old flame going to cost me?'

Then he walks away and I know there's no getting out of this. Tomorrow, I'm going sailing with Carrie. Stuck together in an ever-smaller paradise.

Fan-fucking-tastic.

12

CARRIE

'You feel very tense, Carrie,' Greta says as she digs the heel of her hand into the really painful space between my scapula and spine.

You don't say, is what I'm thinking. But politeness dictates I respond with, 'Oh really?'

I had a dip in the infinity pool whilst the masseuse was setting up in my pod and I was doubled over in hysterics watching Luke get walloped in the face by a soccer ball. I could hear Taylor Swift in my mind bellowing out the lyrics to 'Karma'.

Still, not even that release could untie the knots in my shoulders, which is hardly surprising, since Joe basically told me I'm in Alcatraz for at least the next twenty-four hours until he can get a jet here to pick me up because even if I find some convoluted commercial route to get home, I need him to at least get me to Tortola.

I wince as Greta digs deeper into the irritable muscle. 'You have a myofascial trigger point here,' she says. 'You hold your stress in your shoulders.'

I'm sure I hold it everywhere, I think as I go rigid with each grind of her knuckles deep under my skin. There's not a part of me that isn't trying to curl into the fetal position to stop the pain.

'Greta, would you mind going a little easier on me? I'm a big baby when it comes to pressure. I'm all about the relaxation.'

'Sure, sure. It's your massage; you tell me how you like it.' She softens her touch and adds more oil, now gliding her hands across my back, exposed by the towel that she's folded down to the globes of my ass.

I'm on a massage bed on the veranda of my pod and through my cushioned face cradle, I can see the orange hue from the setting sun reflecting on the edge of my infinity pool. It's a luxury to have an out-door massage, hearing the sound of the ocean and chirping birds, the air still warm on my skin, incense burning around me, hanging in the still, humid air.

'That's amazing,' I mutter, my body finally relenting, relaxing for what feels like the first time in weeks. Possibly months. Suddenly remembering that I haven't taken a break from work in... I can't even remember how long.

My eyes tire of watching the gentle swish of the pool water, my eyelids closing under a hefty yet invisible weight. Greta takes heated stones from somewhere and with one in each hand, slides their hot, smooth surface across my oiled body.

I drift to somewhere semi-lucid. Not awake, nor asleep. *Mmmmmm...* it's so good.

I could count on my fingers the number of massages I've had in my life. I try to place them – the location and when – but my mind is slipping into somewhere it doesn't want to be challenged.

Falling deeper, enjoying being indulged, one memory preys on my weakness. I was lying tummy down on Luke's bed, a sheet barely there between our naked bodies. He was straddling me, his weight across me, as his oiled hands moved down my neck, thumbs teasing my collarbones, across my shoulders, along my spine, around my hips, tantalizingly close to where he was making me hottest.

He was exploring my skin, moving with the ease of silk, the warmth of velvet, and I was relishing his touch. We hadn't been seeing each other long and when he suggested massages, I'd expected to feel exposed, vulnerable, but I didn't. I felt wanted, cherished, when his pupils widened until all but a slither of blue outlined the darkness at the sight of me nude, as his fingers lingered on areas of my body that no one else had ever uncovered.

He brought goosebumps to my skin, my entire nervous system reacting to what felt like a deliciously teasing warm-up to the main event.

His hands moved down to the small of my back, his thumbs rolling over my plump flesh, masked by only his thin cotton sheet. He rolled his hips so that I could feel him against me, feel that he was gearing up for something more too.

As he drew his palms up each of my vertebrae one-by-one, his body followed, until his torso was pressed to my back and his lips connected with the sweet spot just below my ear lobe.

I could feel that he'd hardened against me, I felt his breath like fire on my neck, and I groaned with desire.

'Luke...' As his name leaves my tongue, I remember where I am. Mortified, my eyes fly open and I spring up on the massage bed. 'Holy crap, sorry, Greta. I— Oh God, this is humiliating.'

If I were a man, there'd be a very stiff rod between my legs right now. If there is one thing I can be grateful for in this hideously embarrassing moment, it's that I am *not* a man.

Greta is giggling behind her fingertips. 'Don't worry about it, girl. It happens all the time. You're relaxed and massage can evoke happy memories.'

Happy? More like X-rated.

I hide my face in my hands, now sitting on the bed, hot stones on the floor around us where they've fallen from my back.

'It wasn't... you know... how it sounded,' I bullshit, knowing Greta can see right through me.

She waves a hand. 'Lie back down and have your happy moment, girl.'

I shake my head profusely. 'I can't.'

'Yes, you can. You deserve it. You won't let yourself fall asleep again, anyway. We can talk if you want to.'

'I...' Am sitting on a bed naked but for a towel over my lady parts, so actually, the lesser of evils is to lie back down and spare my further embarrassment. 'Okay.'

If nothing else, I like the happy drawl of her accent, how her words bounce rhythmically and her 'r's are exaggerated. There's a hominess about it.

Greta moves onto my arms and I keep my focus

firmly on what is happening in the present, until she asks with a coy tone, 'So Luke, huh?'

I bite my lip, bringing my free hand to my forehead. 'Please don't tell him.'

She chuckles. 'What happens on the massage table stays on the massage table. Honestly, with the stories I have, I should write a book.'

13

CARRIE

It's Wednesday morning.

The dawn of more enforced fun with Luke et al.

Can't wait. Thought no jaded ex ever.

Said no woman who has ever been dumped on her ass by a man she was head over heels for when being forced onto a boat with zero escape other than jumping overboard. *Ever.*

At least last night I was permitted to dine alone after my simultaneously glorious and hideously awkward massage, then spend an hour soaking in my heated infinity pool, alone, listening to the sound of the sea lapping onto the beach below and splashing against the rocks at the edges of the bay.

Now, though, I need to be seen to be sociable

with my client and his family and friends. While also being seen in business mode.

Joe Hettich might know I had a blip in the past with his best friend, but I was a young woman then. Today, I'm older, significantly wiser and more successful.

I will *not* under any circumstances go there again.

I will *not*, unequivocally will *not*, mess up my chances of partnership by falling for Luke's charm.

So, I'm sitting on a table on the terrace of the main house, drinking coffee from a French press and enjoying a plate of exotic fruits, waiting for a mushroom omelet. My laptop is open on the table in front of me as I work on the tax paper I agreed to prepare for Hettich following yesterday's long meeting with Luke. He is my client, after all, and though I'm reluctant to acknowledge it, for this week, he's sort of my boss, again.

But when it comes to our, *my*, personal life, *I* am 100 percent in control.

Jessie is lying by my feet, intermittently shuffling and rubbing her fur against them, most likely doing what Eddie does and making sure I don't forget she's there if I have any food going spare.

I'm wearing a long white and blue striped linen

dress with capped sleeves. It's one that always makes me feel elegant but is very weather appropriate. So much so, I've rarely worn it since I bought it a couple of years ago.

I plaited my hair wet after showering because even though it's not yet 9 a.m., it's too hot and humid to contemplate a blow dryer. Pointlessly, because I'm wearing large cat's eye shades, I have on a smidge of eye make-up, but I'm otherwise covered in sunscreen all over.

I've been chatting with the staff as they come and go. Henry and Jenny came to the terrace for a light breakfast before heading down to the beach to start preparing for our sailing trip today. I can see them lugging cooler boxes down the steep steps and across the sand, then they jump in a speedboat like the one they drove to collect me from Tortola, and disappear around the rocks, out of sight, presumably to the larger boat we're sailing today.

It all feels very *Below Deck*. If I forgot that Luke would be on the boat too, I could almost be excited. Callum would be utterly giddy with the build-up of it all, I'm sure. I do wish I could treat him to a visit like this for being an insanely great best friend but, truly, even if I make partner, a resort like Joe's *home*, kitted out with all of his toys, would be hugely beyond my or even our means.

I start pulling together a flow diagram of how the new Hettich business structure would look with my suggested changes – navigating those little boxes is not my forte, but I'm managing – intermittently breaking the frustration of tiny text boxes by eating otherworldly sweet slices of mango, and dragon fruit that actually tastes of something, rather than the bland stuff in the stores of Manhattan.

Life ain't too shabby...

Until it's ruined by Luke's arrival, swanning onto the terrace like he doesn't have a care in the world, as if *he* owns the place. All butt-hugging shorts and muscle-stretched t-shirt, sexy aviators and shower-wet hair.

Makes me... sick. Completely, totally and utterly... ogling. I mean, sick.

I watch him surreptitiously, my eyes on him from behind my shades, my body fully angled toward my laptop but the allure of him impossible to ignore.

Unfortunately for him, his lenses aren't dark enough for me to miss his double-take in my direction and I don't miss the falter in his step as, I'd guess, he ponders whether to sit with me.

I nudge my laptop further away from me, so that

it is fully intruding on the space that's set for breakfast opposite me on my table.

No. Thank. You.

I'll eat alone. As I did for weeks, months, after you.

Of course, he does the next worse thing. He sits on the adjacent table and on the opposite side of his table from me, so we're facing each other anyway.

He too sets the laptop I didn't realize he was carrying on the table and opens it to work.

I focus intently on my screen, chastising my eyes every time they betray me and flick his way.

'Morning, Luke. Would you like coffee?' Dionne, the woman asking the question, is something of a waitress, chambermaid and handywoman combined, as far as I can gather, and lives on Charithonia with her husband Glen, who is also a handyman, as well as a gardener. I know this because we've been chatting.

See, I am sociable when I actually have an interest in people. In fact, I'm always sociable, often too polite to avoid conversation even if I'm feeling grouchy. Just not when it comes to my arch enemies.

I'm spared eavesdropping into Luke's breakfast order by my cellphone screen coming to life. Rachel, the big boss, is calling me.

'Rachel, hi,' I say, slipping out from behind my

table and moving farther along the terrace, farther away from Luke. When I've exhausted the space I can put between us, I turn to rest back against the balcony rail and ask Rachel, 'How are you?'

As I do, I see Alisha, looking as glamorous as ever, figuratively gliding on the air toward Luke and pulling out the chair opposite his.

I am such an idiot.

He wasn't sitting on the next table over to put distance between him and me. He was sitting at the next table so that he could enjoy breakfast with his girlfriend.

And more than I hate my own stupidity, I hate the irrational disappointment I feel.

'Carrie? Are you still there?'

'Yes!' I say, too zealously, like I've been caught red-handed doing something... bad. 'It's going well, Rachel. I had a very productive meeting with the CFO yesterday and I'm pulling together a tax report for him and Mr Hettich.'

'Ah, you had a good meeting with Luke Chalmers?' There's something peculiar about her tone, almost like a teenage girl teasing another about a crush.

My mind is really playing tricks on me now.

Rachel knows nothing about my past with Luke. We're friendly colleagues, rather than friends.

I need to get out of this situation asap, before I really lose my mind.

'We had some very sensible discussions about the new rules in the Cayman Islands and I suggested a company restructure. I'll obviously let Eric see the report before it goes to the client. Since, ah, presumably, he'll step back in as soon as he's well and able?'

Please, say yes.

'Great. And are you okay, Carrie?'

'Me?' Bizarre. 'Yes, sure.'

'You know the storm that's heading your way is all over the news here,' she says.

Ah, she means the storm. Of course she does.

'It was never part of the plan that you would get caught up in a storm,' she continues.

'None of this was planned, Rachel. You couldn't have predicted Eric being sick, or the storm. And it's... stunning here. I'm having a, ah, nice time. Lots of business but in a beautiful place.'

If only the man who smashed my heart to smithereens wasn't here too.

'As for the storm,' I continue, 'apparently, it still might not hit the island. Even if it does, I spoke to

Joe about it yesterday, and whether I should, ah, leave the island.'

Because I can't stand another minute in Luke Chalmers's company.

'He assured me that he has a large, reinforced steel and concrete shelter under his house, which is big enough for all of us to weather the storm, so to speak. Animals too, he said. So you've no need to worry. I'll be back in New York and back to the office in no time.'

'Okay, Carrie. It sounds like you have everything in hand. Great work. Keep me posted on how things progress over there, won't you?'

'Sure, will do. Have a great day, Rachel.'

14

LUKE

'It's your call, boss,' Henry is saying, clearly holding back on his true feelings as he speaks – his voice reflective of the position of his shoulders up by his ears, contrary to his words.

I've walked into the bar on the terrace to meet the others and head down to the beach, where we'll tender out to Joe's superyacht.

'Look, Henry...' Joe says, his hand on his shoulder in a rare show of tenderness – not that he isn't a big bundle of gooey soft-center, he is, but he doesn't often show it so openly with his staff. 'The sea's calm today, so let's enjoy her. We have hurricane provisions fully stocked and fuel for the island's generators. If Isabel doesn't change course overnight, then I promise we'll spend all day tomorrow preparing for her visit on Friday.'

Henry nods, clearly still worried about the hurricane. I won't lie, I am too. This morning, the news said Isabel is definitely going to be a category five hurricane when she makes landfall, wherever she makes landfall. They're predicting gusts of up to 285 kilometers per hour, and they still think she's bound for the Leeward Islands.

This won't be like the tropical storms Joe and I have ridden out before during summer breaks from college and work trips to the Far East. They were menacing level get-in-my-path-and-I'll-make-those-unsteady-drunk-legs-even-wobblier, but Isabel, if she comes, wherever she comes, will be menacing level so-much-as-look-at-me-and-I'll-eat-you-alive.

'Okay, boss,' Henry says.

'Henry, everyone on this island is family to me. I won't let anything bad happen. We have one of the safest bunkers in the Caribbean, enough rum to sink a pirate ship and a fresh pack of playing cards. There couldn't be anywhere better than Charithonia to weather this big lady, I'm telling you.'

I clear my throat. 'Sorry to interrupt.'

'Chalmers! You set?' Joe asks, holding out his

arms so that his pineapple and frangipani-emblazoned shirt fully opens to his chest of thick hair.

'Sure am,' I say as Alisha and Ella, four bouncing kids and two tail-wagging dogs come onto the terrace. The women are laden with bags and brightly colored inflatables – crocodile, flamingo, unicorn and dolphin – which they dump down onto the deck with a thud.

'I'll take these down to the tender,' Henry says, already getting on with the task.

'Where's your stuff?' Ella asks me.

I shrug and hold my hands out, proving that I've turned up for the day in a pair of aqua-blue swim shorts, a white t-shirt and a pair of Havaianas. 'The boat's already got everything I could possibly need and the great company is coming with me.'

'Oh, you're having one of your charismatic moods this morning. Your mother really should have spelled your name with an r, shouldn't she, Chalmers?' Alisha jokes. 'Speaking of charming people,' she adds, coming to my side and nodding in the direction of Carrie, who is approaching, wearing a wide-rimmed beige hat and a short black cover up that could just as easily pass for sophisticated or sexy-as-sin. 'Have you told her that we aren't together yet?'

'Huh?' My mind has blanked. I freaking hate myself for it but it's true. In her dress, Carrie's legs go on for days and her plump, firm breasts are framed by the neckline of the material. As much as I wish that Alisha making me realize that Carrie is single yesterday had no effect on me, it seems to have obliterated the dam that was controlling my salacious thoughts. 'I— Ah— Pardon?'

As Carrie slips briefly out of view to come through the arch from the walkway onto the terrace, Alisha places the tip of her finger under my chin and closes my mouth for me. 'Drooling isn't a good look on any man, honey, charming or not.'

I look her way. 'I'm not *drool*ing. I was just—'

'Yeah?'

Carrie briefly stops to ruffle Jessie's – then impatiently attention-seeking Woody's – furry ears before heading our way. *What's so good about her, traitors?* I purse my lips, scowling at the dogs as I silently fume at their betrayal. Just like everyone else around here, they seem to think the sun shines out of her ass.

She duped me once too.

I notice the large, overfilled beach bag she's carrying by her side.

'I was just wondering how much stuff one

woman can need for a day on the ocean,' I end up jibing to spare myself.

Carrie throws daggers at me with her eyes, her cupid's bow tightly creased. 'I didn't know what the itinerary would be, so I brought some options,' she says, looking at the others apologetically as she meekly justifies the excessive luggage. I sort of feel bad. In a very miniscule way.

Alisha steps toward Carrie and loops an arm through hers. 'Don't you know it's rude to ask a lady what's in her bag?' she says, playfully glowering at me. 'Come on, Carrie, let's head on down to the beach now that we're all here.' She takes Carrie's bag and swings it back at me, narrowly missing my crotch with the heavy load, and only because I jump back out of range. 'You can make yourself useful,' she says.

Admonished like a child the same age, I end up with Noah on my back and carting Carrie's ridiculously, needlessly hefty pack-up down to the beach for the tender.

With the help of Henry and Security Dave and Security Thom – two of three security guys who follow Joe and the family wherever they go – we get Ella and the kids, Joe and Alisha, over the inflatable sides and into the dinghy first. Then we wrestle the dogs in and there's no space left, so Carrie and I wait for a second run.

Carrie and me. On a beach. Alone. In paradise. And she looks freaking great. Any other man would be thrilled with this outcome.

But this man, me, is both hated and hates.

'Did you have to try to ridicule me like that?' Carrie snaps once we've waved the tender around the rocks and out of sight.

'I was joking around, Carrie. Jesus, you used to be fun.'

Despite the breeze blowing her long hair in a way that shields her face from me standing next to her, and despite the fact she has big shades covering her eyes, I know she's glaring at me.

'He's my client, Luke. I need to be professional about this whole...' She motions back and forth between us.

'Ghost of girlfriends past?' I offer.

'Shit show,' she corrects.

Now I'm a shit show. *Nice.* 'I see.'

'See what?' she bites, now turning to face me.

'You only have professional boundaries when it suits you. Being professional never bothered you when there were lines you wanted to cross.'

She gasps. '*Me?* Right, because me, your junior,

led you on, flirted and taunted you until you had no self-control and you were forced to cheat on your wife.'

Red mist washes over me instantaneously with her words. '*Cheat?* I would never cheat. *Never.* I've seen the mess that does to a relationship. I saw my own father do it more times than I can count and I am *not* him. And for your information, my *ex*-wife cheated on *me*.'

'Right, sure. Was that a little nugget you were keeping to yourself back then?' She shakes her head. 'Change the narrative to suit you, Luke. Next, you'll say I blew it between us.'

I step closer to her, my heart pounding and my breaths coming thick and fast. *How dare she?*

'God, you got so arrogant and conceited!' I'm shouting, which is wholly uncharacteristic, but Carrie knows how to push all my buttons.

She doesn't back down. If anything, my words make her more brazen. She seems to grow taller, to puff out her chest, until our bodies are almost touching. 'When you've been treated like dirt, Luke, you have to choose fight or flight. I chose *fight*.'

'I treated *you* like dirt?' I scoff. She's unbelievable. 'I ruined my career over you.'

She throws her head back with an ugly laugh.

'Says the man who hangs out on private islands and fancy yachts whenever the hell he wants! It doesn't look like things went so badly for you, does it?'

I feel myself gawking. Incredulous. 'Did you swallow a fucking lemon tree? You're thirty-one and on the cusp of partnership, Carrie. It's impossible to see why you're so bitter and twisted when you've got what you always wanted.'

'Are you kidding?' She throws her hands up in the air and finally steps back, putting some much-needed distance between us. 'I've spent seven years trying to retell a narrative. Seven years trying to show people that I didn't try to sleep my way to the top. I've worked harder and longer than anyone else I know. So yes, I'm fucking bitter and—'

The sound of the tender engine cuts through her words and we both shift to watch Henry coming toward the beach, at the helm.

He kills the engine and hops off the vessel like he's a stunt double in an action movie. Remarkably, keeping his uniform dry. Damn him and his hot man peacocking.

He drags the dinghy until the front is just touching the sand and holds onto the roped edge while the rear bobs up and down with the lapping waves.

'Jump in, guys,' he calls.

I could be chivalrous and take Carrie's oversized pack-up to the boat but I think, *naaah, I'm good.*

Instead, I leave her huffily lugging her bag down to the water's edge with one hand and in the other, holding her sandals.

I feel Henry scrutinizing me but I try to ignore him – what does this charmed kid know? – and toss my flip-flops onto the boat.

'Do you need a leg up?' Henry asks Carrie.

I'm about to jump and pop-up onto the boat as she starts struggling to lift her bag up and over the edge of the tender. *For God's sake.*

Conceding on grounds of not wanting to seem like a total dick, I take the bag from her and set it in the boat.

'Thank you,' she says, though it clearly pains her, which is actually hilarious. 'No, Henry, I'll be fine, thank you.'

This should be fun.

I step aside and motion for her to climb in ahead of me. I watch, not able to help the smirk that tugs on my lips. 'Please, hop in.'

With her brows practically knitted together and muttering something I'm sure I wouldn't care to hear under her breath, she holds on to the rope around the dinghy's edge and grunts as she attempts to heave herself up.

Not nearly high enough, she attempts to flick her leg up and on to the inflated rim of the boat. Her dress blows up until her butt cheek, barely covered by her bikini, is exposed and she's still pulling and grunting and it's all so inelegant and ungraceful, laughter splutters out of me. I don't mean to but she does deserve it.

'Come and hold the boat, Luke; I'll give her a hand,' Henry says.

Okay, okay, I guess I have to help.

I bring my palms, one each side, to her near-naked butt and start to push, but she screams and flings her leg back down from the boat, whacking me in the temple as she does so and sending me crashing into the shallow water.

'Don't touch my ass!' she shouts as I manage to get my feet on the sandy bottom and stand, completely saturated.

'I was helping you out. You didn't have to try to drown me!'

'Drown you?' She rolls her eyes. 'You're such a baby.'

Then she tugs on the rope and tries again, this time swinging her leg a little higher, and though her fine, *fine* behind is exposed, and she looks like a beached whale with a very nice ass flapping around, she eventually tumbles into the dinghy and pops up from the deck like a mole from a hole, straightening her clothes and pulling her hair from her lip gloss.

'Elegant,' I tell her, before pulling myself up and into the boat, making sure I flick water over Carrie in the process.

Henry pushes us off, hops on to the dinghy and stares at Carrie and me. Both disheveled, one of us wet, the other sodden. Uncertain, he ventures, 'Are you guys set?'

'Oh, we're all set,' I say sarcastically, shaking water drops from my shades.

'Just eager to get going,' Carrie says, her expression as smug as someone who bought the last bag of Hershey's kisses in the entire universe.

15

CARRIE

I try not to seem like a woman who's never been around a billionaire's play toys before but as I step onto the concealed swim platform of Joe Hettich's 105-foot catamaran, *Ella II*, I'm gawking. My jaw is literally hanging loose.

Henry has pulled us up to the back of the superyacht and ties on the dinghy as Jenny offers me a hand to climb onto the million-star luxury accommodation.

'What happened to you?' I hear Alisha ask as Joe storms off ahead of me toward a huge lounge area, which has two dining tables either side of a walkway to the inside of the boat – *ship*.

Around the tables are white chairs with blue

padded cushions and in the middle of the tables, surrounded by every snack imaginable, are vases of fresh flowers. Either side of the tables and under the shade of the deck are two lounging sofas, where Joe, Noah and Toby are lying – the boys playing on tablets and leaning back against their dad, who's the epitome of relaxation: eyes closed, hands behind his head.

Alisha asks her question from where she's sitting at one of the tables with what looks like a coffee in a cup and saucer, snacking on canapés.

'Is there a beer?' Luke grumps in response. Now it's *my* turn to laugh at *him*. There's a member of staff, dressed much like Henry and Jenny, whom I haven't seen before, and she moves swiftly to a glass refrigerator on the deck.

'Should I ask?' Jenny whispers to me.

'Just some beaten-up man pride,' I tell her. 'He won't be touching my ass again anytime soon.'

Jenny smirks. 'Welcome to the post-*Barbie* era, Ken.'

As we're sniggering and making our way up to the dining tables, Henry appears at my side. He sets my bag down on a chair and says, 'Come on, I'll show you around before we raise anchor.'

I glance back across my shoulder to see the

steward now has an open bottle of beer and she's handing it to Luke. As she does, Noah says, 'It's noon somewhere, Uncle Luke.'

Ha, the kid's funny.

I'm smiling as I follow Henry up an exterior staircase to what he tells me is the main deck. It's another insanely large hangout area.

'It can seat more than twenty people,' he says. 'Great for entertaining.'

He puffs up one of the pale-grey cushions that decorate the space, as if he can't help himself.

'I told you *Ella*'s one hundred and five feet in length and she's forty-seven and a half feet in beam.'

'Beam? You mean across?' I ask.

He smiles gently. 'Sorry, it's yachty speak. Yeah, in width, if you like.' He's kind, Henry, and he seems smart. I like him.

'Coming off the fly bridge over there is a diving board.' He points in the direction of the white board overhanging the serene waters. I can see fish swimming and much further below, rocks dug into the seabed. 'You'll have some fun on that when we get into deeper water.'

I'm not so sure, but I don't say that. Being chicken isn't really cool. 'Sounds it.'

He gives a short laugh, like he's got my number. I

mean, come on, I'm a thirty-one-year-old tax advisor who spends most of her life between an office and the four walls of her apartment, and the most exciting thing I've done in my life was... Luke.

God, I need to get *out* more.

'There's a rainfall shower on the aft deck for when you get out of the water,' Henry goes on, pointing to the rear of the boat and making his way down another set of stairs toward the front of the catamaran. I follow him and we arrive at what look like two giant trampolines between the two hulls. The ocean glistens beneath them, as if it's lost a fight with an angry pot of glitter.

'You can bounce or lounge on these and you'll have the best view in the house from here once we set sail,' Henry tells me.

I spring toward him, where he's now as far forward as he can get and turning to look back at the boat.

'There's a crow's nest there attached to the forward portion of the mast. You can ride it up to the second spreader and you'll get an incredible view.' Then he looks at me and adds quietly, 'I like to snoop on people on other boats from up there, especially some of the celebs we get sailing around the islands.'

'Now *that* does sound interesting.' If Callum were here, I'd never be able to drag him down. He'd have on his star-spangled Speedos and a shameless super lens hanging around his neck. He is the font of all celeb gossip. My only source, in fact.

'Oh yeah. You wouldn't believe some of the things I've seen from that crow's nest.'

I chuckle. 'I'll look forward to you dishing the dirt.'

'I'd have you up all night,' he says, heading off again toward a glass window through which I can see the steering equipment and a man I assume is the captain fiddling with things inside. I know he didn't mean anything by his statement but Henry has left my cheeks blushing.

It's been a while since I was kept up all night.

A *real* while.

'This is Captain George. Captain, this is Carrie, a friend of Joe's.'

Friend seems a little generous, though I'm not a foe and he seems genuinely nice, just a little weird, and I'm certainly enjoying his hospitality, so... I accept the hand of the man wearing a brilliant white and pristinely pressed uniform, with four gold stripes on his epaulette. He could be front and center of a commercial for laundry detergent.

The captain and I make small talk, mostly because I have zero idea what to ask him after 'where are we headed' and 'how is the weather'. I don't know anything about fancy-pants boats.

The captain introduces me to his engineer as he passes by, then Henry points out the portside navigation station and a stairway down to what is apparently the starboard hull and the crew sleeping area.

'Is the boat crewed all of the time?' I ask, following Henry inside to the main interior area.

He nods. 'Most of the year, yeah. Either Joe books it out for himself, or friends and family, or sometimes she's in port. Regardless, she needs a crew to take care of her.' He has stopped in an opulent passageway, with the kind of walls one might expect of a superyacht – burl veneers punctuated with gold trimmings, and the floor is covered in marble-effect tiles. '*Ella II* is like a beautiful woman; she needs to be treated right.'

Is he...? Is there... like, a thing *happening here?*

Surely not. He's young and hot and really ought not to have any interest in me at all, but the way he's looking at me is... saying he does? Weird. Awkward. Totally inappropriate.

Yet, a little flattering, honestly.

I clear my throat. 'What's this?' I ask, planting my hands on a table in the center of the wide corridor.

'A buffet table,' he says, letting his eyes linger on mine for too long before looking away. 'The four doors you can see lead to state rooms. A master and three queen guest rooms. I think Ella has taken Char and Sanza for a nap in the master but the guest rooms are free. Would you like to see inside?'

I'm curious, so I really want to say yes and see how the other half sleep, but something tells me it wouldn't be a good idea with this strange new dynamic I'm sensing to introduce the thought of beds and bedrooms and what people get up to in beds and bedrooms.

'I'm good,' I say breezily, moving away from Henry and deeper into the salon, as he calls it.

'Starboard side.' I watch him point to the right. 'There's another hangout space.' He's referring to a large L-shaped seating area with a huge wall-mounted flat-screen TV.

Inside, at a bar and preparing drinks, are two more female crew, with beautiful smiles, pearly white teeth, and immaculate chignons.

'Port side.' He points to the left. 'This is the main bar for the stews to serve drinks. I help out on deck when I'm on the yacht but otherwise I'm based on island. There're ten crew, when Jenny and I are onboard. You've got the captain and an engineer, an Officer of the Watch, Chief Stew – that's Brittany, who you saw out on deck – Riley and Daisy here, also interior, Bosun, Jake, who'll be somewhere sorting out the sea toys, probably. Then there's me, acting as deckhand, and Jenny as an extra stewardess. Which leaves the man you'll like most of all... the chef. He'll be prepping lunch in the galley right now, so I wouldn't advise we disturb him. He's a bit of a perfectionist. Aka grumpy as hell.'

I chuckle, thinking of the stern chefs on *Below Deck*, then turning on the spot, taking in the sheer luxury of it all, mulling over his words, all I can say is, 'Wow.' I exhale at the enormity of it all. 'It's quite the enterprise.'

Henry gives a short laugh, eyebrows raised. 'Everything with Joe is.'

Of course it is. He's one of the richest men in the world. I couldn't even conceive of having his kind of money. Not that there's anything wrong with my little Manhattan apartment. It fits me, and Eddie, and Callum is right next door. Plus, I spend most of my life in the office.

But I'll be damned if this trip isn't making me

think there's got to be something more. Not money and things, but time. Time to enjoy *things* and *people*.

I don't know at what point I stopped having time. When I decided to give it up. I wonder if anyone can ever get it back without jeopardizing everything they've worked tirelessly to achieve.

As if playing the role of the devil on my shoulder, the uncontrollable shrieking of Noah travels in from the aft deck. Through the windows, I see Luke pretending to throw the boy overboard, and Noah's infectious delight makes my lips curve up.

Cute.

Sometimes, I think I'd like all of that – family life, happy kids. But I couldn't have it with anyone if I had the slightest doubt about our relationship. Not after what I suffered between my parents.

Maybe that's part of the reason I don't really put myself out there and date a lot. I'm afraid of ending up with the wrong guy and terrified the right guy might not even exist for me.

More than that, logistically, I just don't have the *time*.

'Come on,' Henry says, gesturing with his head toward outside. 'You must be ready for a glass of bubbles.'

I check my watch. 'Sure, why not?' Like Noah

said, it's noon somewhere. In fact, it's almost noon here.

We head out to the deck, where Alisha is drinking champagne, Joe is holding a cocktail and still lounging with Toby, and Luke and Noah are making their way back over to the dining table and snacks.

'Don't have too many of those; your mom won't be happy if you don't eat lunch, buddy,' Luke says, all... paternally.

It thrusts my mind back to one of the questions of our past. *Whatever happened to his baby? Was there ever a baby? Did he just want out between us?*

I realize I'm watching him with a furrowed brow and slip my shades from my head to cover my eyes. Shielding me from him, or the other way around.

Brittany seems extremely nice, not least because she brings me a glass of fizz when I take a seat at the dining table near Alisha.

'How do you like the boat, Carrie?' Joe asks.

'*Like* doesn't cover it. It's incredible, Joe. Thank you for having me here and letting me gatecrash your time with family and friends.'

'It's nothing. I like to know the people I'm working with,' he replies, and I watch him have some peculiar unspoken exchange with Luke. The kind that makes me feel like I'm being talked about behind my back. A feeling I remember from school days.

I never had a lot of friends at school, or growing up. I never felt like people really got me. Not until I thought one person got me completely.

How wrong I was.

Next thing, Henry is standing by me at the table. He strokes my arm – pulling me out of my head – as he says, 'Let me know if you need or want anything, Carrie.' He flashes me what is, admittedly, a most delectable half-smile, though it makes me cast my eyes to Joe warily.

I do *not* want him to think I'm flirting with his staff.

Is that what's happening here?

God, this really is like an episode of *Below Deck*. *Below Deck* meets teen angst.

16

LUKE

If I could force someone overboard with my eyes, Henry would be taking a deep dive to cool off.

What the hell has gotten into him?

I've always thought he's a decent enough guy but today...

Has he thought that maybe Carrie doesn't want him to brush against her every time he walks past her chair? That she doesn't need him to stroke her arm and laugh overzealously at her *un*-funny jokes? And maybe, just fucking maybe, she thinks he's an obnoxious dick when he winks at her from the swim platform while he's rising off the sea toys and splashing enough water on himself that his polo is clinging to his svelte frame? What does he think he is, a Chippendale?

'Are you okay there, Luke?' Carrie asks from where she's sitting opposite me at the dining table, having just set her cutlery down after finishing a dish of grilled mahi-mahi.

She leans back in her seat and her dress pulls across her chest, the neckline opening a fraction wider and giving me a sneak peek at her shimmering, hot-pink bikini beneath. I try not to look. Try not to give her the satisfaction. Because something tells me the subtle shift in position is intended for me; it's supposed to tease me, either because, one, she's had two glasses of champagne and is now sipping from a glass of wine, which always used to make her tantalizingly confident, or, two, because she fecking *knows* Henry is flirting with her and *knows* that it's pissing me off.

Why? Damned if I know. It's not like I have any right over her, or any claim to her. I never did. That's not how we were. It never felt like I was older or in a more senior position or like I had more say in anything we did than she did.

I taught her things by day, and by night she opened my eyes to all kinds of random facts. Like hummingbirds are the only birds that can fly backwards – she whispered that into my neck one night as we were falling asleep and once her breaths had slowed, I whispered back that she was my hummingbird.

She told me that dogs have a unique nose print and no two will ever be the same – she told me that as we lay in my bathtub, her back to my chest, effervescent salts fizzing around us. In response, I kissed her temple and told her I didn't believe there was anyone else quite like her in the world.

She showed me how to laugh at the mundane, the sublime and the ridiculous, in a way I had forgotten – as if I were a teenager again.

We were equals. She wasn't mine.

But for whatever reason, Henry is grating on my very last nerve.

'Why wouldn't I be fine?' I snap without meaning to, my clipped tone betraying my cool façade. Because she might not have been mine, but I was always hers.

She shrugs. Fecking shrugs. Then she smirks, sips from her wine glass, and says, 'You've been tugging on your hair and your nose has been twitching all through lunch, the way it used to after a long day and late night in the office.'

I'm aware of the eyes of everyone else at the table

– Noah and Toby included – on me. I rub the tip of my nose reflexively, irritated that Carrie knows me well enough to spot my stress tells.

The only saving grace is that the skin of her neck is turning crimson and I'm guessing she just thrust herself right back into a memory of *our* late nights in the office. I'd love to see behind the shield of her shades and I'm thankful that my own are in place.

'Maybe you're just wishful thinking.' I fix her with a stare and behind our lenses, I know she's returning the look.

'Ha. My work life got a lot smoother without you in it, Luke.'

'Yet here you are, working for me, again.'

She rolls her jaw tightly and inside, I'm laughing myself to death.

'On that note, and before you two start quarrelling across the table,' Joe says. At his words, I watch Carrie swallow so hard, it's a movement deep in her neck, right down to where her collarbones begin. I have to look away. 'I've been ruminating on something since we got here and I want to run it by you both for your views. Whether you think it's a flier, how we would structure it efficiently if you do.'

'That's our cue to go, Alisha,' Ella says. 'We'll leave this trio to the mundane.'

'I'm all ears,' Carrie says, brightly yet matter-of-fact. Happy to be on professional territory, I think. But... this isn't *her* job; it's mine. I'm Hettich's sounding board. *I'm* his CFO.

'We can chat this through first, buddy,' I tell him. 'Let *Eric* know if there's anything we need to put his way afterward.'

The shape of Carrie's cheek changes and I know she's biting down on her gum. It's one of *her* stress tells.

'I'm more than happy to be a sounding board,' she says, smiling at Joe. 'Off the clock.'

She's playing that card? Throwing him a freebie initial consultation.

'You're sitting on his multi-million dollar, fully catered yacht, Carrie; it's hardly free advice,' I gripe. It's querulous and petulant but also true.

And it has the desired effect. Her professional façade drops as she asks, 'I suppose you're being paid overtime?'

I narrow my eyes on her. 'I have an equity stake in Hettich global; I don't get paid in six-minute units.'

Screw you.

'So the idea?' Hettich says, reminding us he's still

at the table, though it takes long seconds before Carrie and I stop glaring at each other.

Something inside me has tightened and twisted and I think it's loathing, but Carrie must be the only person in the world whom I hate so much, I can't take my eyes off her. She's a witch. Spellbinding and dangerous.

'Go ahead, Joe,' Carrie says, finally breaking our stand-off to reach into her over-packed bag at the side of the dining table and take out her laptop.

'You brought your laptop?' I ask, disbelieving.

'Lucky, too, isn't it?' she says, one side of her lips quirked.

'I suppose it'll stop me needing to make notes.' Then because her sanctimoniousness is eating me alive, I add, 'Just like old times. You taking my notes.'

As the Bosun appears at the table, shielding me from the direct line of Carrie's sight, I chuckle like an adolescent in sex ed.

'Sir, with lunch wrapped up, we thought we'd head on out to our first stop. Drop anchor and get the sea toys out. Are you ready?'

Joe looks my way. 'Are you sure you can play nicely?' He thinks he's funny and honestly, I do too.

Smirking, I tell him, 'I'm always nice.'

As we sail the dazzling blue ocean, Joe explains

his latest wish to diverge. This time into digital media advertising.

'It's a highly regulated space,' I tell him.

'Luke's right,' Carrie adds, though I think it physically pains her to say the words. 'And we'd need to think about intellectual property, which entities are licensing to which within the group. For example, if the Delaware subsidiary...'

At some point, I forget that I'm in one of the most sought after financial advisory positions in the entire North American continent. In fact, I plain forget to advise. Because I'm lost in the poise and elegance of the expert tax advisor sitting across from me. In her knowledge and business acumen. In the way she has complete control of the situation. Command of her billionaire client.

I know that no matter what happened between us, what she did to me afterward, I did the right thing in leaving our firm and giving her fledgling career the chance to thrive.

'What do you think, Chalmers?' Joe is saying. I've a feeling this isn't the first time he's asked.

Shit. Where were we? Where were *they*?

Carrie is watching me and I want to say something smart and insightful. Something full of wisdom, something *she* hasn't thought about. But I'll be damned if I can.

'What would your primary concerns be if Hettich adopted a Delaware Holdco structure?' she asks, for some reason surprisingly, letting me off the hook slightly.

I nod, then give myself another moment of pause, as if I've been pondering the discussion.

The only thing I've been pondering is her.

I'm fucked.

I manage to fumble and stutter my way through some vague musings that I think or hope are loosely related to the discussion Carrie and Joe were having and I'm thankful when we reach our first ocean stop, in a place that feels like the middle of nowhere but is actually a famous site for cave diving: just the menacing peaked rock heads of the structure protruding from the ocean and a small but picturesque sandbank.

'I think I'll go watch them drop anchor,' I say, needing some air because, though I'm sitting on the aft deck of a yacht in the open water, I'm feeling hot and bothered and very claustrophobic.

As I'm watching a deckhand guide the captain above him to the perfect spot and release the anchor from the bow, Alisha appears by my side.

'Have you told her yet, that you and I aren't *you and I*?'

'Not yet.' Nor am I ready to, because the mind screw of emotions I've been feeling for the last thirty minutes while I was supposed to be talking business was, at best, confusing, and at worst, fucking scary. 'I will.'

'Good. Because I think you two are either going to kill each other or shag each other's brains out and either way, I don't want to be caught in the middle.'

Hands in my pockets, I turn sharply to face her. 'You're going to have to think of another option.'

Though throwing Carrie overboard would be much less traumatic for me than delving into our past.

17

CARRIE

It feels odd stripping down to a bikini in front of my client but since everyone else is doing it – not to mention it would look wholly ridiculous were I to jump in the sea fully clothed – I peel my dress over my head, then follow the others down to the concealed swim platforms at the back of the boat.

The children are first into the water – Noah and Toby jumping in, the other two being guided and carried by Ella and Alisha, Sanza inside a rubber ring. There's a yell of 'Cowabungaaaaaaaaaa!', then an almighty splash as Joe does a running bomb into the water from the dive board on the fly bridge. I try not to notice his rainbow-striped Speedos that couldn't be flattering on anyone, though I do chuckle when he asks Henry to hand him a Mexican sombrero, which Joe places on his head, much to Noah's amusement.

As I watch Joe front crawl to share the joke with his aspirational, gorgeous family, I realize Henry has moved to my side.

'He's always like this,' he says, dipping his head in the direction of Joe.

'It's admirable to be able to work as hard as he does and remember to enjoy life,' I say.

I witnessed my parents work incredibly hard to give me the very best platform they could to build my own life and career, but my childhood often felt cash rich and time poor. My parents stayed together, through years of bickering and misery, to save for my future, rather than making happy memories.

I shake my head, no longer laughing, and I don't know why I tell Henry, 'I wish I could take a leaf out of his book.'

I almost threw away everything my parents gave me once.

I cringe when I realize that Luke has stealthily made his way close behind me too, and I can only guess he heard my moment of... self-insight? Weakness? Either way, I don't like it. I don't want him to feel like he knows anything about me. Maybe he did seven years ago. Today, he's nobody to me. A total, complete, utter—

Why must he keep being topless around me? Stupefying me with his naked, obscenely attractive torso?

Whoa. Proverbial slap across the face.

I need to cool off, shake him off, remember what he did to me, how he left me.

I also happen to like the way Henry is looking at me in my bikini. For some peculiar reason, he seems to be *interested*? Even if that is true, the feeling isn't reciprocated, despite his good looks and kindly flirtatious manner, but I do like the confidence boost he's giving me. It's diminutive, but I'll take any enhancement to help counter the ever-present feeling of rejection I have when I'm around Luke.

Screw him. I could be fanciable.

I'm standing on the edge of the platform, building up to jumping in the water, suddenly hyperaware of my posture as I turn to smile at Henry.

Luke makes a show of checking his watch. 'Are you going to dive in, Carrie?'

Yes, actually, I am. All grace, all poise. I lift my hands above my head, suck in my tummy, stick out my butt, bend my knees slightly and—

'Or are you too scared to commit?'

Me?

What the actual fuuuuuuuuck...?

Oh God, the pain hits my torso like a truck has been dropped on my stomach as I slap, tummy first, off the concrete ocean.

Shitake, shitake, shitake.

That absolutely effing killed.

That dick.

That smarmy...

I surface from my blunder, trying to wear it well and pretend that my entire upper body is not in agony, only to find Luke near peeing his board shorts, he's guffawing so loudly. His hands are on his knees and he's folded forward.

'Are you okay?' Henry asks, clearly fighting his own amusement.

Damn it, I thought he was in my corner. Now the only guy to flirt with me since, like, 1993 is mocking me too.

'Totally. Why wouldn't I be?'

I can barely breathe. It. Hurts. So. Bad.

I take deep breaths, my back to the boat and the others already in the sea, treading water that I can appreciate is gorgeously warm as the pain of my belly flop begins to recede.

When eventually I start to feel more human than peanut brittle that just got whacked by a sledgehammer, I turn back around to face the catamaran, where Luke is standing on the edge of the dive board, bouncing gently. Then, arms up, torso pulled delectably taut, he propels himself into the air, summersaults, knees tucked to his chest, then straightens and dives like a bird after fish into the ocean, barely making a splash.

'What an absolute di—' Suddenly a rubber ring with a contented child and its mummy are at my side. '—plodocus.'

Ella laughs. 'Don't worry, Sanza isn't properly talking yet.'

I put a hand across my mouth. 'Sorry. I know you guys are close. I don't mean to...'

Well, actually I do mean to badmouth Luke, I just wouldn't have done it in front of Ella, in an ideal world, where belly flops and insanely egotistical men don't exist.

'We are. He's like the sibling I never wanted, though.' She chuckles warmly. 'He's spent a lot of time out here with us, especially when...' She looks at me in a way that makes me feel like she's considering her next words. 'He's had low times.'

I wonder if she means after he got divorced. It makes sense now how he and Alisha would have met. I wonder how long they've been together. They seem to play off each other, as if they've known each other forever. If I didn't hate Luke, maybe I'd even think their banter is sweet.

The conversation also reminds me that I did once – through other connections – see that Luke was working in the Caribbean for a while, in one of the big accountancy firms that has offices out here. Not that I wanted to see that information, and I tried my best not to, but that would have meant disconnecting from most people in the Finance world on LinkedIn.

'Show me two siblings who don't also think the other one is a diplodocus sometimes,' Ella adds.

I'm still laughing with her when Luke front crawls past us, fleetingly throwing me a wink that, in turn, makes me want to throw up in my mouth.

When he gets to Alisha, he pops up on her shoulders and dunks her under water and I think maybe that belly flop has done lasting damage to my insides because they really feel tightly knotted, twisted and contorted.

I spend the next hour swimming, snorkeling, feeling like an idiot for not being able to drive a sea scooter and hold my breath underwater at the same time, and dipping in and out of conversations with the others. Oh, and ending up in a splashing war with Noah and Toby, who only relent when Luke – much to my annoyance – saves me by sending them both a tidal wave.

There are moments when I forget I'm here for work, that there's a huge storm brewing and very possibly heading our way in forty-eight hours, and that I'm not part of this group. It feels *nice* to feel part of something more.

I've never had loads of friends. Growing up, I never felt like people got me. Until Luke. It was as if every corner of me somehow fit his sphere when we spoke. The allure of him was more than looks or chemistry; it was something I couldn't place, and less resist. Then it was gone and I was a square in a round world again.

If only Callum and Eddie could be here and I weren't trapped in paradise with the man I despise more than anyone else on the entire planet.

When we're rounded up to get back on the boat, I hang back, floating around on a noodle until everyone else is onboard. I might as well savor it because I'll be flying home as soon as Joe confirms the plane for me tonight.

Reluctantly, I swim up to the platform and climb the metal steps. At the top, I follow Henry's feet up to his outstretched arm and take his hand as he helps me up.

'The shower's just there,' he says, inclining his head.

I nod. 'I remember.'

As the crew prepare to set sail, I close my eyes and lean my head back under the shower, rinsing the salt from my body and hair.

18

LUKE

Give me strength.

She's basically in underwear under the head of the shower, her long hair flowing down her back, to the neat arch where her body nips in and subtly curves out again.

I'm not watching her, I'm just... noticing, that's all. Noticing how that body I used to be so familiar with could bring another man to his knees. If I'm honest with myself, irrationally resentful that it could.

One of the interior staff opens the doors to the salon and the dogs come outside, providing a well-timed switch of focus.

'Good dogs,' I say, fussing them as I, discreetly I

hope, take one last look at Carrie over the rim of my shades.

She was different out there, in the water. Swimming, diving, like she didn't have the weight of the world on her shoulders. As if she forgot that Joe was her client. She was smiling and joking, pretending to be a crocodile with Toby attached to her back as she swam, playing along with being a shark out to get Noah's flippers.

I found myself wanting to be part of their fun.

'Are you checking me out?' Carrie gripes, pulling a towel across her front.

Oops.

'What?' I ask, as if I'm incensed, rather than caught in the act. 'Got a pretty big opinion of yourself there, Carrie.'

Even from behind closed lips, it's obvious she grits her teeth. 'Me? *Please*. Why don't you go perform an Olympic dive off the top of the boat again, Greg Louganis?'

I snort. Full-blown snort. And right before she remembers that she cancelled me entirely from her life and hides her face behind her towel, I catch her grin too.

Playful mockery was part of our repartee once. Feisty, charged fun. Like two old friends in a bar. I used to *want* to come to work in the mornings just to find out what smartass remark she'd throw at me. That was long before either of us made so much as a move on the other physically.

But once Carrie has wrapped herself in her towel, she heads to one of the tables on the aft deck, which has been laid out with infused waters and fresh-cut watermelon, and that resting bitch face she wears these days is back in situ.

And why in the good Lord's name is Henry here, again?

'Do you want to change out of your wet stuff in one of the bedrooms?' he asks her.

Oh wouldn't you like to get her in a bedroom, I internally quip, for my own benefit. But they do, in fact, head inside together to a bedroom and I almost snap my spine leaning backward to get a view of the pair of them, counting the seconds that they're behind the door together. One, two, three—

'Luke, we're going for a family siesta,' Ella says, leading the kids and Joe into the salon.

Alisha appears at my side, a book in her hand. 'I'm going to get out of the heat for an hour too.' Then she pats my cheek and tells me, 'Don't do anything I wouldn't do.'

'Is there anything you wouldn't do?' I tease.

'Wouldn't you love to know, Chalmers?' she counters, chortling her way to a bedroom, extra pizazz in her swaying hips as she goes.

Why am I still watching the bedroom door where Carrie is getting changed? Did Henry come back out?

I slip on a t-shirt and surreptitiously switch my wet shorts for a dry pair, then help myself to a bottle of beer and head up to the lounge area on the top of the boat. I tell myself I'm going up to lay out in the shade and relax but there's an insanely annoying devil on my shoulder telling me I'm actually going in search of Henry, to make sure he's not with Carrie.

I don't care, I yell at the devil, though I feel like I exhale some tension when I see Henry in conversation with the Bosun at the bow of the boat.

Irrationally appeased, I lie back on the soft cushions under the canopy of the top deck and take out my phone. I check the latest sports news on ESPN and fall down a rabbit hole with some mindless videos on YouTube – the ten worst shark attacks, the deadliest jellyfish stings, and a video about twin panda bear cubs being born in South Korea.

For the first time since Monday, I feel myself slipping into relaxation mode. I should probably check some emails, do some more work, but the cub thing is kind of sweet. I switch to my news app and see a depiction of the merging storms that have grown into Hurricane Isabel. Sources are predicting Charithonia will be hit by the outer edges of the storm. That's still going to be huge and damaging but it's better than a direct hit.

It suddenly seems absurd that I'm lounging on a boat when, in forty-eight hours, the surrounding islands could be struck by devastation.

It's thinking about the storm that makes me tune in to a voice below, on the trampolines at the front of the yacht.

'Dad, it'll be okay. Mom shouldn't have told you where I am, not if you're going to worry like this. I know that. I love you too. I don't mean to be sharp, I just don't want you to worry. Plus, I've asked my client if I can leave tonight. With any luck, I'll be home in New York well before the hurricane arrives.'

Tonight? She's leaving *tonight?*

I know she asked to leave but Joe blew it off with a massage, didn't he?

The catamaran is on the move again but that's not the reason I feel unsteady on my feet as I over-look the bow, watching Carrie end her call and move off the trampoline to place her phone in her beach bag. Then she's back in the middle of the springy floor, earphones plugged into her ears.

I wonder if she's still obsessed with country music.

It doesn't matter. She's leaving, again.

Just like that. She was in my life, then she was gone and uncontactable. Now, she's back again, and she's going, without anything being resolved, *again*.

I don't know what needs to be resolved or how but there's a tightness in my chest, like something has been reignited since seeing her here and I think maybe if I just knew *why*. **Why** did she ghost me, completely cut me out of her life, ruin any chance for us *ever*? Maybe, if I know, this feeling that's gripping me can rescind.

I'm going to head down there; I just need to take some big-boy deep breaths first and finish my beer.

Carrie has switched out her hot-pink bikini for a backless and front-plunging (if that's the right word) green bathing suit. It sets her hair on fire and I watch as she tilts her head back, then draws her red locks to the top of her head and twists them into a knot.

As I'm doing so – fretting, I mean, rather than gawping – I notice Carrie's back is turning pink in the sun.

Passing through the salon first to grab some SPF 50, I head out to where she's now reclined, eyes closed behind her tortoiseshell shades, legs bent, hands out from her sides and tapping out a beat to what I know will be the voice of a man with a husky southern twang, or some poppy group like Old Dominion.

Despite feeling the enormity of trying to have a *real* conversation with her, I find myself remembering a Sunday afternoon at my place, me picking Carrie up by her waist as she tried to change the track on my music player to something country. Sugarland, I think it was that day. Her squealing as I brought her down to the sofa in my lounge and sobering once I was hovering over her...

My hand moves reflexively to my chin, where she gently nipped me between her teeth, mischief making her irises sparkle.

'Garghhh! Jesus, Luke!' she screams now, startled when she opens her eyes on the trampoline to see that I'm the reason the structure is flexing. 'What are you doing? Why aren't you having a siesta like the others?'

I shrug. 'I'm not tired.'

I'm pretty sure she rolls her eyes behind her large lenses, and I'm fairly certain that over the sound of the boat moving across the ocean I hear her mutter, 'Smartass.'

'Here,' I say, tossing her the bottle of sunscreen. 'Your back is pink.'

She picks up the cream, considers it, then hands it back to me. 'Thanks but there's a reason my back is pink and there's a reason I'm lying on it to shield it from the sun.'

She can't reach.

'For an intelligent woman, I'd have thought you'd know that's not how sun rays work.' I shake the bottle and squeeze the lotion into my hands. 'Turn around,' I instruct. She stares at me stubbornly. 'Turn. Around.'

Eventually, she concedes, shuffling her back toward me. I come to sit behind her and she lifts the fastening of her bathing suit higher on her neck. Her neck that looks long and smooth. I blink back a memory of my lips against her skin – the taste of cocoa butter, salt and home.

'Most of the UV rays we get are indirect,' I say, channeling a dermatologist to distract myself. I place my hands on her shoulders and draw the cream down to her upper arms. She stiffens under my touch and goosebumps form on her skin. 'They reflect off surfaces, which means...' My words catch in my throat as my fingertips reach that enticing curve of her back. Her body feels like silk. As soft, as magnetizing, as it ever was. 'Even if you're trying to shield your back, the sun is bouncing off the sea and the boat to reach you.'

I sweep the cream just lower than the hem of her clothing and hear her sharp intake of breath.

She feels this too. No matter what's gone between us, it's as if there's a spark, a flame, undeniable physical chemistry between us.

I want to talk to her about what happened. I need some closure. But my legs slide further down the sides of hers and I think she nudges back into me. It's a move that's barely there but I don't think I imagine it.

I'm staring at her neck, wondering what she'd do if I just brought my mouth down to touch her, to nibble the lobe of her ear, in the way that used to make her squirm.

'What are you doing?' she shouts, springing up to stand.

Shit. What *was* I doing? I come to stand too and hold up my hands in submission. 'I was just putting your lotion on. No funny business.'

'No funny business? You were shuffling and nudging.' She pokes the air with her fingers. 'Right into me! And I *know* what you were thinking, Luke Chalmers.'

She starts prodding my chest with her finger.

'I was thinking your pasty skin will fry in this heat, Carrie. And, oh yeah, you're welcome.'

'I'm welcome? For your horny little groan and roaming fingers?'

Did I groan? No, she *did. God, did I? Was it me I heard?*

She's forcing me backward, fierce in her prodding until I grab hold of her finger to stop her.

'You know something, Carrie? You need to get over yourself.'

My words bring thunder to her eyes. I've never seen her, or any woman for that matter, as mad as she is in this moment.

'And *you* need to cool the hell off!'

I'm too busy staring at her to respond quickly when she pushes my shoulders and sends me stumbling off the trampoline, onto the sleek, white deck.

My calves hit the catamaran's safety rail – ironic – and next thing I know, I'm flying from the vessel, crashing into the water as the boat continues to slowly sail past me.

'What the hell did you do that for?' I yell to Carrie after I kick and thrash my way to the surface. 'You could have killed me pushing me off a moving boat!'

'We're crawling,' she says, eyes casting up to the

sky. 'Regardless, you were making a move!' She's walking along the deck to keep level with me. 'And you have a girlfriend!'

'What do you think I am, a glutton for rejection?' I slap the water with my palms. 'Christ, Carrie, I wasn't making a move, I was trying to save you from a disgustingly expensive healthcare system.'

She stops moving now that's she's reached the back of the boat and keeps her eyes on me. I'm getting further away from her but I'd love to be able to read the expression on her face as she asks, 'You really weren't?'

'No, for God's sake. Now can you get them to stop the fucking boat?'

'*Oh crap*, yes. Hold on.' She seems to faff on the spot, turning right, then left, not actually doing anything productive.

'It's not like I've got anywhere to go!' I shout, watching the boat move further and further...

Then Henry appears next to Carrie – of course he does – and calls, 'We're turning around. Stay calm. It's best to float on your back. Enjoy the water.'

Enjoy the water. I'll give him enjoy the fucking water.

Nevertheless, I roll onto my back and float while

the catamaran makes sluggish work of coming about.

It gives me time to think... *Was I making a move? If I had been making a move, would she have been receptive? If she didn't think I was dating Alisha, would she have been open to it?*

I've had a lucky break. Carrie was right; I did need to cool off.

I do not need to go there again with her, ever.

This has been a good, though death-defying and unwanted, time out.

A perspective-getting near-drowning.

At last, the boat is moving alongside me. Henry tosses me a life ring and, though I feel like a total ass, I hook my arms over it and let him drag—

'Arghhhhhh! What the hell was that?' I let go of the ring as a burning sensation like fire blazes across my thigh, up my shorts and around my waist where my T-shirt has come up in the water.

I'm thrashing around, frantically trying to work out why I feel like I've fallen into a raging inferno, when I see tentacles. Hundreds. No, *thousands*, of tentacles and the balloon-esque body of a—

'Shit, shit, shit. It's a jellyfish!' I scream. 'It's a fucking jellyfish!'

Jesus. Jesus. I literally just watched the ten deadliest jellyfish stings in the world on YouTube. 'Henry! Carrie! Help me! Help! I've been stung!'

Carrie starts yelling something incomprehensible. Even she, ice-queen, Managing Director of Ghost Your Ex LLC, is afraid for me.

And Henry is... *laughing*?

Correction: doubled-over laughing. 'It's just a bog-standard jellyfish, mate, not a killer. Here...' He tosses me the life ring again and though the pain is searing on my skin, I'm distracted enough by wanting to pinch Henry's nipples *so hard* between my fingers and twist until he squeals like a piglet that I'm rendered capable of hanging on to the life ring and I think, *maybe* I won't die today.

Henry and Carrie make their way down to the swim platforms at the back of the boat, now stationary, and they both help me out of the water.

Tears are filling my eyes. The pain is worse than being punched full force in the nuts.

Henry leaves to go somewhere, probably to split his sides laughing at me some more, leaving only Carrie and me, and damn it, all I can do is beg her... 'Carrie, do something. It's agony. Help me.'

I'm trying my best not to cry. Really. Truly. It's *that* excruciating.

Carrie holds out her hands. 'I don't know what to

do, Luke.' She looks around but there are no staff coming to my rescue. 'What can I do?'

That's when it comes to me. 'You're going to have to pee on me,' I tell her.

She folds her arms across her chest. She's standing over me, where I'm on my knees on the swim platform. 'I outright refuse to pee on you.'

'Carrie, you can go immediately back to hating on me but, please, I'm begging you. Pee on me.'

'I—' Her conviction is wavering, thank heavens. 'If, *if* I do this, how am I even going to pee on your leg and hip?'

I roll up the leg of my shorts and lift up my T-shirt, coming to lie on my side. 'You'll just have to squat. *Please.*'

'What, like this, do you think?' She squats across me, one leg either side of my hip, sincerely trying to figure this out. 'Luke, I can't, it's too disgusting.'

'No, this *pain* is disgusting, Carrie. Come on.'

'Are you sure it's that bad? You would rather be peed on than just... suck it up.'

I glower at her. '*You* can't feel it. And it's your fault this happened!'

Still squatting over me, she points at my face. 'Don't blame me for your idiocy.'

'My *idiocy*?'

'Yes. Imagine what Alisha would have thought if she'd seen that move you pulled.'

'Carrie, I'm not with Alisha.'

She stands, her legs still either side of my body.

'You're not?'

It seems like so many thoughts and emotions wash over her face. I wonder how she feels – bad, embarrassed, like she should just—

'Would you stop gawping and just freaking pee on me?'

The next voice I hear isn't Carrie's, though; it's Alisha's.

'What on earth is happening?' She looks like we just woke her up, a hand across her eyes to shield them from the brightness of the afternoon.

'Oh fudge,' Carrie says, practically jumping away from me. 'It's not what it looks like,' she says.

I'd love to know what the hell she *thinks* this looks like.

'Coming through,' Henry says, walking down to us with a plastic bottle of some kind of liquid in his hand. 'He got stung by a jellyfish,' he tells Alisha. 'Near anaphylaxis, he was.' He's laughing and Alisha laughs with him.

Then Joe appears and he's chortling too, clearly having overheard the story.

'Carrie was about to pee on him,' Henry calls up to Joe and Alisha.

'I wasn't!' Carrie protests, looking as mortified as I feel about this whole damn experience.

'Here, mate,' Henry says, crouching next to me and helping me come up to sit. 'Vinegar works better than urine, trust me; as someone who's been stung as many times as I have fingers, it works. Then I've got you an ice pack. Should bring you back from the brink.'

He trickles vinegar from his bottle over the affected area, while Alisha and Joe hurl banter-cum-outright abuse at me, and Carrie keeps her back to them, her hands on her hips and her eyes fixed on mine like she's lasering me.

Once Henry is done, he helps me to my feet, then heads up to the aft deck.

As I make to follow him off the swim platform, Carrie asks through gritted teeth, 'Will you stop at nothing to make me look like a fool in front of my client?'

I scoff. 'You know, it's sad that the only thing you seem to think about is work. And for the record, I have never, nor will I ever, be the type of man who cheats.'

19

CARRIE

I watch Luke limp away with Noah hot on his heels. 'Uncle Luke, what happened? Did you get stuck in the propellers?'

'No, buddy.'

'Did you get attacked by a shark?'

'No, buddy.'

I see the trail of water running off Luke's clothes as he heads for the salon, then I feel rather than see the eyes of Joe and Alisha on me because I don't dare to look at them. How shameful and childish I've been will be written all over their faces.

Abruptly, I wish my body was shielded with more clothes.

That jet can't pick me up soon enough.

'Joe, I want you to know I'm not normally like this.' Unwillingly, I look at him now. 'I swear to you I'm more professional than this, always. Luke just...' I sigh. 'None of this will affect the work I do for you, I promise.'

Joe smiles. Earnestly, I think. 'Carrie, do you know how many times I've wanted to throw Luke overboard?'

I try to reciprocate his lightheartedness, but I just feel... heavy.

'I've been nothing but impressed with you and your work so far. If anyone should be apologizing, it's me. This trip hasn't exactly gone the way I planned.'

I open my mouth to speak. To protest. The trip *hasn't* gone as planned. I'm ruining his precious time with his family and friends.

But Joe speaks first. 'Now, I'm told afternoon tea is being served in a few minutes. Will you join us?'

I nod, though more food and socializing are pretty much the last things I want. At this stage, even the second stomach I reserve especially for desserts is too stuffed.

'Of course,' I say brightly, because I have to make this right. It's my last act before making partnership, hopefully, and so far, it's a disaster.

Joe starts to move in the direction of the aft deck but I have to check...

'Joe, am I still able to head back to New York tonight?'

'The jet should be on the deck in Tortola when we get back.'

Thank you. *Thank* you. Because above everything else I'm feeling – remorse, embarrassment, guilt – Luke's words are replaying over and over in my mind and giving me a headache. *The only thing you seem to think about is work.* He struck a chord. Callum tells me as much. *Everyone* tells me as much. Even *Rachel* tries to send me home from the office when I'm working all the hours. Though I usually brush *it, everyone*, off. For some reason, Luke's words are taking hold of me.

Maybe because the reason I have had to be work obsessed is Luke, *us*, the mess he left me in, to pick up the pieces alone.

Perhaps even more than that, though, I can hear him as if he's standing right next to me, grinding out the words, again: *I have never, nor will I ever, be the type of man who cheats.*

And I think the problem is, that's exactly how I felt when he went back to his wife.

It felt distinctly as if the man I had fallen offensively in love with had cheated on me. We were done and there was no coming back from it.

I pull on my cover-up dress and go in search of cake and people but before I reach the dining tables on the aft deck, Ella appears in front of me, handing me a glass of champagne.

'We ladies will take tea on the top deck,' she says. *Oh no*, I really have ruined the Hettich's family time. 'I never get a moment's peace from being Mom.'

On grounds that it would make me feel better to believe that's the reason for the forced gender split on the boat, I agree and follow her upstairs. Alisha is already waiting in the lounge area and a coffee table has been laid out with a three-tiered stand of scones and cakes. There's a silver tray of finger sandwiches, and three place settings, each with a decorative china cup and saucer to match a teapot in the middle of the table. Standing to the side of the table is an open bottle of champagne – presumably the same drink as I'm holding – sitting in an ice bucket.

'Wow, this looks incredible. I'm ravenous all of a sudden,' I say. Despite being full to bursting moments ago, I'm salivating at the sight of the rich, decadent cakes, my attention landing on the midnight-blue mirror glaze of one in particular.

We take our seats and Riley and Daisy fuss

around us like they literally cannot do enough to ensure we're having the best time. If I asked, I wonder if they'd throw Luke into a sea full of jelly-fish again, or at least help me hide his body after he gives himself a coronary.

When they leave, I say, 'I've apologized to Joe but I want to say sorry to you both too. You've been nothing but nice to me since I arrived and you don't have to be. This is supposed to be a work trip and Luke and I are just... ruining things for you all.'

The sisters look at each other, then Alisha says, 'Girl, we are *thrilled* you're here.'

'Luke has finally met his match,' Ella says. 'I thought I'd never see the day his cool, calm exterior would be broken. Or again, at least. I've only seen him pull down his rock-solid walls once before.'

'Believe me,' Alisha says, leaning forward to pick up a smoked salmon finger sandwich. 'I try my best to wind up that man but nothing gets to him.'

Ella similarly reaches for a savory snack. 'No one but you,' she says, smirking at the same time as taking a bite of food.

Alisha gives a short laugh. 'If my ex-husband and I acted like you and Luke do, we'd have never split up.'

I feel myself frown. 'All Luke and I do is fight.'

Hardly the foundation for a relationship. 'I think Ella and Joe have it right. You two seem really, genuinely happy in each other's company.'

Ella chuckles. 'We are, but don't think that behind closed doors we don't keep each other on our toes. We bicker incessantly. You need that. It keeps the fire alive. Especially when your husband is a man like Joe with a big idea a minute. He needs reigning in.' She dabs the side of her mouth with a cloth napkin. 'But you're right. All of this stuff means nothing if there's no love. Beneath all the material things, Joe's a good man. The very best.'

'Trust me,' Alisha says. 'You only argue when there's something you care enough about to fight for it.'

The conversation changes and I join in but am only semi-present. Alisha's words have stayed with me. Luke didn't fight for me. I never fought for him. Yet I did care. I cared so much, I would have taken fighting with him every day of my life over him walking away. But he didn't give me a choice.

We finish tea and when it's cleared, Brittany asks us if we'd like a sundowner to drink as we sail back to Charithonia by sunset.

All three of us take a refill of champagne and

head down to the trampolines at the front of the boat as the sun begins its slow descent.

Joe, Luke, four kids and two dogs are already there, sitting and lying on the ginormous beds. Against the almost surreal backdrop, they look like the cover for an LP.

While Ella and Alisha move confidently into the group of *their* people, I hang back a little, approaching tentatively, feeling like an imposter.

I look around for Henry or Jenny, Brittany, Riley, Daisy or Jake. Someone to make me feel less like I'm intruding on the time of this family and their close friend, but there's no one around. *Why now?* They've been non-stop attentive all day. Henry overly so.

Then Jessie spots me and waddles over to me, wagging her tail. There are multiple reasons I love dogs. Their indiscriminate affection being *numero uno*.

As I bend to stroke her, my eyes are drawn to Luke. He beckons me over with a flick of his head – a surprisingly kind gesture, since he's probably cursing me internally for his near-death experience.

I decide to take him up on the offer and, with Jessie's emotional support, I make my way onto the trampoline, accepting, I suppose on some level, a sort of truce for sunset.

Before I come to sit, I spot something on the surface of the water and a voice calls, 'Turtle, starboard side.' I look around for the source of the sound and eventually find Henry and Jake up in the crow's nest above us.

'Turtle!' Noah says, bouncing up and running to the side of the boat, Luke darting after him. Thankfully, all of the kids are wearing life jackets but Luke catches Noah and sweeps him onto his knee, coming to sit on the side of the boat, his legs hanging down the side.

I think I move to get a better look of the elegant creature, gently swaying with the waves, but in doing so, I wind up taking a seat next to Luke and getting Jessie for company again. She flops her head down into my lap.

I'm here in the warm Caribbean, watching the sunset, a mesmerizing turtle floating in front of me, Luke by my side, a child on his lap, a dog on mine. In another time and place, in an alternate universe perhaps, this would have been the stuff dreams are made of.

I chance a glance at Luke and my breath catches when I find him already looking at me.

Six weeks.

We were only together for six weeks.

But these are the things we talked about for our future.

'It's hard to believe there's a storm coming,' Ella says, the others now all standing behind Luke, Noah, Jessie and me.

'Oh, I don't know,' Joe says. 'Life is funny. When you think you're cruising along, the universe throws you a curveball.'

It sure does.

'Thankfully, lightning doesn't strike the same spot twice.'

I only realize I've spoken those words loud enough for someone else to hear when Alisha says, 'I'm not so sure about that. This won't be Charithonia's first hurricane.'

20

LUKE

Something is happening to me. Either I have a tummy bug, or my jellyfish sting – which, for the record, did freaking kill and has left whip marks across my thigh and torso – has caused lasting damage to my internal organs, or I've suddenly developed seasickness after years of sailing. *Or* something far worse has my stomach twisting and flipping and turning.

We're all back on Charithonia, having been dropped to the beach by the tenders, making our way up to the main terrace back at Chateau Hettich, and though I'm talking to Toby, who is perched on my shoulders as I climb the steps up the rock face, I can't help replaying Joe's words to me back on the boat.

I've seen fewer fireworks on New Year's Eve than you and Carrie set off when you're together.

She sure does bring out a hot-headed version of me. In fact, I can't wait until she's gone later and I can resume my peaceful existence.

I'm just *fine* without Carrie in my life.

Totally fine.

I've been *fine* for seven years.

But since Joe asked the question – 'Are you fighting over the past, the present or your future?' – I don't know, it's just sort of stuck with me.

It isn't the future. It can't be the future. There is no future for Carrie and me. She made sure there never could be; that's what wrecked me so much. She's part of a past box that was neatly compartmentalized from my present.

Except now she's here because of flipping Eric's stomach flu and the box is open. Its contents are spilling all over my present.

And like Joe said through a mouthful of banana bread, 'Regardless of which it is, you owe it to yourself to find out.'

He's right, I think.

But I don't know if I have the courage it would take to delve into the depths of the box.

We reach the top of the stairs and there's a shift in the jovial mood of the adults among us.

Henry hands Carrie her heavy bag, which he's carried up for her, and he flashes her the kind of smile a guy would brandish in the middle of a sorority full of chicks on spring break.

You're just a kid, I want to scream. An extremely buff kid.

But actually, he isn't much different in age to Carrie when I fell for her. *Damn it*. The sooner she leaves, the better, if not only to spare me wanting to put superglue on Henry's seat the next time we have dinner together.

Jenny cuts through my spiteful thoughts. 'We'll wait for confirmation from the pilot, then Henry and I will come and get you to take you by boat to Tortola.'

Carrie thanks them both. She starts thanking everyone for making her feel welcome – avoiding looking at me, I'm sure – and damn it, even the dogs look sad.

She wasn't supposed to be here! I want to scream.

But I don't. Instead, I subtly shift away from the group and as soon as I'm through the archway of the terrace and onto the main pathway through the resort, I pick up my walking pace, heading directly for the sanctity of my pod.

I want her to go.

I've wanted nothing more than for her to exit my life as swiftly as she was pulled back into it for the last three days.

But now that she's going... I can't bring myself to say goodbye.

21

LUKE

Seven Years Ago

There's a note on my desk when I come back from my late-morning meeting – as she usually does, Carrie has covered it with a notepad and left a blank pink Post-it note on top to let me know it's there:

MEET ME AT OUR HOTEL. ROOM 252 –
12 p.m.
    HAPPY BIRTHDAY! x

We'd both been in and out of meetings, passing like ships in the night, all morning. Now she's MIA and something tells me I'm going to thoroughly, meticulously, scrupulously enjoy the birthday gift she's planned for me at noon.

I am literally tingling with anticipation.

Carrie and I have been seeing each other for six weeks. We haven't been together in a hotel for three. We spend our time together in my apartment. Locked inside the safety of my four walls, we talk – really talk – we eat, we drink, we laugh – truly laugh – we binge Netflix and we chill – the best, most glorious, head-spinningly hot kind of chilling.

The last time we used our hotel, we'd both been to the same business networking event. I'd had half an ear on conversations with colleagues and associates but the rest of me had been glued to Carrie. Watching her work the room, infiltrate conversations, garner laughs and smiles with her easy manner. I was so desperate to be the person she was entertaining, the man to receive her smiles, I couldn't stand the thought of us leaving the event separately, having to work our way back to my apartment on our own.

It was close but too far away. I needed to be with her sooner. It didn't have to be sex; it just had to be us. So I sent her a message, told her I'd be waiting in our hotel, watched as she read the message and felt my heartrate soar when she glanced up from her phone and found me from beneath hooded eyes.

I pick up her note from my desk and slip it into the pocket of my suit pants and, already breathing heavily, walk as surreptitiously as I can while bursting to run from my office and to Carrie in the hotel.

As I'm midway along the main corridor, flanked by offices either side of me, my phone chimes with a message. Keeping my face as straight as I can, knowing where I'm headed, I look at the message, expecting to see words, maybe even a picture, from Carrie.

But what I receive stops me in my tracks...

Happy birthday, Luke.

The words are accompanied by a picture but neither the words nor the image come from Carrie. Both the birthday wishes and the accompanying image of a baby scan come from my estranged wife.

It feels like my entire body falls from the tenth floor of the office block to the ground.

Anya's pregnant?

We haven't slept together in... There was one time. A last goodbye, the day she moved out of our home for good, to go back to Chicago to where her parents live. It was three months ago.

Three months.

'Everything okay, Luke? You look like you've seen a ghost.' One of the secretaries – not mine – presses a hand to my shoulder as she walks by. She doesn't wait for my answer.

I don't think I could answer. I'm numb. Mindless. Stupefied.

Someone else passes me, our arms colliding as I turn back in the direction of my office, then back toward the exit and Carrie.

God, Carrie. What is she going to think? She's in a hotel room waiting for me and—

'Luke, we need a word.' I look up to Christopher Oakes, partner and head of the entire tax division for the firm. Through the window into his office, I see two other partners and the HR director inside.

To say this doesn't look good is an understatement.

I follow Matt inside.

'Take a seat, Luke.'

I do because I don't have a choice and because my entire world is spinning double time. I'm dizzy, and taking a seat is better than falling on my face.

None of the others say hello and I already know

what's happening. My mushed-up brain is still capable of processing the enormity of the situation, so I'm not surprised when Matt takes a seat behind his desk and tells me, 'We've heard a rumor that you've been having an inappropriate relationship with your associate.' He looks as disappointed in me as he does critical. 'Is it true?'

I don't make it to Carrie in our hotel.

I tell myself I'm doing it to save her career.

I think maybe I also can't bear the thought of telling her that Anya is having my baby, that I've quit the firm, that I have catastrophically fucked everything up. That I can't see any other option than for she and I to be... done.

Present Day

The door to Carrie's pod is open and she's inside, packing her luggage on top of the bed.

I tap a knuckle on the door. She isn't startled. In fact, the smooth way she turns to look at me across her shoulder tells me she expected me to come.

She turns back to her luggage, needlessly rearranging things she's already packed to avoid looking at me.

'How's the leg?' she asks.

'My leg?' *What is she talking ab*— 'Oh. It's fine. Some blistering. I might have overreacted in the moment.'

'I'm sorry. The jellyfish was an unintended consequence.'

'I'm not here to get into the jellyfish incident,' I say, though I do have plenty to say about it.

She inhales so deeply, even by the door, I hear it.

I take a tentative step forward.

She eventually turns to face me and rises to full height, folding her arms across her like a shield. 'Why are you here?'

'I have to know before you leave...' I hear uncertainty in my voice – as much as I feel. 'Why did you ghost me? Why did you cut me out of your life completely?'

Her eyes rise to meet mine. For a second, I think she won't answer.

'I need to know,' I tell her, almost pleading.

Eventually, she speaks. 'You broke my heart, Luke, and I couldn't stand the thought of watching your relationship with your family through social media.' She tugs her lip between her teeth and shakes her head, killing our connection. She raises her hands from her sides, as if to ask, *What do you want from me?* Then she says, 'I did it to protect myself. You went back to someone you told me you didn't love. What did that say about your feelings for me?'

The first thing that hits me is the way her body seems to deflate with her words, as if holding them inside had been holding her up and now, she's... making me question myself, making me second guess the narrative I thought I knew.

'But you left us with no chance of ever coming back or, I don't know, being friends, even. I still— I still wanted you in my life, I just hadn't figured out how to make that happen. By the time I did—'

She scoffs. 'Was I supposed to sit around and wait, Luke? Wait for what? For you to want to be my *buddy*? To come to dinner with you and your family?'

'I don't know. I don't know what I should or could have done differently.' I drag my hands over my face. This isn't what I was expecting. I have zero clue what I *was* expecting.

I don't get the chance to pull all the pieces together, though, because Joe seems to appear from nowhere, and he's standing by my side in the doorway of the pod, clearing his throat to announce his arrival.

I wonder how long he's been listening, and clearly Carrie does too. She's suddenly straighter, taller, mindful her client is in the vicinity, but her cheeks pinken, like she's ashamed to have let her professional armor slip.

'Sorry to interrupt,' Joe says.

'Not at all,' Carrie says jumpily.

I know I can't go back to our conversation. I asked my question, at long last. The question that's haunted me is out in the wild and it has an answer.

Joe's come to collect her and take her out of my life, again. Maybe for another seven years. Maybe forever this time.

It's a good thing, I think.

Yet I can't shake the sense that when I process her words, I'm going to be left with a void somewhere deep inside me. I hope it will only be a bareness where a long-pondered question is now answered.

I fear it's not.

'I'm just about packed,' I hear Carrie say as I slip away into the night, feeling like there are a million things I should stay and say to her if this is the last time I'm going to see her, but not knowing what they are, or not able to find the words.

So, I leave without saying goodbye.

22

CARRIE

He's just going to leave? No goodnight, no goodbye?

I can feel my eyes stinging but I'm pinning my shoulders back. Joe is my client. Luke is my ghost.

He's haunting me now like he did in a past life. Nothing has changed. *He* hasn't changed.

Why did I tell him the truth? Why did I let those words tumble out of me?

I can't unsay them, how it felt for him to leave me dressed in lingerie I'd picked out especially for his birthday, lying on the bed in our hotel, waiting for the man I was insanely, incomprehensibly in love with to come to me.

But I'm not fighting tears because of a memory.

I'm willing myself to be strong, stoic, because he's done it again. Just sloped off into the night. Gone.

In seven years' time, he might even throw at me that he wished we could have stayed in touch, so that we could be... *friends? Friends!*

I only have myself to blame for feeling like this. I've done it again. Bared myself, made myself vulnerable for him. To be left feeling hollow.

God, I hate him, I hate him, I *hate* him.

I'm so consumed by my dark thoughts that I have to ask Joe to repeat himself as he stands in my doorway and tells me, 'The jet would have been able to land in Tortola but it wouldn't have been able to take back off, Carrie, so it had to turn back. I'm sorry.'

Can I ask him to say it for a third time? Because maybe lucky number three will be the time it sinks in.

'I can't leave?' I'm trying not to be hysterical but my brain is about to explode.

'I'm really sorry, Carrie. I've pleaded with air traffic control. Or, you know, my pilot has on my behalf, but the military have taken over the airport. As of two hours ago, nothing but essential flights can land or take off.'

'But... I... The storm isn't even here yet.'

Joe nods. 'If there was anything I could do, I swear to you, I would.'

As the reality sinks in, I lose my professional composure and sink onto the edge of the bed behind me.

I'm stuck here, in paradise, with a superstorm heading my way. With *Luke*.

Joe crosses the room to me and I sense his awkwardness as he places a hand on the top of my head. Sense it and *feel* it. Because this is a bizarre way to comfort someone for anyone who isn't a clergyman.

'What if... I go to Tortola and stay in a hotel near the airport? Maybe we can keep trying?' I suggest, knowing this is an unlikely plan, but it would get me off this island and away from Luke.

Finally, his holiness removes his hand from my head, then in another peculiar move, bends to his hunkers in front of me. *Am I acting like an eight-year-old child?* Joe's certainly making me think so.

'If you're worried about the hurricane, Carrie, try not to be. You'll be safer here than in Tortola, I assure you. We have an abundance of hurricane provisions. Troy will be in the bunker with us and he'll rustle up some great food. We have generators and appliances down there. It's geared up to be a safe room for many eventualities.'

I exhale slowly, nodding. 'Thank you.'

This whole mess isn't Joe's fault. It's also crazy that he needs a panic room but now that he's said it, he's probably a significant ransom risk.

'I'll leave you to unpack.' He makes to leave the room. I can't wait to be grumpy alone, in my pajamas. 'Oh, Troy will cook breakfast in the morning at the usual time but some of us will be heading out early to Virgin Gorda, so you might not see us.'

'Another island?' I ask, coming to stand.

He nods. 'Most of the staff are from Virgin Gorda and their families live on the island. We'll head out first thing, before the sea gets too choppy, so we can help secure their properties and bring their families here if they want to weather the storm with us, so to speak. We'll be back as soon as we can get the job done to prepare Charithonia.'

There's a sadness about him that I haven't seen before. For all his eccentricity, I can see what Ella sees. Joe is a compassionate man.

Suddenly, the sound of the ocean and the light of the moon in the dark sky beyond my pod seem less beautiful and more ominous. 'It's going to be bad, isn't it?' I ask.

Joe twists his lips with, I think, a heavy heart. 'It

looks that way. I'll leave you to it. Ask the staff if you'd like anything cooking up for supper.'

'Thank you.' He steps out of my pod, into the night, and I call, 'Joe? Could I come with you tomorrow, to Virgin Gorda? I'd like to help, if I can.'

'The more hands, the better. Troy will make a quick bite for us at dawn and we'll set off after sunrise.'

'Goodnight, Joe.'

'Sweet dreams, Carrie.'

I close the door behind him and press my forehead to the wood.

The Atlantic is out to get me.

I'm starting to see this storm as a metaphor – it's going to hit. It's going to be a direct hit and it's going to alter life as I know it.

There's a dull ache in my chest, beneath my breastbone, and it definitely feels like fear. I *am* afraid.

I just don't know if it's the hurricane or my proximity to Luke that's most terrifying.

Where does he get off messing with my head and my heart?

Turning, I press my back against the door and slide down until my butt hits the floor. On top of everything else, I now have three important calls to make and a fur baby to let down, again.

23

LUKE

She cut me out to protect herself.

I'm walking along the beach, cool sand falling between my toes and soft under my feet. There are lights on in the resort – in Carrie's pod too, though I know she must be gone by now – and security briefly cast a torch light in my direction when I came down here, but my path is mostly illuminated by the blue light of the moon.

I broke her heart?

She cut me off and tore mine to shreds.

I've always thought she did it as a reaction to us ending. Not that break-ups tend to be nice but I do appreciate ours was abrupt, and I guess I thought she took it badly and reacted impulsively.

Us ending was hard enough to take, but what was harder was thinking that she didn't even care enough, had never cared enough, to want to *know* me afterwards.

I could be bitter, even hateful, because she didn't care as much for me as I did about her.

Argh, I don't know. *Did I think that? Did I truly believe that all this time?*

I'm starting to question everything I've always thought and that's a dangerous place to be.

Carrie is compartmentalized. In the past. I've moved on.

I needed to ask one question, to get closure. Now I have it.

So why am I walking up and down this beach, too restless to sleep, feeling like someone is crushing my internal organs?

I sink down onto the sand, bending my knees and wrapping my arms around them as I sit.

Was this all on me? Did I honestly expect her to wait for me? To wait for what? I didn't even know how things would pan out with Anya.

The moon is beautiful. Big, bright, full, its light dancing on the gentle ebb and flow of the ocean as it teases the shore. It feels implausible that a storm meteorologists are predicting will be the greatest to ever make landfall in the Atlantic is imminent.

Yet as mystifying as the night feels, something about the calm of it makes everything so clear to me.

She loved me.

For seven years, I've thought that my feelings were unrequited. That to her, we were a thrill, a rush, a forbidden relationship that was fueled by adrenaline. All the while, I had been in love.

But it wasn't one-sided at all.

She ghosted me for the same reason I couldn't bring myself to say goodbye to her in person and end us properly back then.

She was in love with me. I was in love with her.

And we fucking blew it. *I* blew it.

* * *

At some point, in the early hours of the morning, I fell into a restless sleep, tossing and turning between erratic and unreasoned dreams that seemed pertinent in the moment but that now, pulling on my workout clothes, I can't clearly remember.

It's around five thirty in the morning, the sky is grey and lightening by the minute. I pull on my sneakers and a black baseball cap, clean my teeth and head in the direction of the terrace.

From my vantage point at the top of the rock, I can easily see the change in the sea. The usual blue hue looks closer to a shade of grey. Last night, it looked like a millpond but this morning, it's etched by an infinite number of white caps. The chop bears the imminent reality.

I stop on the walkway at a midpoint between my pod and the main house, watching the waves. The air has changed too. It's denser. The smell has changed. It's saltier, tinged with the smell of aquatic life.

We need to get to Virgin Gorda and back quickly. Soon, the rough sea will be menacing. The weather bods are predicting waves up to 100 feet when Isabel hits – something like eighteen or nineteen men tall. Wind gusts up to 285 kilometers per hour.

I can admit to myself, I'm apprehensive. This is *big*.

I will also admit, only to myself, that I'm pleased Carrie left the island last night, even if I never see her again, because I know she's safe.

Though, as I think that, there's an unwelcome pressure behind my eyes and I take off my cap to drag a hand through my thick hair.

She was within my grasp, after *all* the empty time that spanned between us. Now she's gone, again.

A guttural noise escapes me. The sound of frustration. Maybe anger. At her. At myself.

Not the focus of today, I remind myself.

Today is about preparing this island and Virgin Gorda and the homes of as many family members of Joe's staff as we can for the hurricane.

When I get to the terrace, Joe, Henry, Jenny, Dave (one of the security guys), Glen (one of the gardeners), Dionne (one of the housemaids), Monique (one of the kitchen staff) and Roy (a handyman) are all sitting around one large table, having pulled a bunch of smaller ones together.

The tables aren't set as usual with cloths and flowers in vases. Instead, they're bare carcasses and on top of them are a basket of breads, a bowl filled with what look like hard-boiled eggs, a plate of bacon and sausages, and a board of sliced cheeses. A delicious and wholesome but nonetheless fuss-free breakfast of necessity before a long day.

'Morning, all,' I say, making my way into the group and accepting a mug of coffee Monique pours for me from a French press on the table. I tell her she needn't but she asks me, 'What else would I do?'

There's an atmosphere about the place that's somewhere between anticipation and adrenaline.

It's really bizarre to think this, so there's no way in hell I'll confess it out loud, but I have a strange sense of excited nervousness. Like, I really don't want a hurricane to hit the islands, or anywhere for that matter, but if it's coming, I sort of want to see it, feel it, breathe it, live it.

I know, when I look at Joe, that he's feeling the same. It's like standing at the top of the hardest, fastest black slope and knowing that, no matter how treacherous the run is, you're skiing down it and you're going to feel the buzz of danger.

'I appreciate it, thank you,' I tell Monique, accepting the mug of coffee but not taking one of the spare seats at the table. Instead, I walk around to grab my own plate of food, which I set down at my spot between Joe and Jenny. I still don't sit. I can't. I'm fidgety.

I take a bite of sourdough bread and stand by the table, coffee in hand, waiting for it to cool enough so that I can take a much-needed hit of caffeine.

There's not much conversation at the table besides some discussions of which boat we're taking to the island and how many tools and chip boards we can bring with us. Then there are dead moments, where you could literally hear a pin drop. Even the dogs are lying under the table quietly, not begging for food or wanting to play.

It's in one of these long silences that I get the shock of my life.

'Good morning,' Carrie says.

I think I've heard a ghost but when I turn around, she's here, she's real and she's standing right behind me.

I jump, startled, and splash scalding hot coffee over my hand, which in turn makes me drop the mug, and the boiling hot liquid spills onto the crotch of my shorts.

'Jesus, shit, bastard and mother-fucking fuck!' I jump on the spot, legs wide and gangly, pulling on the material of my shorts, trying to fan the burning of my cock.

'Oh my God!' Carrie shouts.

I'm still dancing and holding the bridge of my nose when Carrie grabs a jug of ice-water, pulls out the waistband of my shorts, and pours the water – cubes and all – down my crotch.

As the last ice cubes drop – one, *pop*, then two, *pop* – from my shorts onto the decking, I look up to Carrie and ask, 'Are you *effing* kidding me?'

'It didn't help?' she says sweetly. But I know that look. It's not innocent at all.

'Enjoy that, did you?' I ask.

Someone at the table sniggers, someone else snorts, then all the tension of the morning fades into raucous laughter from everyone except me – I'm livid and worried how many blisters I'm going to get on my dick – and Carrie, who looks really damn pleased with herself.

'I didn't *not* enjoy it.' She shrugs. *Shrugs.* Lieutenant Chalmers may have been caused irreparable damage and Carrie *shrugs.*

As I'm scowling at her, she swings her hips, making her firm butt cheeks look outrageously attractive in her blue yoga leggings.

Eyes up, Luke, she's not a piece of meat.

Only as she bends across the table to pick up food – I'm fairly certain she folds forward, hips high for my further torture – do I realize...

'What are you still doing here?'

Everyone has calmed again and Carrie shifts to face me, food in hand. 'The airport is closed, so it looks like I'm staying.'

My head shoots to Joe. 'She's stuck here?' I'm irrationally livid with him. The storm isn't Joe's fault but the very last place on earth I want Carrie to be right now is the Caribbean. Not because her presence is like a slow torture to me – except when it's a boiling hot drink, or dangerous sea creature, or kick to the face kind of pain – because… 'There's a cat five hurricane coming, Joe!' I state the obvious.

Give him his due, Joe looks needlessly apologetic, but I don't know who else to take this out on. Any fear that I've been harboring internally just increased a million-fold.

'We're all aware, matey,' he says calmly. 'I tried my best but the military has commandeered the ports.'

'But—' I stop myself as I consider the space, all the faces at the table whose families and friends will be here too. *Joe's* family and friends.

'I want to be here,' Carrie says, and if she's lying, it doesn't show. 'I'm glad I can help.'

'Sorry. It's a shit situation for everyone,' I say to the group rather than anyone in particular. To Carrie, I add, 'You're right. More bodies will make faster work.' I try to sound airy but I stuff my hands in my now soggy pockets and clench my fists.

'On that note.' Joe stands and drains the coffee that's left in his mug. 'We should load up the boat and get going.'

Everyone moves on Joe's instruction – not that he

meant it as an order, but this is Joe; he has silent control of, well, *everything*.

I hang back a beat, feeling the muscles in my cheeks twitch with the tension in my jaw.

I don't want Carrie to be here. For one thing, she's a gigantic pain in my ass – correction, burnt crotch. But I also don't want her anywhere near this storm.

And the reason my jaw is stiff and my fists are clenched in frustration is because despite both those things, I do want her here.

I'm so damn thrilled she hasn't gone, that last night isn't how it ended between us.

Because something has shifted in me. I'm not sure how or what, but when I saw her on the terrace, it was as if she sent a surge of energy through my entire body. I can still feel a tingling under my skin from her presence.

I'm drawn to her like a moth to a flame, knowing the ending could be fatal. Unable to deny that I haven't felt anything like this electricity in my veins before or since *her*.

24

CARRIE

I'm scared.

The boat crossing to Virgin Gorda is rough, the swell is as big as I've ever seen from a boat and Henry tells me this is only the very beginning of what's to come. The sky is increasingly cloudy, not like the beautiful sunshine that's been around since I arrived – it's hard to fathom that was only Monday and now Thursday looks so different.

There are ten of us squished onto the speedboat, holding down wood and tools while trying to root ourselves to the boat as it crashes up and down, water spraying back at us from the bow.

Yet I'm pretty sure it's not the journey or the storm that are making me afraid. Or not more so than being on the boat with Luke, after I bared all to him.

I'd vowed to myself, if I ever saw him again, not to let him know how much he hurt me and last night, I don't know why the words fell out of me.

I was angry, frustrated, upset. I was supposed to be leaving.

Until I wasn't.

This morning, he reacted to me as if I was a pane of fragile glass, waiting to be shattered. All jumpy and protective.

Well, I don't need his pity. He's seven years too late to show remorse.

I'm pleased he dropped his coffee and I hope he found my little trick with the iced water to be more feisty than wilting flower.

When he looks my way, I realize I've been scowling at him. *Damn it*. I don't want him to think I'm looking at him. Though, I have to admit, wet from the spray, his workout gear sticking to everywhere it touches on his torso, cap in hand and dragging a hand through his wet hair to tug it back from his face. He's... well, I can see why twenty-four-year-old me would have been turned by him.

Okay, okay, why even thirty-one-year-old me would be rapt.

But why is *he* staring at *me*? He has no right and I narrow my eyes to let him know it.

Thankfully, our destination is dead ahead. When Henry drives us up to it, Luke and Jenny jump onto the dock, each taking a line and tying the boat to it. I watch Luke twist and turn the rope like he's done it every day since he was born, and I watch the muscles of his arms twist and turn too.

What's *wrong* with me? Am I greedy for punishment? Has the lack of clothes, the sea, sand, sun and alcohol of the last few days made me certifiably nuts?

The man *left* me, *ditched* me, made me fall in love with him, then *dumped* me.

We get off the vessel at a place called Leverick Bay. There are other boats, a restaurant and hotel. The water is much calmer in the bay, sheltered by surrounding islands.

I can imagine, on a different day, it's even more beautiful here, a hive of tourist activity, laughter and rum.

Today, surprisingly, people still seem jovial. Deep bellowing laughs can be heard around the marina from men and women, though many of them are securing boats and premises.

There are two trucks waiting for us – a black one

and an electric blue one. Yup, I'm that stereotypical gal when it comes to cars. They move, they have four wheels, I'm going to be sitting on a bench seat in the back, no roof over my head. That's all I care to know.

One of the truck drivers is Dionne's brother and the other is Roy's father-in-law. The decision is made to split the group, half in each truck, and go off in different directions, to get as much done as possible, as quickly as possible.

Henry seems to have been appointed chief weather watcher and he determines we need to head back to Charithonia no later than 2 p.m., otherwise we risk the journey being too dangerous. We also need to pitch in with the guys left on Charithonia to tie down and protect everything on Joe's island as best we can.

It's going to be a long day but I'm glad of it. Pleased that I can help somehow and delighted to not have dead time on my hands to worry about what's to come.

I messaged Callum and my mom last night, telling them both that I'd be here for the storm, playing it down as much as I could, lying to them that Joe has basically declared the island a safe haven with a ginormous panic room. But, of course, I had to confess I didn't know when I'd next be in touch, that the rumors are that the phone lines could be brought down in the storm, and power supplies could be thwarted.

I couldn't face speaking to them, so I let their follow-up calls ring out. It wasn't just about the storm. More that my head was absolute mush from the day's sail, from my declaration to Luke, then the day being rounded off by me being trapped in the path of a mahoosive storm.

My mom must have passed on the message to my dad because, by current count, he's tried to call me sixteen times since 9 p.m. last night.

At this moment, I have a legitimate excuse to bury my head in the sand.

There are ten people – twelve including the drivers – and two trucks. Eight men and four women, so when Jenny and Monique head for the black truck and Dionne to the blue, it makes sense for me to follow Dionne, Glen, Henry and Dave, to even out the sexes. Much like women are from Venus and men are from Mars, women bring multitasking and strategic thinking to a team scenario. Men bring brute strength. Not to typecast but trying to be practical here.

I'm last to climb into the back of the truck. Henry reaches down a hand to give me a tug up. I lift my sneaker-clad foot to the vehicle but before I push up from the ground, I hear a voice I will never fail to recognize, up close behind me.

'Monique is riding in this truck. You're with us, Carrie.'

Releasing Henry's hand, I spin around to find Luke speaking to me but glaring at Henry as the words leave his mouth. In response to Luke's near growling, one side of Henry's lips quirk up, like a teenage boy who just doesn't know when to quit.

'To balance numbers,' Luke adds, briefly glancing my way before turning his back on me and going back to the blue ride.

I've no problem switching places with Monique; I was only trying to balance the numbers myself, though if I'm honest, I'd rather not spend time with Luke today, or ever again in my life.

The eye roll Monique gives, arms folded across her chest as she approaches me, suggests she got told to change trucks.

I smile apologetically, without knowing why she's been switched.

'Honey, you need to put that man out of his misery,' she tells me, winking as she accepts a hand up from Henry.

25

LUKE

'I'd appreciate it if you didn't manhandle me,' Carrie gripes as I hoist her up and swing her onto the back of the Mitsubishi pick up.

'We're under a time pressure,' I tell her, though kind of enjoying pissing her off.

I didn't *manhandle* her, I just picked her up and put her onto the truck where she was going anyway. It had nothing to do with the fact she followed Henry to *his* truck, or that Henry keeps flashing her hot-girl-bod smiles and flexing his muscles in her direction. It had nothing to do with the fact that if she's here in the British Virgin Islands for this storm, I want her to be right next to me at all times, in my eye line, where I can at least attempt to protect her.

'We've got a lot of work to do and you were dilly-dallying.'

She's sitting and we're pulling away, but she still pouts at me, her eyes like a scorned cat's. 'I was on the other truck already.'

'Yeah, and Monique wanted to ride with Jenny,' I lie.

I follow Carrie's pointed finger as she asks, 'Jenny, who is sitting right there?'

Oops. Dumbass.

'Fine. Dionne.' I roll my eyes as if *she's* being the petulant one, and diagonally opposite me, bobbing up and down on the bench seat as we drive across uneven tarmac and divots in the road, Jenny is fighting back laughter.

'Who says dilly-dallying, anyway?' Carrie says.

'Joe.' It comes out sulkier than intended but the big guy's name seems to put a nail in that one.

'Have you seen this?' Roy, thankfully, breaks into Carrie's and my latest bickerfest. He's holding out his phone, though I can't make out what's on the screen. 'They're calling Isabel equivalent to a category seven hurricane, if such a thing existed. She's a monster.'

I'm not laughing anymore. I glance up to Carrie and see the same concern in her eyes as I'm trying to keep out of mine.

I want to tell her it's going to be fine, that I'll look after her. In truth, all I know for sure is that I'm going to try my damnedest. Because I haven't figured out what the pull is between us in these islands, why I feel like I can't be more than six yards away from her without my insides searching for her, but I think it has something to do with her confession last night.

Shifting my gaze from Carrie to Joe, who's been uncharacteristically quiet all morning, I see what I never see in his expression, not even when he's making decisions to put billions of dollars on the line. I see worry. And maybe, remorse? For what, I've no idea. He couldn't help this any more than God himself. Still, Joe looks at me like he's sorry.

Our first stop is Roy's sister's home. It's a small one-story place with wood paneling on the walls, with a peach-painted exterior. I consider the roof and the already loose tiles here and there. The wood-framed windows look old and flimsy. Floral fabric blows out from the inside where the strips of glass are set to open, probably on account of the humidity today.

Though I've already dried out from the boat in

the heat of the morning, the air is sticky, it feels claggy against my skin, and the dust that kicked up from the road as we drove feels like it's stuck to me.

We've brought some boards of plywood but Roy's sister, bouncing a tiny, crying baby on her chest, tells us she already has boards; she needs help attaching them across the windows.

'We should leave some space for airflow,' Roy tells us. 'Otherwise the pressure will blow the roof off the house.'

I have no idea if that's fact or myth but I'm already out of the truck and taking tools from the front passenger seat next to Roy's father-in-law, pleased for the distraction because all I can think is, boards won't make a drop of difference. This mother and baby are going to lose the roof of their home regardless, and I get my first real taste of how emotional the next few days are going to be.

When I turn back to the task in hand, Roy's father-in-law is giving the group instructions about another house, along the street, that belongs to Roy's mother. The screaming baby has stopped crying – because Carrie is now cradling it in her arms while Roy's sister focuses on the work we're here to do.

I don't know why but the sight of Carrie with the newborn stops me in my tracks, freezes me dead, steals the air from my lungs. She just looks so... natural at it, I guess, swaying and shushing the little one, gently stroking his cheek.

I'd be lying to myself if I denied ever imagining Carrie with a child. I have, I did. When we were together, and after, when we weren't, when I was trying to make something work with my ex-wife for the sake of what I thought was our baby. No amount of guilt stopped me lying in the spare room of Anya's new home, wishing the woman in the adjacent room, carrying my child, wasn't her but Carrie. I didn't only think about it; I tormented myself with the idea of the life that I'd held in my grasp.

Our relationship had been against the unwritten rules of our firm, particularly with my partnership imminent, but I knew in those weeks we were together, I knew the first night we kissed in the office because I had already thought long and hard about the consequences of not holding back, that I would have given it all up for her.

Ironically, I did.

I've thought for years that I was an idiot, an unquestionable fool to have rolled the dice on my career, because the feelings I had for Carrie weren't reciprocal.

I've supposed as much all this time. Until last night.

'Luke? The drill?' I snap out of my reverie, finding Joe and following him past a bumped and dented old car parked next to the house and round to the yard.

The back of the house is as unkempt as the old car. Roy told us his sister is a single mom. I was raised by one, too, and I know how hard she worked to give my brother and me everything we needed.

Once the storm has been and gone, I'd like to come back here and clean up the garden.

For now, I hoist a wood board over one of three rear windows and Joe gets to work drilling it in place.

I'm stuck, otherwise I'd have leapt to help Jenny and Carrie as I see them jointly carrying a board to the farthest window along from mine. They lift it together against the window, then Jenny says she's got it.

'Are you sure?' Carrie asks her. That board is heavy for anybody, even me.

'Wait and I'll come help,' I call, but Carrie speaks across me.

'I'll grab the driver drill and some screws,' she tells Jenny.

The next thing that happens renders me more dumbstruck than seeing Carrie cradling a baby. She picks up a drill, flips an old crate against the wall, climbs onto it and starts to fix the board onto the window.

I'm not old-fashioned and I try not to stereotype. I'm even the head of the D&I Committee at work. But I had no idea Carrie knew the name of any man-tools, let alone had the ability to use them.

Even more unexpected still is how incredibly hot I find it. Not just the way her body moves and tenses in her form-fitting workout gear, but the independence of it. She doesn't need a man; she doesn't need me.

I have zero clue what is happening to me today; I can only put it down to storm hormones or something, because I am as hot for her as I have ever been.

That's a lot hot. Heaps hot. Near desperate.

'All set,' Joe says, patting our now boarded window as if he knows he needs to knock me back into real time.

He shifts his focus between Carrie and me, then shakes his head and laughs.

Yeah, I'm as easy to read as an open book. I know it and I need to shut it down. Better yet, I need to get my venom back on because that woman who seems to be driving me crazy in every respect *really* hates me.

26

CARRIE

We're onto the third home. Joe and Luke are finishing boarding the windows, while the rest of us pack sandbags around the entrances to the house. There's an unspoken sense of pointlessness about this one. The colorfully painted yellow one-story is set so close to the beach – only a thin, uneven road between the sand and the house – that when the storm brings a water surge with it, the house will stand no chance.

Once the last of the sandbags are in place, hot, sweaty and dirty, I slump down onto the sack, knees bent up to my chest, and listen to my stomach grumble. We've been at it for a few hours already and there's still a lot to do. More than we can get done, truth be told. Not because my watch is telling me it's late morning but because the sea is showing that our time on Virgin Gorda is running out. The stunning blues of the ocean are currently shades of grey, much like the thick-set sky, and the waves are playing an angry song, crashing at the shoreline, each one looking like it's capped with snow.

'Hey.' I glance up to see Luke rubbing his dirty hands on an old rag, his mouth twisted into a smile that's directed at me but which doesn't set my pulse racing like his true one. His voice is soft, calm, slightly husked – the kind of tone that in an instant thrusts me back to twenty-four-year-old me.

I'd forgotten, or scrubbed from my mind, maybe, the day Luke sent me home from the office.

* * *

Seven Years Ago

This isn't just a cold; it's a flu. Not the man kind of flu, but the actual limb-shaking, hot sweats, puffy face, streaming nose, excruciating throat, zero energy kind of flu. Woman flu.

It also came on from nowhere. I swear I was fine when I woke this morning – tired and sort of heavy feeling, but not riddled with germs.

By 3 p.m., when Luke sent me home, ordering me to bed with a book, a hot water bottle and over-the-counter meds he picked up for me from the local pharmacy, I was feverish. The light of my computer felt like it was piercing my eyes.

Now, I'm lying on the fold-down bed of my studio apartment in Midtown, wearing my thickest pajamas, not knowing whether I'm too hot or too cold. The sun is falling behind the skyscrapers I can see from my window.

A knock on my apartment door drags me out of my self-pitying, helpless state. It can't be for me; I don't know anyone else in the building. I'm always working and, lately, when I'm not, I'm with Luke, at his place.

Not seeing him tonight, tomorrow, however long it takes for this stupid virus to disappear is contributing to why I feel so sorry for myself.

The knock comes again and I think, despite the fact this is clearly a mistake-of-door scenario, I'm going to have to answer.

Forcing myself up as slowly as I have only ever

seen my grandmother rise – and she has two false hips – I slip my feet into my slippers and shuffle toward the door.

'Carrie? It's Luke.'

I stop midway between my bed and the door, surveying the used tissues scattered around the floor, the half-eaten bowl of soup on the kitchen counter and the dirty pan to accompany it, my work clothes thrown over the back of my two-seater sofa, rather than hung back up in the wardrobe.

Damn it, damn it.

And the apartment is nothing compared to how truly awful I look, I realize, when I catch my reflection in my lounge mirror.

Mustering strength I don't feel, I quickly throw the soup and pan in the sink, collect the tissues and trash them, drag my hair into a hair-tie and cover it mostly with a wide, fabric hairband. I wipe smudged make-up from under my eyes but there's no time to do anything about the baby-pink, button-down fleece pajamas.

My little exertion has whacked me and when I eventually open the door, I'm panting like I've run a half hour on the treadmill.

And there is Luke, still wearing the dark-blue

suit and crisp pink shirt he had on in the office earlier – actually matchy-matchy with my bedwear, except he looks... divine. I like him later in the day, once his fresh-pressed-ness of the morning has turned into something more relaxed, a little more rugged, like the Luke I get to see in the evenings. Exactly how he looks now.

His arm is wrapped around a brown paper bag with a baguette poking out of the top – if it's fresh, I can't smell it because I can't smell a thing with my bunged-up nose. His other hand is resting in the pocket of his tailored pants. He considers me, from my toes to my head, his focus eventually resting on my face, and he leans his head to the side, one half of his mouth teasing upward.

He says softly, calmly, with a slight husk to his voice, 'Hey.'

I knew before he cooked for me that night, before he gave me drugs at the right time, before he ran me a warm bath full of bubbles and sponged my back as he talked to me, before he lay on my bed and read to me from my book as I drifted to sleep on his chest... I knew before any of that... I was in love with him.

* * *

Present Day

I shove those memories from my mind, knowing that even if I could forgive, I can never forget, and I say back, simply, 'Hey.'

The problem is, I wish I could forget all of it, the good stuff too. Because he's dirty and sweaty, his hair is rugged, and he's driving me insane with this irrational need to have me in his sights at all times, like I'm a porcelain doll that's going to break at just the sniff of a storm. Yet the only reason I know he's been watching me is because I've been watching him too.

'Are you okay?' he asks.

I nod. 'Fine.'

He shakes his head, eyes to the heavens. 'Don't be too expressive, will you?'

I'm about to raise my middle finger and tell him to *express this* but Joe walks into my field of vision and I remember I'm here in my capacity as a professional, not just someone Luke had a fling with once and ditched on her ass without warning.

I jump up to standing and Joe pats the air with a hand. 'Sit, rest, you deserve a break.'

'I'm good, I was just taking two.' I gesture with my head toward what I can only assume from the extremely good smells coming from the place is a bakery, a few buildings along from where we are. 'In fact, I was just about to grab us all some sustenance for the next place.'

'Here, take my wallet; you know what I like,' Luke says, holding it out for me, the way he has in the past, implicitly trusting me to make his decisions for him.

I stare at it. 'I have money; I'm sure I can stretch to picking you something up.'

He scoffs. 'It would pain you to do something nice for me, so here, take it.'

I have no intention of taking his money but I do accept the wallet, if only because to continue the discussion would make me appear even more obstinate in front of my client than Luke is trying to make me seem, and in the grand scheme of what is happening around us... better to take the wallet and not the bait!

As I get closer to the building, which looks similar to the homes we've been prepping this morning, the smell of sweet bread has my tummy not just rumbling but screaming at me to fill it.

I step inside what feels like a front lounge – floral upholstery hangs over the windows, rugs cover the otherwise concrete floor, a few tables and chairs and a two-seat sofa fill the open space opposite the counter – and the aromas from the baskets of baked goods have me instantly salivating.

A lady wearing a colorful apron that's trimmed with decorative white cotton walks into the space carrying a crate of food. She wears a net over a mass of tightly curled and grey-flecked black hair and her lips are painted bright red. When she spots me, she beams.

'Good mornin' and good timin'. This is the last batch of fresh baked banana bread. My *famous* banana bread, you know?'

Her voice is so loud and full of happiness that I could forget the reason I'm on the island. 'Well, if it's famous, I'll take two, please.'

She nods. 'Still warm, too.'

'Even better. Do you think you could slice it for me? Just I'm sharing.' I loosely gesture out of the door, diagonally across the street to where the others are packing up the truck.

'Sure t'ing,' she says, setting about the task and leaving the remainder of the loaf breads on the countertop. 'I've seen what you've all been doing over there. It's good to see.' Her smile is gentler now as she looks at me, rather than the bread she is slicing, making my nerves jitter. 'We've got to help each other in these times. It's all part of God's message, see. He's telling us we aren't doing good enough at caring for each other and our islands. He's teaching us a lesson.' She holds the slices together and slides them into two brown paper bags, which she hands across the counter to me with a wad of napkins. 'We'll all come together, love each other, like he wants us to. He'll forgive us.'

Her words steal mine from me. Her belief and hope are so strong it – *she* – makes me want to be a better person. *Forgiveness*, that's what she thinks the whole storm is about. She isn't angry or sad, she doesn't even seem apprehensive, though she has every reason to be; she's simply accepting. Ready to move on. To forgive and be forgiven.

The strength of her faith is almost palpable. All I can say in response is, 'Thank you.'

Something tells me I'm thanking her for more than just banana bread but in this moment, I can't put my finger on what.

I notice a large clock on the wall behind the woman and watch it tick the last few seconds until eleven thirty. We'll be leaving the island in two and a half hours, our rendezvous time, before the sea gets too rough to get back to Charithonia, where we'll be sheltered and safe, where there's a chef and endless hurricane provisions.

I look at the entire counter full of food that might never be bought. 'How much do I owe you?'

She waves a hand. 'On the house for helping my neighbors. I didn't know what else to do with myself today, so I did what I always do. I baked and baked in case people want it. You know, some people still don't believe the hurricane will come and when they change their minds, they'll have no supplies. They'll need what I've made.' She shrugs and sets about pouring a coffee from a ready-filtered pot into a polystyrene cup, which she hands to me. 'Milk and sugar?'

'Oh, ah, yes please to milk. A sweetener too, please, if you have one.'

She busies herself with turning my black coffee white. 'You might as well choose somethin' else to take with you. All this won't keep much longer and at some point, I'll have to lock up. But I'll be here as long as I can be, as long as someone might need me.'

'Can I at least pay for the coffee?' I ask.

She just pffts. Despite everything going on around her, this woman is full of kindness. And that thought gives me an idea.

I set down my paper bags next to my takeout

coffee and count the cash I have in my pocket, then I open Luke's wallet and see he has a lot more than I do.

'How much for everything else?' I ask. 'I'm willing to accept your gifts but I won't take no for an answer on everything else.'

27

LUKE

Carrie has been gone a while. As I'm beginning to think I'll go to the bakery and check on her, she comes walking back to us with a spring in her step that she didn't have when she went. She's carrying multiple brown paper bags and sets them down on the hood of the truck.

'Help yourselves, guys, the banana bread smells insanely good and it's still warm. There're cinnamon rolls, pizza slices and almond loaf cake too.'

She turns to me and smiles. It's a beaming smile, the kind I haven't seen enough on her since she got here. Wide and dazzling, it brings dimples to the sides of her mouth and creases of happiness around her eyes. The sort that makes my chest tighten and my breathing pick up pace.

'Here's your wallet,' she tells me.

I take it, noticing immediately how much thinner it is since her trip. I open it up to find there are no notes inside.

'You spent all my money on baked goods?' I ask in disbelief. *Surely not.*

'That baker drives a hard bargain, Chalmers. But one whiff of that banana bread and you'll understand how she got me.'

She turns away but I can tell she's still grinning.

'A hard bargain? Carrie, there was over two hundred bucks in there.'

She shifts, coming at me so fast with a piece of banana bread that I can do nothing except open my mouth and let her stuff it. 'See. Incredible, right?'

The food is good. Insanely so. But two hundred bucks?

Then I see Joe, mouth full but still managing to smirk as he nods his head, telling me to turn around and look at something. I do a one-eighty to look at the bakery, and I see a very happy lady wearing a rainbow of colors and stacking crates of food on plastic tables. Squinting, I make out a sign stuck to them, stating in bold marker pen:

FREE TO A GOOD HOME

If my chest was tight and my breathing speedy a moment ago, that's nothing compared to the way my entire body aches as I watch Carrie laughing with Jenny and Roy, tearing into a cinnamon roll, white icing stuck to the end of her nose.

I remember exactly how I fell for her the first time. I know because it's happening all over again.

When Jenny whispers something to her and Carrie raises her head in my direction, I imagine she can see it written all over my face. I'm falling as hard, as fast, as I ever have for her. I expect her to look away, to throw out a jibe or to run away, the way she has a tendency to do. But she surprises me, holding on to whatever is passing between us, and as twisted as the idea of anything happening between us is, I can't shake the voice in my mind telling me to just screw it, because I'm already in too deep.

* * *

Reloaded with carbs, we pack up the truck and head to the next location. By chance, I wind up sitting next to Carrie and as the vehicle turns and bounces through uneven surfaces, our knees end up touching, our thighs sliding against each other, our shoulders pressing together. The circumstances are innocuous, they should certainly be uncomfortable, but there's a charge that comes from our connection coursing through me, and if she doesn't feel it too, she isn't alive.

When we stop at the next place, part way up a hillside, a two-story property with undisturbed views out to sea, I'm sorry for the loss of contact with Carrie. Maybe that's the reason my hand grazes the small of her back as she comes up to stand. Maybe it's also the reason she's slightly off balance in a stationary vehicle in the first place.

We're the last two people off the truck and consequently fall into working as a pair. The elderly couple who own the home have metal shutters over the windows on the second floor and boards for the ground floor windows stacked on their lawn.

Carrie and I get straight to work – I lift the boards and she drills in the screws. We're quick and efficient, so while everyone else helps bring loose items from the lawn inside and shuffles furniture to more protective positions, we fly through the boards.

At 1 p.m., I check my watch and round everyone up. 'We need to finish the last house and get down to the harbor.'

That's what we do, riding higher into the hillside for the last property, adopting the same roles here as we did in the last place. At every home, we've offered to take the residents back to the island with us, to ride out the storm in relative safety, but I'm not surprised they turn us down. There's an overwhelming sense of community here, as if they're all in it together.

Only Roy's sister has agreed to come with us with her newborn and we're picking her up on the way back to the boat.

Carrie and I are boarding up the penultimate window when I realize I'm enjoying this, oddly. Enjoying doing something together, watching her work, us work. Surprised by how adaptable she is.

In my fixation, I let the final board slip right before she tries to screw it into place. She glances up to me from her crouched position under my up-stretched body.

'Help me out here, Luke,' she gripes, though I don't think there's any malice to it; I think she's tired. As am I.

'Sorry, it's been a long day already.'

She nods. 'We still have Charithonia to prepare when we get back.'

I watch her drill. 'You know, you didn't have to

come over here today. You could have stayed back with Alisha and Ella.'

'I know but they have the justification of looking after the kids. I wanted to help here.'

'It's really decent of you.'

She scoffs. 'Despite your apparent hatred of me, Luke, I'm not a bad person. At least, I try not to be.'

She finishes the last screw and we're standing in front of each other, a power drill the only thing between us.

'Is that what you think?' I ask. 'That I hate you?'

Her jaw tenses but she doesn't speak. I can only shake my head at how wrong she is. Though, maybe just days ago, I could understand her reaction. There might have even been some truth to it. Today...

'You couldn't be further from the truth.'

I feel and see her sharp intake of breath. The way her chest rises and her green eyes fix on me, widening, then softening, until there's something in them I like, that I know from long ago, that I want to see in her eyes. A tenderness.

My arm aches by my side and my hand twitches until I need to reach out and touch her. I'm wary, my heart is hammering in my chest, but as my arm begins to rise, I think her expression is telling me she wants the connection too.

When her gaze falls to my mouth, I know I need it.

'Here they are. The dream team.' Joe's words cut into my mind like an unwelcome axe. Carrie jerks her body away from me so fast, anyone would think I was trying to set her alight. Just like that, she's not my Carrie; she's Hettich's tax advisor.

Joe's attention flicks between us and I could honestly scream at him for bursting the bubble, bringing Carrie and me back to reality.

'I've got to tell you, watching you two work together like a Granny Smith and cheddar cheese, I know my finances are in good hands. You're the perfect pairing.' Hands on his hips, Joe lets out a long, steady whistle as he surveys the windows.

Carrie raises a brow and asks me, 'Granny Smith?'

'Apple, as opposed to an elderly relative,' I say, not missing the pinkening of her skin around her long, very, *very* enticing neck.

I feel myself drifting again, to some place where I'm caressing and kissing the skin I see heating now, then Joe asks, 'How did you get so good with a drill, Carrie? You know your way around power tools better than Luke and me put together.'

She gives him a gentle turn of her lips. 'My mom.

When my dad left her, she vowed never to rely on a man again.' I feel like she's looking my way through the corner of her eye. 'She took courses in just about everything she ever relied on Dad for and she taught me whatever she knew. Including how important it is to not need a man.'

This time, she full-blown glares in my direction. I guess I did nothing seven years ago to change that perception for her. Slowly, surely, I'm starting to get a picture of what happened between us – at least Carrie's version of it all. Maybe it's more that I'm slowly prizing off the blinkers I put on to protect myself. To lie to myself. Because admitting that *I'm* to blame for everything that could have been and never was is painful.

'Good on your mom, that's what I say.' Joe puffs out his next breath. 'We should get going. Henry called and said the other crew are almost done and the ocean is already fighting back against Isabel.'

'Right behind you,' I tell him, watching him walk away. Then I turn to Carrie, our moment gone but not wanting to fall right back to griping at each other. 'There are *some* things you need a man for,' I venture, trying to joke into a better place with her.

She pouts, her eyes narrowed, and I'm pretty

sure my attempt has failed. 'For *that*, there's always sex toys and artificial insemination.'

Then she sets about packing up our tools. Despite myself, I laugh, and I'm fairly sure she's wearing the trace of amusement about her lips as she focuses on clamping the drill box shut.

28

CARRIE

It's been *a day* already, and when we get back to Joe's island, we still have work to do. Yet I can't say it's been entirely unenjoyable. Jenny is great company, Joe is bizarre in a truly warm-spirited way – in fact, everyone I've spoken with today has been bubbly, unexpectedly light and happy, and they've made the day fly.

More than anything – though I despise myself for even admitting it – I've enjoyed moments with Joe. Like flashbacks into the past, the way we used to laugh and joke together, torment each other. I've found myself wanting to be around him.

I know it isn't him now that I'm interested in. It can't be. Too much hurt and pain have passed between us. But the *old* him, the old *us*, before every-thing imploded, *God*, I'm pining after him.

We pull into Leverick Bay and the water is much calmer here than I was expecting. From Joe's relay of Henry's call, I was anticipating a tsunami or some-thing. Don't get me wrong, it's choppy enough to test my constitution, but it's not horrific here in the bay.

Our group has left the truck and waved goodbye to Roy's father-in-law, whose sentimental moment with Roy amounted to a stoic pat on the back and telling him, 'I'll see you for dominoes and a rum when the fat lady passes.'

We've increased our numbers by one mom and an adorable baby and we're all standing around, making small talk, waiting for the other truck to ar-rive. The docked boats look different to when we turned up this morning and I can't quite put my finger on why, but I think it's more lines between the boats and the dock, the boats and the boats. Every-thing seems more secure.

Though it defies belief, with my sweaty clothes sticking to me, the wind picking up and the thick cloud cover, I'm actually cold in the Caribbean.

'Are you okay?' Luke asks, coming to my side, so close as he speaks, his chest is grazing my shoulder.

For an insane nanosecond, I want to tell him I'm

cold, to ask him to fold me into his arms and warm me up, the way I would have when we slipped beneath the cold covers in his apartment at night. The way I used to.

Instead, I nod, but the way his deep brown eyes penetrate me is as much of an embrace as if I had asked for him to hold me.

For the first time today, I'm grateful when my cellphone starts to ring in my pocket. Taking it out, more of me rubs against Luke and I try hard to ignore the sparks my body remembers, that my mind wants to forget.

'You should get that,' Luke tells me, glancing at my screen. 'You've been ignoring calls all day and we might lose signal tomorrow. Who knows for how long. Things out here don't repair quickly and Charithonia won't be a priority for the local handymen.'

I lick my dry lips, swallow against my dry throat and I think I manage a stiff nod before accepting my boss's call.

'Rachel, hi.' Holding the phone to my ear, I move away from the group, holding my hand over the handset to shield from the noise of the wind. 'How are you?'

'How am *I*, Carrie? How am I? How are *you*?'

Rachel is usually calm and composed, not fazed by much in my experience, so to hear the frantic tone of her voice instantly puts me on edge.

'Rachel, I'm fine, I promise. I'm sorry I haven't been very responsive on emails and answering calls; I've been helping with storm preparations all day and—'

'Carrie, I don't give two hoots about your emails. I can deal with those from here. I care about *you*.'

'You do?' Perhaps I shouldn't be surprised. A category five hurricane is sort of bad. Understatement of the century. And I am her employee. Yet I am surprised, because work is work. I've never been asked how I am and the person actually mean the question in the office. All I've done is fight to be heard, to set my story straight. This is new.

'Of course I do.' I feel like she's pacing. I don't know why, I just get the sense she's walking lines up and down her very plush corner office. 'I feel like this is all my fault, Carrie. I'm so sorry, I should never have sent you there.'

'Rachel, this is my *job*; I'm pleased you sent me here.' For some reason, my eyes flick across to Luke and I find him already looking at me. 'You weren't to know about the storm and you weren't to know I'd get stuck here. In any event, Joe's assured me everything is going to be fine and I genuinely believe him. He has a safe bunker, which I think is probably more like a kidnap hideaway, but I'm told it's a concrete basement that's half the size of a house and done out like a bachelor dungeon. I won't be alone.'

Rachel's sigh is so loud, I hear it above the island's breeze. 'Let's talk when you get back to New York. I need to explain a few things. But for now, Joe is looking after you, right?'

'One hundred percent. He's great.'

'And... and Luke? How are things with him? Is he looking out for you?'

I feel a frown crease the skin between my eyes and glance back across to Luke, who is now in conversation with Roy. He has been looking out for me, actually, more than I would have expected, given how much we rile each other up and the fact he walked away from any want to enter into a relationship where we would care for each other once upon a time. But as I'm thinking that, I'm also wondering why Rachel is asking.

Of course, he's the CFO of the Hettich group. She asked about Joe. I'm reading something into something that doesn't exist.

Unless Joe has told her about Luke and me, but why would he? And she's never, not in all the time

I've been at the firm, mentioned that she'd heard anything on the grapevine, though it's possible.

'Ah, yeah, he's keeping an eye on things, too, I guess.'

'Carrie, stay safe, okay? We're going to talk properly in a couple of days. If there's anything I can do for you...'

'Maybe just keep an eye on my inbox, please, Rachel. I'm going to set an automatic reply for my emails but if the phonelines go down here, then—'

'I'm not referring to work, Carrie. I'm asking as a friend, not your boss.'

Huh.

'That's—' A friend? At work? Who's my boss? Well, today is full of lots of unintended consequences; what's one more? 'Thank you. Maybe that catch up should be over a glass of wine.'

'I can't think of any better way to hear all about it.'

When I head back to the group, the second truck is arriving with the others.

'Everything okay?' Luke asks.

I can feel confusion in my expression that morphs into something much more contented when his arm kisses my shoulder.

'Yeah, actually. More than okay.'

* * *

I was wrong. The water isn't reasonably calm. It's rough as hell.

As soon as Henry navigates us out of the bay, the waves become fierce, rocking Monique into me and me into Joe, like we're dominoes.

The sound alone is like the ocean is angry with us for being here. Despite the number of bodies onboard and Henry's experience driving, each rise over water brings the boat crashing down the other side.

Luke and Roy have flanked Henry at the steering wheel and I can make out above the sound of the water and the engine that they're helping him navigate the treacherous path back to Charithonia.

I hear them without looking because my hands are glued to the bench seat either side of my hips; my knuckles must be white, my grip is so tight, and I'm immensely grateful for the life vest Luke made me wear, though I'd looked to the sky when he gave me what felt like an order.

Make sure Joe and Luke look after you, Rachel told me on the phone. Her words are the main reason I didn't have some sarcastic retort to Luke.

My hair and body are saturated with sea spray and from wild sloshes of water coming across the bow and over the sides of the boat. I'm wearing shades, not because it's sunny – it isn't, the sky is dark and threatening – but to try to keep the salt water from hitting my eyes directly.

Through the fogged and wet lenses, my attention is fixed on Lola, Roy's sister, and her newborn baby. I'm terrified for them, so I can't imagine how Lola is feeling. She's sitting on the opposite side of the boat, directly across from me, and I'm mentally figuring out how to safely take the steps between us to sit with her and help her, somehow. Help cradle the baby. Help pin down Lola to the seat.

With the next wave, Lola is lifted into the air an inch or two and she lets out a short scream. I don't have time to think about the how, I just rise from my seat and try to step forward. But I stumble, the boat thrashing around in the water, and I fall back into my spot. Thankfully, Dave – big Dave, the security guy – side shuffles closer to Lola, and though it doesn't stop her from crying, it must make her feel safer that he wraps an arm around her and tucks her and her baby into his big frame. Just the sight of it has made me feel better.

I'm so busy watching Lola, I don't notice that Joe has switched places with Luke, not until Luke is sitting next to me and sliding his arm around my waist.

Just like Dave did for Lola, Luke tugs me against him and as I reposition myself to see his face, I find wide brown eyes piercing mine, so intense and full of concern that even the unruly sea seems to still for a moment.

Where Luke's body holds mine, there's an undeniable connection that's way beyond physical. A chemical reaction. A fusion by which the sum of our parts is vastly more than just him and me. He brings his hand to my sodden cheek, rubbing away soaked hair from my skin with his thumb.

'Don't try that again, do you hear me?'

I swallow deeply because, despite how sopping wet every part of my body is, my throat is parched.

There is no impending storm, no rough seas, no background noise. Just *us*. Luke and me, caught in a moment I don't want to get out of, even if it scares me more than any of those other things.

Because there is something in his hold, in his demand and his urgency, in the way he looks at me, that's reminiscent of the way he used to look at me. The way he could make me feel like nothing and no one else in the world mattered.

I want it back. In these still seconds, I want us back, I want *him* back.

I want it all so much, it physically hurts beneath my ribcage.

I don't think I can breathe as I watch his Adam's apple move when he swallows, his chest rise and fall where he should be wearing a life vest, the way he doesn't let go of my face but his gaze falls to my lips.

And I think... *kiss me, Luke. Kiss me.*

The next wave lifts the boat into the air and crashes us down, turning us sideways from where we started. It throws Luke's hand from my face to my body and he holds me down into my seat.

'We're nearly back,' he reassures me. 'You're doing great.'

'I'm not a novice,' I tell him, forcing a tight turn of my lips. 'I've been on a sunset sail before, I've been on a glass-bottomed boat, even a boat club on the Hudson. This is a walk in the park.'

But when he full blown beams at me and tugs my head under his chin, I do feel happier, lighter, less afraid.

29

LUKE

I only know because I am physically moving, helping everyone down from the boat back on Charithonia, that my heart hasn't stopped beating. The way Carrie held me on the way back across the ocean, the way she let me hold her. That look in her eyes, like I'd done something right, as if I was exactly who she needed me to be, at exactly the right time.

It feels like one of those images a person commits to memory, the kind that will sneak out and make you feel like the world has stopped turning when you least expect it. One I'll never forget.

I've helped Jenny, Monique and Dionne down from the boat. I'm standing knees deep in the water while Dave and Roy try their best to hold the vessel as steady as possible, but it's too rough to use a ladder. Henry and Joe are still at the helm, in case they need to turn on the engine and fight against the waves.

Carrie helps Lola to the back of the boat and as the waves bounce everything and everyone around, she takes the baby from her. Once I get Lola safely ashore, I come back for the baby. Carrie hands him to me, our fingers connecting as the small bundle moves between us, barely murmuring, and it's unfathomable, in the circumstances, that I feel a spark pass between us. I don't think it's from touch alone but of some kind of déjà vu from an alternate universe. One where we didn't mess each other up.

Having handed Baby back to Mom, I come back for Carrie.

'I'm good,' she tells me, yelling to be heard above the crashing and smashing of the sea. 'I can jump down.'

I shake my head in exasperation. 'Carrie, could you just *not* be difficult. For once?' I hold my arms up and despite her scowl, she slips down into them. Her chest is pressed to mine and with what little clothing that's between us wet, I feel every inch of her body as it slides against mine. I remember the sensation of her hips in my hands. I could never forget the way her lips part as she watches my own mouth. Suddenly, the chaos around us drifts away to nothing because I finally have her in my arms again.

I can feel my chest and hers rising and falling so hard they're pushing each other, and the split seconds we're locked together feel like long, indulgent minutes.

I want her so badly. In every possible sense of the word, I need her.

Then she pats my back like a boy scout who did a good deed and the moment dies with her camaraderie. 'Thanks. I can make it from here.'

I clear my throat. 'Right.' Then I watch her move onto the beach.

She really felt nothing? Nothing? Seismometers were tripped by what I just felt and all it tripped for her was an unaffectionate pat?

Jesus, what am I tearing myself up about here?

Leave the past in the past, Luke.

Or you're going to end up ruined all over again.

* * *

Henry and I take the boat back out to sea, navigating around rocks while hugging the island as closely as we safely can to get her protection, to the boat house on the western point of the island. The boat house is tucked into a small indent in Charithonia's natural shape, shielded somewhat from the elements. Nevertheless, we secure the boat as best we can.

The superyacht we sailed yesterday was taken to a dockyard, where the hope is she'll be safe from the storm. The crew will be staying in a nearby hotel, hoping to sail back in a few days.

You've got to love insurance when you actually need it. Don't get me started on what a waste of money it is when you never call upon it. Wasting money on insurance, just like getting your heart broken by the girl of your dreams, is as certain as death and taxes.

With the boat tied up with extra lines, we hike back up to the main Hettich residence, filling the time by talking about Henry's plans to go back to college and do a postgrad. I've got to admit, I like the guy, I always have. He's worked for Joe for a couple of years now and I've watched him grow up a lot in that time.

Correction: I don't mind him when he isn't flirting with Carrie.

What I really want to do is tell him to back off, to stake some kind of claim to Carrie. But me not liking the idea of her finding someone else attractive – especially an objectively, though annoyingly, buff and handsome guy like Henry – doesn't qualify as a right over Carrie or any woman.

I grew up with a misogynistic father and I won't become him. I made it one of my life's objectives when he eventually left Mom, my younger brother and me.

With the overcast sky and the humidity rocketing, my clothes that were drenched from the boat are still wet and sticking to me, making me uncomfortable and, in the increasing breeze, cold.

'I'm going to throw on some dry clothes before heading to the house,' I tell Henry.

After peeling off to go to my pod, I change into dry shorts, a t-shirt and a hooded sweatshirt. I'd kill for a shower but I need to grab a bite and a hot drink with the others, then we need to get the last of the jobs done on the island before the wind picks up and picks up some more and keeps on going.

I tug on a clean cap and tighten it before making my way to the others. As I'm walking along the hilltop, looking out to the foam-lined tips of the increasingly murky water, it strikes me just how dangerous that boat crossing was. Carrie should never have been out there. None of us should.

I'd be burying my head in the sand if I said I'm not nervous about what tomorrow will bring.

I reach the terrace and see Carrie laughing with Alisha, one hand wrapped around a mug of something that's steaming and a sandwich in her other. Her laughter flows through my ears, dragging me from my reverie but stilling my feet. I'm powerless to do anything but watch the way her head falls back, the way her wet hair, no longer tied back, hangs down her back, exposing the skin of her neck, around her collarbones, exactly where she tastes and smells impossibly good.

As I take her in, committing to memory the sight of her, every inch of her, even more beautiful now than then, if that's possible, two wide, stunningly beautiful green eyes find mine.

I'm lying. I'm not nervous about what tomorrow will bring. I'm terrified.

'Luke, honey, there are sandwiches and hot tea,' Ella says. Her words reach me while I'm still lost to the view. Then she's right beside me, her hands on my forearm as she leans toward my ear. 'That is, if you can work out how to use your jaw again.' She places her fingertips under my chin and tickles me. 'You're gawping, honey. It's not attractive. Jessie has less sloppy chops than you do.'

I scowl at her from the corner of my eyes but I'm also fighting the twitch at the sides of my mouth. 'Well, like your dog, I'm salivating because of hunger, Ella.'

'Mmmhmm,' she sings. 'Hungry for what, darling?'

All right, now a short sound of humor escapes me. She isn't wrong; I am hungry, I'm starving, and I think the only thing that's going to sate my appetite is a woman who can't stand me, who is my tax advisor, and who broke my heart once and I would be well-advised to stay away from.

But what is it about knowing what's bad for us and wanting it all the more because of it?

I head over to the table where Dave and Jenny have now joined Carrie and Alisha and they're all joking around. There's only one long buffet table still out – the other tables and chairs must have been stowed away inside already. Carrie is actually holding court. She's confident and vivacious, slick with it. She's finally relaxing, maybe. Whatever the reason, it looks good on her. I can see how this woman is on the cusp of partnership at her firm. She's impressive.

As I think that, my mind jumps back to her patting my back when I helped her down from the boat.

While I was lost in the feel of her body against mine, she was friend-zoning me. Except, I don't even think she likes me as a friend. She was just zoning me out?

I raise my chin as I near the group, trying to seem aloof and, I think, coming off like a dorky kid trying to hang out with the in-crowd. What is *actually* happening to me?

I'm usually the self-assured one, maybe even a bit cool? Not here. Not on this island. Not since Carrie arrived. She's going to be my undoing.

'What's up?' I try to ask casually, but it ties around my tongue and comes out like *whassuuup*, as if I'm some goof on a naughties commercial for Budweiser.

'You changed,' Carrie says.

What do you know, she does acknowledge that I exist.

I plate up some sandwiches and a handful of fries. 'You should, too; you'll get cold.'

'I'm fine,' she says. Her words are followed by a shiver. 'I'll be fine. I don't have any spare clothes. I didn't actually pack for a hurricane.'

'Carrie, you should have said,' Jenny says. 'Let me get you something of mine. I'll be back in a flash.'

While Jenny literally runs off, I get the distinct

impression I'm not welcome near Carrie so I go back to find someone who is my friend.

As I get closer to Joe and Ella, I can hear them griping at each other in hushed tones.

'Honey, I know your heart is in the right place but I think you have to tell him. It's getting serious now, I can see it,' Ella says. 'I think the stakes are higher than we realized and it isn't right to keep meddling like this. What with tomorrow and the storm, too, I just think—'

'Isn't serious what we wanted?' Joe asks. 'Isn't that where we were trying to get to?'

'Is everything okay?' I ask, heading over to them. 'I didn't mean to eavesdrop but—'

'But you did?' Joe says, grinning. Happy to be rescued from his ticking off, most likely.

'Joe,' Ella says, giving him a warning look.

Joe holds up two hands. 'All right. I'll deal with it.'

Ella clamps his cheeks between his palms. 'You better had. Today.' Then she kisses him and they're both smiling again, the way I like them.

30

CARRIE

Jenny has got to be joking.

I'm standing in the washroom adjacent to the terrace with my hands over my face, fingertips shielding my eyes, not daring to look and see myself in what could be Jenny's spring-break clothes.

Why didn't I take the clothes she loaned me and get changed in my pod? At least then I could have aborted the idea and dressed in something inappropriate but dry of my own.

I sigh. Because it's already four thirty in the afternoon and we need to get going. The wind is increasing constantly and the sun will go down in a couple of hours, that's why.

Could I just put my wet, dirty clothes back on? No.

That's ridiculous. I need to pull up my proverbial big-girl panties. Or Jenny's Ariana Grande wannabe pants.

I part my fingers like it's Halloween and I'm home alone watching the scariest movie in the world. Peering through the gaps, I gasp again on seeing my body tucked into the most hip-pinching, thigh-hugging shorts I've ever worn. I take a deep breath. At least they fit, they're dry, they're black, which maybe makes them ever so slightly more subtle, and they're high-rise. There are some positives.

Sadly, they aren't high rise enough to bridge the gap between the matching black tank top – no, correction, *bra* – and the shorts. My bust is pushed up and my midriff is bared.

Slowly, tentatively, I peel my fingers away and plant my hands on my waist. If I wasn't me and I wasn't here, with my client and his family, friends and staff preparing for a storm, maybe, *maybe* I'd feel kind of... a smidge... sexy?

But I *am* here, on Charithonia, as Joe Hettich's tax advisor.

'This is a disaster,' I tell my reflection, though my subconscious is making a gentle note that I could invest in some new gym gear when I get home. *If* I ever get off this godforsaken island.

I open the washroom door an inch and peek out to the terrace. Everyone seems preoccupied. If I could just slip out of here, run the gauntlet of the entire width of the terrace, then along the pathway to my pod without being seen, I could find a modesty-preserving top to pull over this outfit. An inappropriate beach top would be better than this sorority costume dress I'm wearing.

Here goes...

I push open the washroom door, braced like Sha'Carri Richardson about to break the world record for the 100-meter sprint.

But... *crap*. The door is pushed right back and as I dive out of the collision path, Noah bursts past me, running with a football in his hands, Toby chasing after him and yelling, 'Give it back!'

While the brothers exit the terrace as swiftly as they entered, I'm left standing in the open space, practically naked, with the attention of everyone out here trained on me.

I look around the faces, which feel like they've multiplied all of a sudden.

'They fit you perfectly!' Jenny calls, drawing even more attention and clearly oblivious to the intense awkwardness I feel.

'Oh... Ah... Yeah, thanks.' Some of the faces get

back to their conversations but there are two men amongst the group who blatantly don't. I'm vaguely aware that Henry is... *ogling me*? I'm acutely aware of the way Luke's jaw stiffens, the muscle in his cheek twitches and the slow movement of his neck as he swallows.

I'm embarrassing him in front of his friends and co-workers. Not that... I mean, how can *I* embarrass *him*? It's not as if he has ownership of me or something. Yet that's the sense I get and it makes me bring one hand to my abdomen and the other to my collarbone, both covering as much of my exposed body as I can.

I need to get to my pod.

Before I can take a step in that direction, Luke reaches for the hem of his hoodie to take it off. Henry also starts to unzip his sweater but Joe places a hand on his shoulder and shakes his head, then directs him away.

Meanwhile, it's my turn to swallow deeply as Luke peels his hoodie over his body, his t-shirt underneath rising with it, fully exposing, inch by devastating inch, his solid torso. Luke was always in good shape but this... *this* is something projected by men's health and fitness magazines. An attempt to make men believe they can look like *this*.

I can feel my heartrate soaring and I hope, in this equivalent of a negligée I'm wearing, that Luke won't witness it hammering out of my chest.

When did I last breathe? Have I forgotten how to do it? I think I feel lightheaded. Nope, I definitely feel lightheaded and weak legged, and also really annoyed with my superficial brain for being unable to take my eyes off the divine example of a male body in front of me.

The show is over. Luke pulls down his t-shirt as he walks toward me, hoodie in hand, and offers it to me.

'Here, you'll get chilly in the wind once the sun goes down,' he says. He doesn't mention how obviously uncomfortable, gauche and inappropriate I must look too.

I open my mouth to thank him but it just sort of hangs there, stuck in gawping mode, and as if I wasn't angry enough with my treacherous self, Luke makes it a million times worse when his mouth turns up at just one side. Smug and hot as hell.

I want to give him some smart or sarcastic one-liner but it's like the music has stopped while I'm playing a game of statues.

He steps closer to me. So close, I can feel the warmth of his body, the heat of his breath. His fingertips rest on my hip and I inhale sharply when his thumb grazes the flesh of my waist. He leans into my ear and I feel his words against my skin. 'If you keep looking at me like that, I won't be able to keep my distance anymore.'

My breath leaves me, hot, heavy, wanton. *What's wrong with me?* After everything he did, *why* does my body still want to betray me?

I turn my head to look at him and it's a mistake. Our eyes meet and in his, I see a reflection of my lust. He's serious. And though I shouldn't, I can't stop myself from wondering what it would be like to go there one last time. *Would the flames between us still burn?*

His mouth is dangerously close to mine and if he moves toward me, I don't know if I'll stop him.

One set of abs and toned pecs and all sensible thoughts have evaded me.

Luke straightens, winks at me. Not a cringewor-thy, sleazy kind of wink, rather, a panty-melting, su-per-attractive, confident kind of wink.

Too sure of himself, delicious, jackass.

'Put that on, *buddy*,' he says, and he pats me on the back. Actually pats me on the back.

Of course. When we got off the boat, I did the same thing to him, though I had been reacting to my own panic. This act of Luke's is all about one-up-manship and I goddamn fell for it.

Oh it's on, Luke Chalmers. Two can play that game.

* * *

Quite how those who stayed on Charithonia today managed to get through as many storm preparations as they have, while also being chef, cleaner, waitstaff, mom, aunt, security and generally human beings, is beyond me.

A bunch of us head down to the staff housing, which is closer to sea level, so a bigger flood risk from the high water levels. Apparently, the glass in the windows is the same level of hurricane proof that the main residence is, so the decision is made not to board the windows. The roofs already have storm clips in place and the various plant pots and pieces of furniture outside the studios have already been taken inside.

So our job – mine, Luke's, Joe's and Alisha's – is to create a wall of sandbags as high as feasibly possible, while the staff carry bags of possessions and clothes that they want to make sure stay safe up to the main house and down to the bunker.

Luke is flirting with Alisha. I know they aren't

together now but it seems like he's upped the ante for some reason. *Is he trying to make me jealous?*

I watch him as I lug sandbags, boring holes in his offensively moreish back, ignoring the way his muscles work beneath his t-shirt, or trying to at least, focusing on how childish he's being and how mad it's making me.

Mad enough that when Henry returns from taking his luggage to the bunker, I decide to play Luke at his own dirty tricks.

'So, Henry, what can I expect tomorrow?' I ask, closing in on him as he heaves up two bags and I take one, too, following by his side, as close as the job will allow, to the nearest studio.

Okay, it's hardly flirtatious chatter but Luke can't hear us; he doesn't know that we're genuinely talking about the weather.

'Well, it's all about humidity and air pressure,' Henry says, seeming sincerely excited by the topic. 'See, hurricanes happen when warm seas heat the air.' He places down his sandbags, his slender muscles working hard, but not a patch on—

Nope. Not going there. Not now. Not ever.

Now, Henry uses his hands to demonstrate. 'Humidity rises and meets low pressure. That creates clouds.' With one hand in the air, presumably acting as low pressure, Henry rotates his other beneath it. 'The clouds start to rotate, and that's the basis for the movement of the storm.'

I glance sideways to Luke and find him sporting the most supercilious look, which I'd like to pat right off his face.

I rest a hand on Henry's bicep and give him more attention than the weather deserves.

'Wow. And what was it you said about air pressure?' Henry doesn't seem to flinch at my touch, though in my defense, not that there's much of one to this level of teenage prank, he has been fairly handsy with me since I arrived on the island.

'The eye of the storm is where the pressure is lowest. Incredibly low, in fact. Because the moist air is rising from the ocean, it leaves an area of low pressure on the surface.' He's using his hands again to gesticulate, leaving no room for Luke to think we might be discussing how sexy Henry is or how much he'd like to get me naked. Nope. We're still talking about meteorology.

My attention is zapped from Henry telling me about high pressure moving into the low-pressure area or something along those lines, because Luke and Alisha suddenly let out a joint, gargantuan laugh, and they're touching, him folded forward, her head thrown back, and they look happy and really quite beautiful together, and... I'm jealous.

Jealous? Jealous of what? That Alisha and Luke might have chemistry, that they might like each other, that even if they aren't together now, one day they might be?

Ouch, there's an ache in my chest that makes me hold my fist to it.

'Are you okay?' Henry asks, finally having completed his explanation. He reaches out to my arm, I think genuinely concerned.

Me too. *Am I having a heart attack? What is this dull but unrelenting pressure behind my sternum?*

I nod. 'Mmmhmm, yeah, great.' I take a slow and steadying breath and move to the truckload of sandbags left to be positioned, distracting my mind, changing my line of vision, moving away from the sound of Luke and Alisha's happiness. 'I think I ate those sandwiches too quickly. Indigestion.'

God, could I be any *less* sexy? I'm dirty, I probably smell, my hair is as frizzy as it ever gets, I'm wearing Jenny's tiny sorority shorts and Luke's sweater, and I'm using indigestion as a tool to avoid being honest with myself and anyone else who can see how my body is physically aching for Luke. A man I should absolutely not want.

But damn it, I do.

I leave Henry to the last couple of sandbags on one studio and make a start on another. At the truck, as I'm wiggling a bag off the top of the pile, I sense Luke behind me before I see his arms reach across me to help, pulling down the bag as if it isn't weighted at all. His shoulder brushes mine and even through clothes, I feel that lightning strike again, like I did when he helped me down from the boat, his hands on my hips, my pelvis sliding down his front, his dangerously dark eyes fixed on mine.

I mumble to myself, 'They say lightning doesn't strike the same spot twice.' *But in paradise it seems there are no rules.*

Is the way I'm feeling nonsensical, make-believe, or *special*?

Not in seven years and a multitude of dates and failed, doomed-from-the-off relationships have I felt the pull, the draw, the irresistible smolder of a man the way I do now, in the most absurd circumstances, with Luke.

I realize, to my sheer mortification, that I muttered my words loud enough for Luke to hear. When I take the sandbag from him, his fingers coming to rest over mine and staying there, urging me to look up into those brown pools, he says, 'Maybe it isn't supposed to but we both know it is.'

I'm acutely aware of his touch and how it's penetrating my skin; it's in my bloodstream and coursing to every part of my body. My eyes fall to his lips. The same lips I've kissed so many times before.

He moves his face closer to mine, his eyes narrowing, hooded and dark, and I watch his attention fall to my mouth too.

'I like you wearing my clothes,' he says. 'I always did.'

It would be so easy to move up an inch, closer an inch, to let him fill the space between us, to take my mouth closer to his.

Luke's hand comes toward my face and I watch it as if his movement is happening in slow motion, the anticipation of his fingertips caressing my cheek, his thumb stroking my neck, has my insides spinning and flipping in unbearable turmoil.

'We're nearly done,' Joe says, his voice coming from behind me somewhere. He's blowing air like he's been working out. We have, really, all day.

I dart back from Luke, hot and flustered. A lucky, lucky, lucky save.

Yep, wholly fortuitous.

Joe is my client and honestly, even if he wasn't, I

can't just forget what Luke did to me. My job is a layer of protection I need because clearly my head, my heart and my freaking libido can't be trusted.

I panic-grab the sandbag and tell Joe, 'Great!' an octave higher than my voice ought to be.

Luke doesn't move. He holds a long blink and I watch his chest rise and fall, then his jaw is stiff as his focus shifts to Joe. 'Yeah, great.' His words are gruff.

Did we almost kiss?

Whatever games we're playing with each other, the temptation is real.

31

LUKE

'Is there a reason you're literally watching my every move?' I ask Joe. He's not stopped staring at me the whole time we've been layering the last wall of bags, not since he interrupted whatever that was between Carrie and me.

What was that? Was she going to kiss me? Was I going to kiss her? I fucking wanted to.

Joe pouts, plants his hands on his waist, and remains silent, his gaze flicking to Carrie then back to me.

Would it bother him if something happened between the two of us? She's the business advisor, sure, but it hasn't occurred to me before now that Joe would care.

Not that anything is going to happen. No matter how sold on the idea I might be – *am I?* – Carrie is dead against it.

I think.

Like a magnet, she drags me to her, again. She's finished, at last, and she stands back to assess the work we've done, reaching up her arms to stretch out. Her hoodie, *my* hoodie, creeps up, exposing her hips in those sprayed-on pants. Hips that fit perfectly the shape of my hands. When I've trailed my fingers across her skin just there, bumps have risen on her skin. She's shivered, the way she did under my touch on the boat yesterday.

That's how I know there's hope.

I swallow, wetting my dry throat. We've been there before and it ended in disaster. It almost ended me. But goddammit, I don't know how to be around her and not *want* her.

I hope I haven't been watching her for as long as it feels I have because Joe is still staring at me.

Hoping he didn't notice how my skin heated watching Carrie, how it chilled thinking about how badly it ended last time, I stack the last sandbag on the wall we've erected and slap my hands together to rid them of grit.

'Can't read your mind, Hettich,' I tell him.

He scratches the back of his head. 'Right. Ah, I need to speak with you about something.'

I shrug, coming to stand by his side. 'Shoot.'

'Not here.' He side-eyes Carrie. 'When there's just the two of us.'

So it is about Carrie. I need someone else's thoughts on whatever is going on with me like a hole in the head. I'm confused enough without having to think about my boss, or my best friend, whichever capacity he wants to speak with me in.

As my boss, okay, if something happened between Carrie and me, it would be taboo. But not the end of the world. As my best friend, well, he had me hiding out here for almost a month when the shit really hit the fan last time, so, yeah, to spare his life disruption, he probably wants to caution against it.

Maybe it's nothing to do with any of that and I'm imagining that it is because for the last four days, all my mind seems capable of doing is thinking about Carrie.

Carrie, Carrie, incredible, beautiful, *annoying-as-hell*, no good for me Carrie.

So instead of telling him not to worry, that I've got this, I know what I'm doing, I give him one curt nod.

Then that switch that so often flips in my

chameleon friend flips. He bounces on the spot, then does knee-ups like he's a football player about to go into a big game, claps his hands like a snapping crocodile and says, 'All right, folks, that's a wrap. Let's head on back to the house.' He starts walking up the hill, the sun setting behind the clouds, and despite the thickening sky, there's a glow of orange, a hue of pink seeping into the murk. 'Leave the truck down here. If it isn't tied down, I don't want it near the house.'

For the first time, I sense his nerves. This storm is going to be big. None of us know what to expect. Yet that isn't what's making me nervous.

I hang back as everyone else makes their way up the hill. Maybe it's the storm; it's heightening every-thing, upping the stakes. But I suddenly have an overwhelming sense that I can't let the sun set on today without... I don't know. Without something. Without speaking to Carrie one more time. Without being in front of her again, as close as we were by the truck, and finding out what would happen. *Would she have leaned in? Would we have kissed?* Maybe all I need is more answers to why, but some-thing tells me that won't satisfy the thunder rolling inside me.

'Lost your legs, old boy?' Joe calls back down to

me. His words seem to remind my body how to perform the basic motion of putting one foot in front of the other.

Hands in my pockets, head down, I follow the group, wondering, if I had one question, what would I ask her?

If I had one action, what would I do?

Jesus, I'm a mess. But I don't know which kind of mess: the way I was right before we got together, when nothing else in the world seemed to matter if I couldn't kiss the neck I watched from my desk each day, pull my fingers through her long red hair, feel her body against mine. Or the kind of mess I was when it all imploded.

Probably something between the two but I do know that my judgment is clouded, my vision blinkered, and I need to get her alone.

The hill flattens out to the pathway through the pods, heading toward the main house.

'Chef has made Italiano, apparently,' Joe says. 'Very informal. All welcome.'

Food couldn't be further from my mind, so thank fuck Carrie says, 'I think I'm going to shower and change, Joe. Please don't wait for me; I might make some calls.'

Joe nods. 'It's there if you want it.'

Carrie tapers off for her pod and I swear I could be hallucinating but if I'm not, she casts a look back across her shoulder in my direction. It's subtle, barely there, but the way her gaze falls to her feet afterward makes me think it was real.

And she's going in the shower? Kill me now. Put me out of my misery, because the thought of her naked under a hot waterfall is a form of slow and painful torture.

'So that we're all on the same page, I want everyone in the bunker before daylight breaks,' Joe says. 'That's when the wind really starts to pick up.'

The others walk toward the main residence. Carrie has moved out of sight, her pod between us, and Joe hangs back.

'Luke, is now good for that talk?'

'Huh?' His word pulls my mind to him, or the small part that's willing to not focus on Carrie. 'What talk?'

My feet are moving and they aren't following the others. They aren't even going to my own pod. I'm not sure what Joe says next but I tell him, 'Later. There's something I've got to do first.'

I think I hear him mutter, 'Oh boy,' but honestly, I couldn't say anything for sure, except that I'm heading to Carrie's pod.

My heart is jackhammering in my chest, my palms are sweating, my stomach is rotating like a jet in a flat spin.

Her door is open. She's expecting me.

In the middle of the pod, she watches me approach, not at all perturbed, as if she knew I would. And she's lifting up the hem of my hooded sweater.

Hell, no, I want to be the only person who takes her out of my clothes.

I'm so tightly wound, I could burst out of my own. So I surprise even myself when I stay in the doorway and ask her, 'Did you love me, Carrie?'

Her hands drop from my hoodie. This time, I have caught her off guard. As her hands fall to her sides, she watches an invisible spot on my chest. Her voice is barely a whisper when she tells me, 'Yes.'

I don't know what I expected but that word seeps into my skin, into my veins, and it warms my entire body, making me weak with the heat of it, the heart of it.

'Then why did you return my letters? I get that you might have been hurt, I can see that now. But I wrote six letters to you, Carrie. I explained everything. I apologized for everything. I told you how much I wished...' My words catch in my throat.

'Every single letter was returned to sender, all but the first unopened. *Why?*'

'You wrote to me?'

She didn't know?

'Every month for six months. I told you in my very last letter that if you didn't reply, I'd leave you to get on with your life. So that's what I did. Even when I came back to New York, I didn't look for you, I didn't try to get in touch. Nothing. Until you showed up here.'

'Luke, I never got any letters. Not one.'

'You didn't? But they were returned to sender. The first one had been opened and resealed with tape. It wasn't you who returned them?'

She shakes her head. 'My lease was coming up anyway and I just... I needed a change from everything when you left. As much as I could change.'

She didn't send them back? She didn't even get them?

She loved me and she didn't get any fucking explanation as to why I left? She didn't even know I'd attempted to explain?

Christ.

The enormity of it hits me and knocks the air from my lungs. Outside, the wind is picking up, creating background noise that wasn't there earlier today. The sky is purple and darkening further.

And the woman in front of me looks broken and sexy as hell in equal measure. I want to take her in my arms and hold her, then make love to her, the way I know we can.

What a mess we made.

I drag a hand through my hair in frustration and replace my cap on my head. This feels like a crossroads and every route feels like the wrong way, but looking at her, seeing the way she's looking at me, through her lashes, her breasts pushed up and round beneath my hoodie, in that sinful workout bra...

'I've got to... I'm going to...' *Jesus, I just need to get out of here before I start something that won't be good for either of us.*

I practically run for the door and hear Carrie turn on the outdoor shower before I'm even off her front deck. I look to the sky, asking the universe if it's having a laugh at my expense.

SEALs training would be easier than walking away from this.

I force myself back to my own pod and, like Carrie, I turn on my own outdoor shower. I need to wash away the day. The dirt on my clothes, the grime on my skin, every confused thought and emotion in my mind.

I kick off my sneakers and step under the monsoon head fully clothed, leaning my head back and asking whoever's listening up there for mercy.

I feel Carrie's presence before I even open my eyes into her hooded ones. She's right in front of me, wearing just those tight pants and bra, staring at me through the mist and steam of the shower water.

This could be a really bad idea for so many reasons. It always was.

It could be the second-worst decision I've ever made, but the first was walking away from Carrie, so I'll be damned if I can stop it.

32

CARRIE

'You're so fucking beautiful, Carrie.'

The way my name sounds on his lips, the husk in his voice, it's visceral. I want him as much now as I did before the first time we ever made love. Urgently. Potently.

I can't hear it. I can't hear him speak and I don't want to risk hearing anything else that I can't handle tonight.

This is a horrible idea, I know that with certainty, but he's like fire to my gasoline and I feel this explosion between us with every single part of me.

So I release a long breath and tell him, 'No talking. Please.'

His deep brown eyes seem to question me, but he nods. 'No talking.'

I step under the head of the shower with him, our clothed bodies close but not touching. Keeping my eyes down, I bring my hands to his firm chest, the chest I've been yearning to touch since I saw him naked on the beach my first morning here. I dig my fingers into him, bunching his wet t-shirt into my fists, frustration and desperation a toxic mix of emotions.

He places a hand over mine and inches closer, closing the gap between us until I can feel the hardness of him against my naked stomach. As his other hand comes to my neck, his thumb tracing my jawline, his pelvis rocks harder against me and shifts with it all my inhibitions. I'm lost to him.

'Is this what you want?' he asks.

God knows it shouldn't be, but it is. I move my hands, showing him my response because I don't dare voice it. I'm afraid my words will bring me to the reality of what we're doing, what tomorrow could bring. So I bring one hand to his nape, fingering the thick hair I love the feel of, and with my other hand, I mirror his action, sliding my palm up his wet neck, feeling his strong jaw, landing on his cheek. Though the water is cascading over us, I open my eyes briefly to his, in time to see his breath hitch and his pupils enlarge.

I don't know who makes the first move but our mouths meet in a blaze of furious want. Nibbling, biting, his tongue turning against mine. I don't want us to speak but I'm for sure turned on by the sound of his groan into my mouth, an echo of the sound that comes from me.

God, I've missed him. I've missed us so much. How can that even be possible after so long? After so much has happened between us? It's like our bodies don't recognize time; they only remember what to do.

Six weeks was all we had and it was six weeks that wrecked the rest of my life.

Because of this. Because of the way our bodies know exactly what to do, even if our minds don't. The way my mouth takes everything he gives and I feel it all throughout my body. The way his touch alone brings bright light to my vision behind closed eyelids.

'Jesus, Carrie.' He leans his forehead on mine and with my eyes closed, I see everything I feel, the overwhelm of it all, in the pools of his eyes, in the strained expression of his face. It isn't enough. I need all of him.

My fingertips slide under his shirt, feeling his hips, his obliques, as I ride the top up his body and he helps me take it over his head, then brings his arms back down behind me, to my ass, nudging us closer together, holding us here, pulsating, wanting, as he tugs my bottom lip through his teeth. The things that move does to me register in a completely different part of my body.

I've put everything I've ever felt for Luke on ice, and now our flames are liquifying me. I melt into him, my head dropping forward until I'm biting his neck, sucking his collarbone, nibbling the muscles of his chest.

'Carrie...' My name leaves him as a whisper. A beg. A plea. One that makes me respond by pressing my mouth to his, relishing the sound of his response. Urged on by it, feeling sexier than ever hearing how much he wants me.

He drops his shirt and scoops me up, his forearm under my thighs. When I wrap my legs around him, he rotates us, pressing my back to the tiled wall with a thud, his crotch following, putting pressure right where I want him, *need* him, to be.

'Are you okay?' he asks. I can barely utter my response.

'I'm fine.' I sigh. 'Fine. Don't stop.'

But the fact that he managed to pause in the moment, that he cared enough to stop and ask the question, spurs me on more.

We're a rush of mouths and limbs, grunts and groans, hair tugging, ear biting, rolling and grinding. I need him closer, all the while knowing he won't be able to get close enough.

I need more and I show him, pushing his shorts as far as I can down his thighs until he has to set me down to let me finish the job.

The sight of him, free, exposed, in all his glory, all for me, has my breaths coming thicker, faster. I take hold of him but he covers my hand with his palm, forehead to mine, and grinds out, 'If you want me to last, you can't touch me. I swear, Carrie, I'm too far gone already.'

He looks into my eyes and I see so much in those two worlds. So much, I could forget – I *have* forgotten – all reason. All sensibility.

'The things you do to me,' he says.

Though I don't want to hear words and I'm afraid of my own, of how deep they might be, how vulnerable they'd make me sound if I voiced them, I know exactly what he's saying. No one has ever compared to what Luke makes me feel.

I can't speak but he always said he could read

everything from my eyes, as if they tell a story, so I know, as he's looking at me now, he's in no doubt as to how much I want him, *this*. He responds by sliding my underwear down my legs, taking them down to the ground until he's on his knees for me. *Me.*

As his fingers and tongue draw me like a road map, making my head roll back against the tiles, water spilling down my breasts, my hips rising toward him, begging for him to keep working me the way only he can, stars shoot behind my eyelids, and I pant and moan. And when he asks me, 'Come for me, Carrie,' I have no choice but to give us both the release we're craving.

I'm catching my breath, eyes closed, feeling the water between us, feeling Luke's hands glide up my body, leaving a tremor in his wake, despite the warmth of the shower. When I open my eyes, above us I see a twilight sky, then an even more stunning view as Luke's heavy, dilated eyes are on mine. I pull on his hair as he grinds his even harder length against me, then scoops me up, turning off the shower, and leads us into his pod, where he lays me down on his bed.

He takes a condom from his suitcase and I'm here for it. I'm ready for him. I'm desperate for him.

When he crawls onto the bed and over me, one side of his mouth curves up. He strokes wet hair from my temple, kisses the tip of my nose, then my lips, and his restraint, his kindness, make me fall even deeper.

'I don't want this to be quick,' he says. 'It's been a long time coming.'

The sincerity in his expression, the gentleness of his touch, erases from my mind all the things I've hidden behind for seven years. Leaving only the truth – I've wished for this moment all the time we've been apart.

When someone turns your world upside down the way Luke did mine, there's no way to flip it back again.

But I can't say that. I can't tell him that. Because tomorrow will be the time for talking. Tonight, I keep the words on the tip of my tongue exactly there. I swallow them down and respond only with a kiss and a gasp when he finally slides inside me, finally making me complete again.

33

CARRIE

I know as soon as I wake in the middle of the night, though my body has betrayed me by falling into a sated sleep wrapped around Luke – my leg across his, my arm around his waist, my head on his chest – that my regret is fierce. Dread turns in my head and in my torso, which has nothing to do with the wind raging outside Luke's pod. No, this feeling is one I know too well, and it's worse than the fear of any weather.

He looks so peaceful, so calm, but there's a storm brewing and it isn't a hurricane. We shouldn't have slept together. We shouldn't have kissed.

Why do we do this to each other? Why do we make

such a fucking mess of everything? And why am I crying?

I cover my mouth with my hand, begging my emotions to stay quiet as I slip out of Luke's hold and out of his bed. I see one of his t-shirts, or some kind of garment, it's hard to tell in the darkness of the room, hanging over a chair. Whatever it is will have to do because I need to get out of here.

It's a long-sleeved top, I realize as I pull it on, tiptoeing from his pod and closing the door as quietly as I can behind me. The wind is intense outside; it takes me by surprise, pausing my tears for a moment as I run from Luke's pod to my own. Inside, I shut the door, press my back to it and slide down to the floor, my silent tears now flowing freely.

What have I done? I can't be back here. I can't.

In the darkness, I move to my bed and find my phone on the dresser. It's after four in the morning and shortly, I'll have to move to the basement at the main house, where I'm going to spend the rest of the day with my client and a group of people who all love Luke, the man who just broke me apart all over again.

And I let him. I did more than let him; I begged him to do it. *I* walked to *his* pod.

Why? Was it the letters he told me he wrote? I don't

even know what they did or didn't say. *Did I fantasize that they declared some kind of undying love, a fire that would never be put out?*

What an idiot I am. What a glutton for punishment.

Worse still, I've done it all right under the nose of my client, risked my reputation again, and for what? A one-night stand for old times' sake?

My tears come thick and fast, again. I only have myself to blame. None of this is on Luke. Not this time. I walked into this with my mind closed but my eyes open.

I do the only thing I can think to do: I call Callum. Though it's an ungodly hour of the morning, I beg into the night that he'll answer.

When he doesn't pick up the first ring, I dial again, and again. I feel needy. I'm *being* needy, and needy is *not* the kind of woman I am or want to be, but my best friend's counsel feels like the only thing that might help me at this juncture because I am… lost.

'Carrie,' Callum blurts, panting. *Did he run for the phone?* 'Are you okay?'

The storm. I'll have scared him to death. 'Shit.' I sniff and wipe my nose inelegantly against the back of my hand. 'Sorry, yes, I'm...' A sob escapes me, muffling the sound of the word 'fine'.

'Whoa, whoa, wait, wait. Hold that thought and definitely hold that action, I've got to take this,' Callum says to someone who is not me. Now, I hear music playing in the background... *Usher? Oh.*

'You're with someone.' I sniff. 'I'm sorry, Callum. This doesn't matter. Go back to whoever you're with and whatever you were doing.'

'Baby girl, when did you last call me at four in the morning? This matters.' The music disappears and I imagine he's left one room and moved into another.

'Eddie can't see what you're doing, can he?' I ask, trying and failing to sound playful.

'He's asleep in his bed in the lounge but the man in my bedroom is big enough that Eddie might just catch a glimpse from there.'

'Too much information, Callum.' His usual crudeness about his sex life doesn't manage to amuse me as much as it normally would but it does pause my tears.

I hear a thud and think he just plopped down onto his leather sofa – I must remember to wipe that down before I sit there next. 'Let's get serious, what's wrong? Are you okay? I'm worried to death about you over there.'

'Ha, and Mr Huge is just there to take your mind off things, right?'

'Hey, don't belittle how much I care about you.'

I know he does. I know because I care about him just as much. He's been a staple in my life for... well, since Luke broke my heart and I moved in to my current apartment, which I couldn't really afford then, next door to Callum. Speaking of which...

'Callum, I've done something stupid.'

He sighs. 'You kissed Luke.'

His statement is emphatic. Not surprised or perturbed. Resigned.

'More like fourth base,' I confess, bringing the palm of my hand to my forehead.

'Wh— Hold up. You? *You* screwed him? *Luke?*'

'Please don't call it that and stop with the judgy-judgisome. Though I totally deserve it.' I groan, looking to the ceiling to fight more tears but unable to prevent another sniff of my nose.

'No, I— Carrie, I'm not judging you, babes. Zero judgment. I have a hunk waiting in my bedsheets next door.'

'Right.' I shake my head, knowing it's so far from

the same thing. 'You do this all the time. Means nothing.'

'Yeah, but that's because I do it all the time, Carrie. That's my lifestyle choice. If you take a man to bed—'

'Please don't finish that sentence.'

'It means something, babes. The question is, what did it mean to you and why are you calling me at this time in the morning crying your heart out?'

'I'm not crying. You're crying,' I say, repeating words we say to each other when we're both bleary-eyed after a Nicholas Sparks movie. But they aren't funny in this moment because another silent drip falls down my cheek. 'I don't know, Callum. I don't know why I did it, I don't know what it meant, and I don't know how to face him again today.'

'Did you do a sneak out?'

I blow out so hard, my lips almost raspberry. 'Yes. I'm a wreck. He can't see me like this. And I'm stuck here, trapped. The storm is nearly on top of us and I need to clean up and get to Joe Hettich's hurricane room to ride it out with a bunch of people who are all Team Luke, and *Luke*. Oh yeah, and the client who is probably the last person who stands between me and my partnership case at the firm that I've busted my ass for.'

I expect some kind of told you so or witty remark, but it troubles me more when Callum speaks with the kind of sincerity I rarely see on him. 'I wish I was there to help you through this one, baby girl.'

His words, his tone, only confirm how much of a disaster this is.

'What do I do, Callum?'

'Build yourself a time machine?'

I shake my head. 'If I can't do that?'

'Get yourself a shower. Get dressed. Put your war paint on. And while you're doing all of that, decide how you want to play this thing.'

'What if I don't know how?'

I imagine him rubbing his gruff chin, the way he does when he's thinking, because it's long seconds before he asks, 'Do you want to be with him? Is that what screw— sleeping with him was about?'

'No! It can't be. He's my client. Joe Hettich is my client. I'm not putting my career on the line again for Luke or any man. But even if that weren't the case...' I press my finger and thumb into the corners of my eyes as pressure builds again. 'Nothing's changed. He still walked away from me once before for someone he wanted more.'

I think about the letters Luke spoke of. Letters I never received. I wish I knew what was inside those pages. But the fact is, they were words. He may have written to me to explain a few things, to apologize, but ultimately, he still went back to his wife. Now, it seems, truly his ex-wife, too. I don't even know how long they've been apart and divorced, whether there's been anyone serious since. None of it even matters. It can't.

'I can't go back there, Callum. I can't go back to being in a thousand pieces the way I was.' Pieces that Callum helped pick up and put back together. He knows how shattered I was. How I had to rebuild my life and career.

'Callum? Are you still there?'

'I'm here,' he says. 'Just thinking. So maybe, what happened between the two of you last night, or this morning, was closure, right? It was one last rodeo to say goodbye, or get each other out of your systems, you know? Closing the door on the past rather than opening the door to the future.'

I nod into the darkness. 'You're right. I have to see it that way, don't I?' The tightness that brings to my chest is painful. Am I going to do this again? Set off on the path to the rest of my life with Luke just a memory that eases with time but is always there, always present, like a dull ache in my bones that never ceases?

'You don't have to do anything, Carrie.'

Except, I do. I don't forgive Luke. I haven't forgotten. How can I when I've never had an explanation for what he did to me, to us, the way we ended? We got so wrapped up in the crazy sexual chemistry between us that we, *I*, let it cloud my judgment.

'A mistake,' I mutter. 'Closure.'

'If that's what you want it to be,' Callum says.

There's such a fine line between want and need.

34

LUKE

No, no, fucking no.

It's the bellowing wind outside, wildly chiming the dangling ornament I forgot to bring inside last night that wakes me, but before I even open my eyes, it's the lack of Carrie that has me thumping the bed in frustration.

She's run, again. Gone without a trace.

The worst part is, I should have expected it. I should have known better. Desire got the better of me and here I am, again, with a fucking vortex under my ribcage where my heart should be.

Why did I go there? Why let her in? For this body-crushing feeling all over again?

I roll onto my back and let my forearms fall across my eyes, willing whatever sensation is trying to be present there to just *do one.*

'Idiot,' I chastise myself, roughly dragging my hands up and down my face like it might rub some sense into me. Unfortunately, it's not going to do that retrospectively.

Who am I kidding? Even if I turned back the clock ten hours, I would be powerless to stop what happened last night.

Damn it, even now, lying here alone, devastated, I don't know if I would want to.

Last night was... Christ, it was intense, hot, sexy. Incredible. But not just because there's an unexplainable and unbeatable magnetism between Carrie and me that no one in the world could deny. Not because she's the most stunningly attractive woman to have ever consumed every single one of my senses.

It's because being with her, over her, on her, inside her, is a feeling like nothing else I've experienced in my life. She can blow my world apart, make me feel ecstasy, and make it feel like we're one person, as if she's the other half of me. I felt more alive last night than I've ever felt.

I shake my head, reminding myself that I am in

this pod, in this bed, solo. As I do, I notice the first light of the day is trying to peek through the thick dark clouds, through the slatted blinds covering my window.

I need to get up and move. To spend the entire day with the woman who shatters me like a mirror, for fun.

Or maybe, I just lie here, wait out the storm and take my chances in this pod, because that would be easier than enduring a day with Carrie, asking myself over and over, why did she even come to me last night? I'd walked away. It took more willpower than I knew I had but I walked away from her pod.

Then she was here. In mine. Standing in the doorway to my shower, begging me to make love to her under the setting sun.

Goddammit, it had felt like that. I'd felt the rush of being with the woman I love.

Fuck, fuck, fuck.

I drop my arms across my face again. *I love her*.

And I really fucking hate her too.

Reluctantly, I come to sit on the edge of the bed, feeling tired and deflated. I've hit rock bottom once before and this feeling isn't it, but it sure as hell feels reminiscent.

Regardless, I have three friends who are as close

to me as family and who would probably want to slap me around the head if they knew I walked right into the mess they all helped pick me up from seven years ago, again. I've got four energetic but pretty amazing god kids who need me today. Uncle Luke needs to take his head out of his ass and turn up to play and distract.

I dig out a pair of shorts, a t-shirt and a sweater from my drawers and shove some staple bits into my duffle bag to take with me. Not because I think my things are at risk in the pod – this place is solid as a rock – but because I don't know how long the storm will take to pass and if I'll be communal sleeping tonight.

One thing's for sure: if the kids want to nap to-day, I'll be a willing cuddler.

Yawning, I sling my bag over my shoulder and head outside.

The hurricane isn't due to hit for hours but the wind is already ferocious, the white foam capping the sea is plentiful, and I'm fighting against the drag to get to the pathway.

Where is Carrie? Is she already there? Is she in her pod?

There's no way I'm letting her walk alone in this.

I make a detour. There are no lights on in her

pod, the slats have been drawn across the windows and when I try her door, it's locked.

'Carrie, are you in there?' I call, receiving no reply. Though even if she was inside, I probably wouldn't be able to hear her response for the howling in my ears.

Relieved to be able to put off seeing her a little longer, I turn back in the direction of Hettich House. The main door is closed but not locked. I let myself in, my ears feeling the relief of filtering out some of the anger of the weather. Seeing no sign of anyone still on the first floor, I head down to the basement.

When I say basement, this is like no ordinary basement, no rickety wooden door leading down an unsafe staircase into a dark pit with a concrete floor and things that remind you of the most tense scenes in a horror movie. The Hettich *basement* is as big as my loft apartment in Tribeca.

Leaving my luggage in the main lounge, I make my way through the security door that's been left open, though I know Dave won't be far away, despite the fact a kidnap risk seems slim to non-existent in the current climate. I hear the lyrics to 'I Just Can't Wait To Be King' coming through a sound system that's barely registrable over the sound of Noah and Toby belting out the song.

Oh boy. I guess this is close to normal wake-up time for the sprogs.

I'm going to need a strong coffee.

Sure enough, Dave is hovering at the bottom of the staircase and holds out his fist to me in welcome. 'You good, man?' he asks.

'Yeah, all good. You?'

'Ready for whatever the day brings.' Dave is ex-SAS. I'm close to certain nothing fazes this hunk of man.

Scanning the room and the many faces scattered around the enormous open-plan living space, before anyone else has noticed my arrival and before Noah has had a chance to dive on me, I ask, 'Am I last to get here?'

'Pretty much,' Dave says, checking his watch. 'Just waiting for Carrie, then I'll close everything up.'

'She isn't here?' *Shit. Where is she?*

'We thought she'd be with you,' Alisha says, noting my arrival and calling over from the large wood dining table, where she's sitting with Jenny, Ella and Monique, taking advantage of a lull in the sing-shouting session. She's grinning, her expression alive with mischief, teasing me.

Normally, I'd give as good as I get, but right now,

I'm not finding anything funny, especially the fact that Carrie isn't here.

'Why would she be with me?' My tone is too clipped, unintentionally so.

Alisha doesn't catch my tone, or does and doesn't care, because she looks to the ceiling and says, 'Oh I don't know, maybe because neither of you turned up to dinner last night and you're the last two people to—'

Something in the way I respond to her now, though, makes her pause. That, or Ella has kicked her sister under the table. The almost last thing I need this morning is for people to be gossiping and throwing around jovial innuendos. The very last thing I need is to not know where Carrie is when there's a storm raging outside.

'Morning!' Carrie's voice comes from behind me, too close behind me. I'm grateful she's here but I'm frozen to the spot. Ridiculously, I wasn't ready for her. I'm *not* ready for her.

And the overriding emotion I'm left with is fury. Not even because Alisha is looking at me like *I told you so* but because I woke up this morning, after an earth-shatteringly incredible night with Carrie, alone. Gutted.

She did it to me all over again.

She left.

Now she's singing good morning to everyone as if nothing happened.

I really wasn't ready for this. Not for the rage making my fingers tremble, or the unmistakable stabbing in my chest.

Thankfully, Carrie's lively arrival has notified Noah of mine. He and Toby – dressed in their *Cars* franchise pyjamas – call me over to where they're set up on a karaoke machine and, by the looks of things, draining the life from their dad, Roy and Henry, who are sitting around them on a huge U-shaped sofa.

After the way he's behaved the last two days, I'm not surprised when Henry seems to be the only person in the room either not able to connect the dots or not caring what picture they draw. He stands from the sofa and it's clear that Carrie is in his sights, but Joe places a hand on his arm and mutters something to Henry that makes him retake his seat. *Yeah, back off, hotshot. I'm making a big enough mess of this without turning what's going on between Carrie and me into a love triangle.*

Remarkably, Char and Sanza are both lying fast asleep in portable cribs. The dogs, Jessie and Woody, are lying on the rug next to them, ever the protectors. Roy's sister, Lola, is feeding her newborn in a nursing chair that looks like it might have been brought down here especially. Ella literally gets everything right when it comes to kids.

In another area, sitting along two sofas and starting a game of dominoes on the table between them, are Dionne, Glen, Thom, Troy and Kevin.

'Give me a beat to grab a coffee, boys, then you can subject me to whatever Disney performance you want,' I tell the kids.

I notice adult eyes are watching something behind my back, then Joe's flick to me, questions written there that I'm not ready to answer. So I act like I don't see it and move to the coffee machine in the kitchen area. There are two filter pots freshly brewed on two separate machines. There's also a large fancy coffee maker – beans, milk foamer and all – but if I touch that thing, I'll break it, so I pour myself a steaming mug of black coffee and take it over to the guys on the sofa.

Only when I sit near Joe, facing toward the dining table and the staircase I walked down, do I finally look at Carrie and see that, though she's tried to cover up with make-up, her eyes are red and puffy, not just from tiredness but from tears.

She's been crying.

'Well, that must have been some night,' Joe says

for my ears only. 'Because you both look like *sh*— Like you didn't catch a wink of sleep.'

She walked out of *my* bed, yet she's the one who gets to cry about it? Where's the justice in that?

Nevertheless, it tugs on the heart I'm desperate to turn to iron. How much easier this day would be if I just didn't feel. Unfortunately, I'm not the guy who's going to make love to a woman and not ask if she's okay the next day when her eyes are showing me she's not.

Jessie and Woody have that sixth sense dogs have because as I push up from the sofa, the dogs get up from near the sleeping girls and head over to Carrie, who strokes them and hugs their heads against hers.

How? How can a woman as warm as Carrie be a total and utter... ice queen?

Instead of causing a scene and going to her directly – probably to be embarrassingly brushed off with some callous remark – I go where I know she'll head next: the kitchen for coffee. Not before I give Henry a look that says, *If this storm doesn't kill you, I might.*

Though I still get the sense there are prying eyes in the room, general chit chat resumes. Kevin, the other security guy alongside Dave and Thom, must have locked us in now, as he comes into the basement and starts chatting in work mode with Dave. The group is complete and ready for the storm. Little do they know, I'm waiting for my own thunder to arrive in the kitchen.

I set about filling the machine with ground coffee for a double shot, a drop of foaming milk and a sweetener for Carrie's drink. Less because I want to make her a drink, or do anything particularly kind for her, than because I need a diversion, something to do with my hands. The uncertainty I felt as soon as I woke alone is back, and seeing her coming my way in my peripheral vision only makes it worse.

In the time it takes me to find some backbone and look at her, she's already grabbed herself a mug. 'This is for you,' I tell her.

She doesn't look at me as she says, 'I don't need you to make my coffee and I don't need you for anything else, for that matter.' She speaks quietly, in hushed but wrathful tones.

She's got a nerve. 'That's not what you were saying last night.'

'Last night was a blip. A complete lapse in judgment.' She reaches to take the milk jug from me. When her fingers meet mine, she finally looks at me. 'Trust me, it won't happen again.'

'You've got that right,' I snap back, speaking close

to her ear. 'You've ghosted me for the last time, Carrie Briggs.'

I don't know why I call her by her full name. I guess because my mom used to use my full name when I was in the doghouse as a kid. And Carrie is 100 percent in the doghouse with me.

Yet what has me seething even more than the woman herself is the way my pulse rate just surged with her sharp intake of breath, the way something jumped inside me when her pupils widened at my use of her full name. The way my fingers tingled under her touch.

Because, if I'm honest, I'd have taken the pain of today to have last night with her. I think. Maybe.

'*I* ghosted *you*?' she bites, pointing at herself then me as she snarls. 'Do you think whispering a few sweet nothings against my earlobe last night undoes the last seven years and what you did to me?'

I thought I was riled. This woman is furious. Her face looks like that of a Scotsman who's been lying on the equator without sunscreen for a decade.

'You want to know why I snuck out this morning, Luke? Because last night was a stupid, idiotic mistake.'

I don't like the insinuation in her words and

somehow, we wind up squared to each other, chest to chest. 'You came to me!'

'I know. It's on me and I'm sorry.' Her next breath presses her chest against mine and though my mind is screaming at her, my hands are itching to take hold of her, placate her and smooth this over. I don't want her to be sorry. I wasn't. At least, not last night.

I don't want to fight with you. Those are the words spinning around in my head but I know they are, doubtless, not the right words to speak.

'I shouldn't have come to your pod but the rest of it is on *us*. We messed up, again. Foolishly thought that sex is enough when we both know it isn't. Last night was...' She blows out like she's blowing a raspberry and I want to tell her, *Yeah, I'm with you, it was beyond words.* But she adds, 'It didn't answer any questions, it wasn't an explanation for what you did to me.'

'That's what you want? An explanation?'

'That's what I've wanted all this time, Luke.' She looks around the room, as if she's just remembered we're not alone, that we're in a storm bunker with a ton of other people and two dogs. 'Look,' she says, calmer. 'What's done is done. We need to get through today, then go our separate ways.'

No. I don't even think about why I want to say

that word but it seems to fit. Yet something stops me from saying it aloud. Something heavy. A weight I can't describe.

Instead, hurt and frustration have me shaking my head and as I drag a hand through my dark hair, I say, 'Fine. I just wanted to make sure you're okay, for some reason, and I have my answer. You're great. You've moved on.' I start moving back to the kids and Joe. 'Enjoy your coffee, Carrie.'

'I will,' she says huffily.

'Great. Maybe you'll be functioning like a normal human being once you're caffeinated,' I say, turning back to her and raising my arms from my sides.

She scowls, rolling her jaw. 'If, by that, you mean someone like you, I'd rather not, thanks.'

I scoff. 'Fine, so don't drink the coffee.'

'Maybe I won't.'

'Fine.'

'Fine.'

God, the woman drives me crazy. Is there anyone in the world as stubborn as she is?

I slump down on the sofa next to Joe, who is wide-eyed and sort of looks like a GIF asking, *What the fuck?*

'I take it everything's fine?' he says, amusement toying with the creases around his mouth.

I feel the muscles around my own face twitch for entirely different reasons as I bite down on my gums to prevent me dignifying his question with a response.

Joe nods. 'Looks like this is going to be a really long day. I might as well go ahead and fess up to a thing or two...'

35

CARRIE

I genuinely can't believe I wasted any more tears over that... that... *ape*. That *man child*. That total, complete *ass* of an excuse for a human being.

'Honey, come sit with us,' Ella says, and though she doesn't *say* it like one of the Mean Girls asking me to sit with the Plastics for lunch, the way every woman around the table – Ella, Alisha, Jenny, Monique and now Lola – is watching, it feels a little like I'm the new girl in the high-school diner.

Beaming outwardly, sighing inwardly, I realize this is *precisely* why I don't want to, didn't, or shouldn't have, gotten sucked in by Luke's charm again.

Throwing one last scowl in the direction of my

ex, I find him slumped huffily on a sofa next to Joe – my billionaire client, my last gig before partnership, best friend of my nemesis who, despite every smart cell in my warped brain, I'm unable to stay away from. Apparently, distance and time are a cure for absolutely nothing.

Because even while we were arguing by the coffee machine, I was watching his lips move, seeing the signs of last night's passion in the plump skin. I felt the skin of my neck tingle where he kissed it just hours ago, remembering how the day-old growth around his chin deliciously grazed my cheeks, my stomach, my inner thighs.

I sit at the table and find the silent curiosity has turned brazen... 'So you and Luke slept together, huh?' Alisha says.

Either my imagination is playing tricks on me or there is a genuine twinkle of mischievousness about her irises.

Horrified, I try to buy myself time to think of a response to Alisha's outrageously invasive— *Oh screw it.* It's written all over my face, evident from that blow-up Luke and I just had.

'I'm not surprised,' Lola says. 'That man was looking at you all day yesterday like he was going to devour you.'

He was? I hate myself for the way the idea turns me on. Maybe I was too busy looking at him like I wanted to devour him to notice whether it was reciprocal.

But I'm not stupid. There's insane chemistry between Luke and me. A lack of sexual chemistry was never the problem.

Still, I'm not used to this level of direct questioning from anyone other than Callum and, honestly, there's rarely anything I have to tell on the romance front. So I fumble a response. 'I— Ah—' Blowing a raspberry like someone far younger than even a high-school girl, I shrug. 'Yes. But look, I'm here for work, and I swear it doesn't change anyth—'

'You're not speaking to my husband now,' Ella says, wafting a hand. 'What's said in girl talk stays in girl talk. But I will tell you, Luke is a good man, and we *all* approve, not that you need our approval or blessing or anything like it. I'll also say this: Joe, whose business this really oughtn't to be, won't be angry or sad or whatever you're worried he'll be thinking, Carrie. In fact, I didn't want to be the one tell you this but here goes—'

Ella doesn't have a chance to finish her sentence because Luke has leapt up off the sofa, Joe has followed, and they're facing each other down like boxers before fight night.

Luke is yelling. 'You did what? Why in the hell would you do that?'

'Oh boy,' Ella says, pulling my attention back to her from the show of testosterone. 'He finally told him.'

'What am I missing?' I ask, my head spinning back and forth like a boomerang between Ella and Luke and Joe.

'I'd just like to flag,' Alisha says, 'I didn't know about this until I was already on island and embroiled against my will.'

'Know about what?' I ask, getting the distinct feeling there's something I really should know that I definitely don't.

But no one replies before Luke runs like an NFL player into Joe's waist, propelling him over the back of the sofa, both men landing on the wood floor with a thud and the kind of groans that generally come from aging, aching bones.

Ella and I move closer to the action, where we can see both men rolling onto all fours to come up to stand. 'I think, if you just take a pause, you'll see this as a good thing,' Joe is saying.

'A good thing?' Luke near screams, unsexily

high-pitched, before diving across Joe's back. Joe crawls around, thrashing like an animal under attack to throw Luke off him.

'I feel worse this morning than I ever did!' Luke shouts.

'So it was a make-or-break situation,' Joe defends. 'Either way, you can move forward.'

Though I have no idea what they're arguing about, his words strike a chord in my brain that I might be able to consider if I weren't watching this display of adolescence, a little horrified on both their behalves, honestly, but also grateful that the attention is no longer on my sex life.

Dave and Thom glance to Ella and me. 'Should we step in here?' Dave asks in a *Peaky Blinders* accent.

'It wouldn't be the first time they've gone at it,' Thom adds in his Michael Caine-esque accent. 'It's your call, Ella; you're the matriarch.'

Ella holds up a hand in instruction. 'Give them a minute.'

Joe manages to roll over and pin Luke to the floor, Joe's back to Luke's stomach.

'You had no right to interfere,' Luke is saying, struggling beneath Joe until somehow Luke is on top of him and they seem to be running through a playbook of sex positions. So much so, I'm biting my lip to stop myself laughing.

'I did it to make you happy, Luke. You're my friend and I'm tired of seeing you miserable.'

Joe's words seem to tame Luke for a moment. He stills, still straddling Joe's waist and pinning his arms to the ground. 'I'm not miserable.'

'You can be, honey,' Ella shouts, receiving a glare from Luke in return. 'Sorry, not my business.'

'You knew about this?' Luke asks, his eyes flicking to mine briefly then back to Ella.

'I... You know what he's like, Luke. When Joey sets his mind on something...'

Luke moves to... *slap???* Joe. Joe slaps back and they're having some kind of purses-at-dawn-type slapping wrestle.

'You know I'm a black belt,' Joe says.

'Black belt or not, Hettich, we're in the middle of a goddamned hurricane! What were you *thinking*?' Luke shouts, with, I think, genuine fury in his expression.

Joe holds up his palms. 'Now that I do feel bad about.'

Luke swipes at Joe's palms and they're rolling around the floor again.

Noah and Toby have left their games to come

and watch whatever the heck is happening on the floor between their father and godfather. 'Mom, is Dad okay?' Noah asks.

'Oh, yeah, honey. They're just, ah, play fighting, that's all.'

'Play fiiiiiiiiight!!!' Noah yells.

Then Toby is yelling too and they're charging toward the wrestlers, leaping into the fight. Then the four boys – two probably more mature mentally despite being younger in age than the others – are all piled up and shouting and laughing and I swear, I still have no clue what this whole hullaballoo is about.

Somehow, between the madness of it all, Luke is looking at me and I'm looking back at him and I think, maybe, he's apologizing.

His apology could be for one thing or a thousand. I have no idea.

All I'm left feeling is... sad.

Why is life never straight forward?

As if Planet Earth herself wants to let me in on something, there's a roar outside that cuts through all the noise inside. There's a crash and a bang of the magnitude I've never heard so close. Through the thin slatted windows that sit high in the wall on one side of the basement, the sky has grown darker.

Thick grey clouds interspersed with darts of color and debris. The sound of corrugated iron screeching, scraping, coming loose is the worst symphony I've ever had the misfortune to hear.

The men and boys all pause in their brawling positions on the floor, until Toby clings to his dad and says, 'I don't like it.'

'It's okay, buddy, nothing can hurt us down here. It's just wind,' Joe reassures him. I wish his words could reassure me too.

I follow Luke and Henry to a side table up against the one wall with windows and tentatively climb on top of it alongside them, hoping it's made well enough to withstand the weight of three adult – *meh, two and a half* – humans. As I peer through the thin, wide window, I can't believe what I'm seeing is real. The sea's waves are menacingly huge – significantly higher than when we were making our way back to Charithonia in the boat yesterday. They're washing onto the shore so far that most of the beach is underwater.

Palm trees are swaying from left to right at such angles, they defy gravity, their branches thrashing against one another. There's so much debris in the air – leaves, tree branches, metal, plastic, God knows what else – that the sky looks as busy as a trash heap.

Is that a flying door?

The island is going to be destroyed.

I look back at the faces in the room, at the kids cuddling their parents. Suddenly, the fight between Joe and Luke, whatever it was about, the animosity between Luke and me, it fades into the background of what really matters and that is keeping the people in this space safe.

'Should we close the shutters?' I ask.

'I think that's sensible,' Henry says. 'She's only going to get worse until the eye of the storm is around us.'

'Isabel is a bizarrely pretty name for something so grumpy,' Jenny says behind us. I have to agree and I'm about to say as much when the lights in the basement flicker, then, together with the television, they go out. Right at the same time, the shutters close over all the windows.

'It's a default setting when the electricity goes out,' someone, maybe Kevin, says.

I can't tell because the space is in complete darkness and my eyes are struggling to adjust. Feeling unsteady on my feet, I reach a hand out to the wall and I'm about to crouch down to get off the tabletop when two big hands are on my sides.

I do recognize the next voice I hear. Even if I hadn't, I would have known it was Luke who is steadying me, simply from the way he holds me. I lean into him and he lifts me down from the table to the floor but doesn't let me go. Our torsos are touching, my hands are on his biceps, his scent is all around me and I don't need light to know he's looking at me, that he's also been thrust back into a memory of last night.

The fire between us, the familiarity of every stroke, each nip and nibble, the tenderness of his teeth against my skin, the softness of his lips against mine. Despite the cries of children in the room, I feel as if I can hear the beating of his heart, the fast, rhythmic beating that's in tune with mine.

When there's a loud click and the lights come back on, for the briefest of moments, we're still alone in the room, the bad stuff forgotten for the second it takes me to proverbially step back onto the brighter side of sanity.

Luke asks me, 'Are you okay?'

I nod because that's all I feel capable of. The room becomes louder as I fully tune in to the distress of the kids, the soothing and shushing of their families in response, the booms, the crashes, and the thunderous roar of the wind outside.

'What can I do to help?' I ask Ella, who's holding Toby against her chest and stroking his hair.

'The lights are back now, sweetie, you're fine,' she's saying on repeat. 'Distractions,' she says to me.

I look around the space. 'Distractions, got it!' My eyes land on a large toy chest, so I make a beeline for it. Inside, there's a wealth of boxed games. Some I recognize, others I don't. I do remember the one with four hippos and a stash of marbles, so I take that one out. 'Who would like to play this with me?'

The response isn't immediate but eventually, Noah and Toby head my way and I set up the game on the coffee table.

'Ah, I used to love this one,' Luke says, also coming to sit on the floor with us. 'Can I be the blue hippo?'

'No,' Toby says emphatically. 'You can be yellow, Uncle Luke. Aunty Carrie, you can be green.'

I don't hear which of the boys takes the other two hippos because I'm too distracted by becoming Aunty Carrie. I should tell them it's not the case. I'm just their father's tax advisor, temporarily at that, but the way everyone in this room has accepted me into this safe haven and made me feel welcome – Luke aside – makes me accept the comment and the green hippo instead.

We play two rounds of the hippopotamus game, I think – it's hard to know where one game ends and another begins. There's squabbling and shouting, lots of flying marbles and slamming of animals. I'm not entirely sure which of the boys won. But I judge the success on the fact that neither boy is worried about the storm, even though the generator trips in and out multiple times as we play.

It's going well, until the roaring outside gets louder and the walls of this apparently fail-safe basement begin to tremble as if we're in an earthquake. I know the air pressure has increased because my ears have popped as if I'm on an airplane and with all of this going on, I can't stop myself from looking around the space, seeing the worry on the faces of everyone else too, and wondering if this is really as safe as Joe has made out.

'Hey,' Luke whispers. He reaches his hand toward mine on the coffee table then stops himself. 'We're good down here. It's going to be fine.'

'It's not going to be fine, Luke,' I say quietly. 'We might be but the islands are going to be ruined by this.'

I wait for him to argue, to tell me I'm wrong, and

when he simply nods, my spirits drop further still, as if this day hadn't started at rock bottom in any event.

'Mom, my ears hurt,' Noah says, and Ella and Joe replace Luke and me at the coffee table so their family of six is sitting around the hippo game. Ella mouths *thank you* to me as I uncross my legs and stand, rubbing my own ears where the pressure is starting to be painful.

'How about it?' Luke asks. He's standing by the toy chest with a wooden chess board in his hands.

'With you?' I ask, knowing the answer. 'No, thanks.'

'Don't you play, Carrie?' Joe asks.

'She plays,' Luke tells him, his eyes still fixed on me. 'She's never beaten me, though.'

We've played multiple times, in fact. Always by the light of his wall fire in his New York apartment. We'd play, we'd drink wine, eat food, talk into the early hours of the morning, and wake up in each other's arms. But he's right. It was a game he always won, just like in life. Except... 'I've only never beaten you because you don't play fair. You're dishonest.' I scowl at him, knowing he understands the double meaning of my words. 'The one time I had you in check, you flipped the board.'

'Ha. That sounds like Luke. Sore loser,' Joe says, receiving a murderous look from Luke in response.

It's true, Luke flipped the board. He couldn't stand not getting his own way. So he turned the board and then crawled across the floor of his lounge and turned me on until I surrendered.

'He certainly never played fair,' I say. He didn't play fair that night and he definitely didn't play fair when he led me on, made me fall in love with him, showed me the kind of highs I'd never, *have* never, known with anyone else, then left me.

'I promise I will, if you give me a chance,' Luke says, already manipulating the situation. Already making me wonder if he's also making me an offer of something that's nothing to do with the game.

'No.' I won't fall for it.

'Are you that afraid?' he asks.

You're damn right I am. Terrified, in fact. Because last night, I was right back there. I was falling.

'You don't scare me, Luke. To be afraid, I'd have to care, and I don't. It's all just a game.'

We seem to have moved closer to each other. Me to him, or him to me, I'm not sure how but we're facing each other, staring each other down, just a fraction of air between us.

'If it's just a game, you might as well play and

have some fun. Unless you can't because it isn't *just* a game.'

I feel my eyes narrow, my brow crease, and I sense the others in the basement wondering what the hell is going on. I'm curious myself. 'Fine.'

'Fine.'

'Oh great,' Joe says. 'Everyone's fine again.'

From the corner of my eye, I see Ella flick him with the back of her hand, though I won't be first to blink or take my focus from Luke. When his eyelids eventually close for a nanosecond, I feel myself grin like the Wicked Queen after Snow White takes a bite of her poisonous apple.

36

LUKE

I'm still reeling about what Joe just told me. This whole damn thing, Carrie being here, my soul being in tatters, again, is his doing.

Yet, somehow, Carrie and I are going to play chess, as if my mind isn't whirring at a billion thoughts per hour. I'm not sure why I suggested it, whether I saw the box and the memories of us playing together made me want to be right back there, to remind her of great nights we spent together, or if I just wanted to distract her from the storm that I can see is scaring her, making her increasingly anxious. She was great with Noah and Toby, amazing. I'm not surprised everyone loves her. She's extremely lovable.

Now, it's my turn to take care of her, try to put her at ease, to the extent she'll let me. After all, isn't it my fault she's here in the first place? My idiotic friend playing creator of the universe and delving into things he has no business messing with to get her here?

I have a lot of questions about Joe arranging Carrie's being here on Charithonia – like why, after all these years, did Joe think it was necessary to force Carrie and me to spend a week together on his island? What did he possibly think this could achieve except more heartache for one or both of us?

But I can't focus on that at the moment because I need to concentrate on Carrie, getting her through this storm calmly and safely. Getting her back to New York in one piece physically and mentally.

Shit, she's going to think I was involved in this whole thing. That I've set her up somehow. She'll never believe that her being here has all been constructed by Joe and his ludicrous ideas and I had no idea it was happening.

Then I go and sleep with her. *Double shit*. She'll think I was in on it all and then I conned her into going to bed with me.

No. Far from it. *She* came to *my* pod.

But as she sits across from me at this table, looking up to me through her eyelashes, smoldering, I won't be sorry for what happened last night. I can't be. Even though she ripped out my fucking heart, again, and I'm pissed beyond measure at Joe for this entire thing, I can't be sorry about the way it felt to be with her again, to have her in my arms, in my bed. To be inside her, connected to her. To be *us* again.

I'm playing white and I choose to move the pawn in front of my king forward two squares. Carrie scoffs. 'Of course, move your pawn first. You do love a pawn in your games, don't you?'

Animosity is literally dripping off her. If I had any doubt as to whether there was an ulterior meaning to her words about playing this game, it's gone. She put her resting bitch on ice for the sake of the kids and now, it's back with extra zest.

'It's the safest first move in the game book,' I tell her.

'Ah, yes, because you always play by the rules.' She doesn't even look at me as she speaks. Not until she moves her knight to F6.

I tsk. She's bold. 'There's a fine line between confidence and recklessness, Carrie.'

The lids of her eyes partially cover her bright

irises as her jaw stiffens. 'Don't I know it,' she says. 'I've crossed it too much recently.'

I'm fairly certain she means just hours ago. She thinks what happened between us last night was reckless. She's probably right. Yet her words hurt. Irrationally so. I shouldn't care if she thought last night was a mistake. It was. I knew that the moment I woke up alone in my pod.

And this is all the fault of my supposed best friend, who, for the record, I'd like to loathe right now, but he's cuddling his scared kids and I don't have the capability.

I should tell Carrie about it. Come clean on Joe's behalf. But she's going to be livid. Her client set this whole thing up and who knows who else was in on it. She'll think I was and I know how much her career means to her, how much it has always meant to her. So much more than me, evidently, and I don't dare tell her the truth she deserves.

I move my rook to E3. As I do, there's another fierce gust of wind, more hurtling of debris outside, and the pressure in the air climbs.

Carrie brings her hands to her ears, wincing with discomfort I know she's feeling because I feel it too. Jessie and Woody start howling, crying at either the noise or their own ear pain. Carrie gets out of her seat like a lightning bolt, rushing to the dogs and hugging Jessie, who's a willing recipient of her affection. I'm not a dog lover the way Carrie clearly is but the dogs' distress is making the kids' tears worse, so I follow Carrie's lead and hold Woody in the same way she's cradling Jessie.

I don't know how long the four of us – Carrie, me and the two dogs – sit on the floor like this until the pressure finally dissipates. The noise outside subsides.

Henry opens the shutters on the windows, jumping back up on the tabletop to look out. The sun is shining for the first time in what feels like days.

'We're in the eye of the storm,' Henry says, and I follow his lead to see out of the narrow window. 'I'm going out to take a look.'

'Is that wise?' Roy asks.

'Are you crazy?' Alisha adds.

'This is a once-in-a-lifetime experience; I can't not go,' Henry tells them. 'I'll close the doors behind me and I'll only be a minute or two. The eye is so wide, we've got a while before Isabel comes back full strength.'

I don't want to be a fool but the guy's got a point. I wish there wasn't a hurricane. I wish none of us were stuck down here and afraid, that these stunning Caribbean islands wouldn't be hit. But since it *is* happening, I sort of want to see it.

Whether it's adrenaline or excitement, or just morbid curiosity, I follow Henry to the staircase to leave the basement.

'Mom, can we go?' Noah asks.

'One hundred percent no!' Ella replies. 'Uncle Luke has a death wish.'

'I won't be long, buddy,' I tell Noah, unwilling to relent.

Dave types in the code to open the door at the top of the stairs and Henry moves up first. As I climb, Carrie follows. I turn to her. 'Absolutely not. You're staying.'

'Excuse me?' she says, looking like she might actually slap my face. 'As if you have any right to tell me what I can and can't—'

'Damnit, Carrie, I can't be doing with this. You're exhausting.' I sigh. I really am tired of this back and forth with the woman I can't stop goddamn thinking about.

'*I'm* exhausting?' Nostrils flaring, she pushes past me. 'You should listen to yourself, Luke. All chivalrous and caring. Which, by the way, actually comes across as domineering on you.'

'I do care whether you get hurt, Carrie. I'm not a monster.'

She spins so fast to face me that I walk right into her on my next step up. 'Seven years too late.'

'You think I didn't care?' My words lose all their strength. I cared. I cared so much, it ripped me to pieces. *How* could she fail to see this?

I wait for her next retort, the one that opens my final wound and has me as injured as I was back then. Instead, I see the fight drain from her, her shoulders drop and her face soften. I think she'll speak. Maybe tell me she knows I cared. Of course she knows.

Silence.

She sets back up the stairs and into the lounge of the main house. I'm amazed it looks intact. That the windows haven't broken.

I look beyond the glass and I'm speechless as we make our way outside. The landscape looks wholly different. The lush green of the hills, the palm trees, the blooming frangipanes, they're all gone, replaced by what looks like barren land. The terrace has been destroyed – the wood frame and the roof that used to be decorated in tea lights are halfway down the rockface to the beach.

The beach that *was*, because I can't see the beach

for the grey, brown murky sea water that's covering it entirely. The steps that led down to the sand are gone without trace and some of the pods – Carrie's included – have partially lost their roofs.

'Jesus,' is all I can say.

'If it's like this here, imagine what it's like on the other islands,' Henry says. 'Local homes aren't built like Charithonia. They'll be destroyed.'

The three of us look around in silence at the devastation, a strange contrast to the chirping birds, blue sky and beaming sun. It's a trip, completely.

'There's still the other half to come,' I say in disbelief.

'The worst half,' Henry adds.

I watch Carrie now, observing everything I can see in silence, her eyes wet. I want to go to her, to put an arm around her, but despite the enormity of what's in front of us, I can't forget her words of minutes ago. She doesn't think I care or that I ever cared.

'We should probably head back inside,' Henry says, moving to Carrie and putting his arm around her, where mine ought to be. 'People get caught out in the eye of the storm. She'll come back with vengeance.'

'All right, Dr Meteorology,' I mutter for my own ears.

'I'll follow,' Carrie says, her voice hoarse. 'I just want another minute.'

Henry nods and walks back into the house. I linger behind her, out of her view but with her firmly in mine. There's no chance I'm leaving her out here alone.

I give her minutes, wondering what she's thinking, wanting to ask but also knowing she doesn't want me to be here with her. Eventually, she speaks, as if she knew I would be right here the whole time.

'It's perspective getting, isn't it?' she says.

Yeah, I suppose it is. It makes me feel like this is no time to leave things unsaid.

On that note...

'Come on, let's get back inside.' As I speak, I hear a distant rumble like thunder and I know it's the return of Isabel. 'Carrie, let's go,' I tell her, more urgently now.

She nods, eventually shifting to come inside. I hold open the door to the house for her as the thunder of the wind grows louder, the sky grows darker again, and hell, I confess that I'm afraid now too. But Carrie halts, staring at the storm, watching it draw closer, hypnotized by it.

'Carrie!'

It's as if she doesn't hear my words at all. She's lost to the storm, mesmerized.

'Luke!' Dave hollers from the top of the basement staircase, holding the door open for us.

'Carrie!' I yell louder, finally making her jump, startling her out of her transfixion.

'It's incredible,' she says. 'I've never seen anything like it.'

'And it's a killer, Carrie! Inside, now!'

She nods, thank *fuck*, and steps toward the door, but her path is blocked as Jessie dashes out of the house as fast as I've ever seen her run. Terrified.

'Jessie!' Carrie shouts.

Before I have a chance to even consider my next move, Carrie is running after the dog.

'Carrie, leave her! You need to get inside!'

I'm not even sure she can hear me now over the sound of the wind that's almost upon us.

'It's my fault she got out!' Carrie shouts back without slowing down.

'Shit!' I have to go with them.

I'm chasing her, closing in on her over the cliff top as the wind is back, almost bowling me over. I can barely keep running, and Carrie is struggling too.

She shouts something and she's pointing down

at something on the other side of the hill. I follow blindly over the peak, fighting the storm, as a small concrete building comes into view. At best guess, it's some kind of pump house or utilities store.

As I see it, the wind blows Carrie off her feet. She falls in slow motion, the force of the elements keeping her from hitting the ground.

I'm right next to her and grab her waist with one arm as the hurricane fights us both. Together, we manage to open the steel slatted doors to the building and as we're dragging them shut, Jessie bursts inside with us, barking.

It's a utility room, with laundry machines, a heavy work bench and tools inside. Carrie and I wrestle the doors shut, pushing back against the wind, and pull down a steel slat to lock them in place.

I doubt that alone will hold in the force of Isabel, so I drag one of the machines out from under the counter and ram it against the doors. As I do, Carrie finds a flashlight in a drawer and shines it as I try to lift the worktop, which, unexpectedly, comes loose with ease. She helps me lean the heavy load against the machine and the doors.

Finally safe, she lights two chunky candles with matches and preserves the flashlight battery.

I move around to her. 'Are you fucking crazy?' I scream, grabbing her face in my hands. 'You could have gotten yourself killed.'

'I couldn't leave her out here alone,' Carrie says, gesturing to Jessie and bursting into tears that, despite my anger, make me pull her against my chest and hold on to her as tightly as I possibly can.

'I only just got you back, Carrie, for fuck's sake,' I grind out through my teeth. 'I only just got you back.'

Then I'm kissing her hair, her head, her cheeks, her lips, anywhere I can to somehow tell my mind she's real and she's fine. She's here.

To somehow tell her that she's safe and I've got her and I want to look after her.

'I'm sorry,' she sobs.

Behind her, Jessie is lying on the concrete ground, whimpering and scratching her ears. She's in pain.

'It's okay,' I say, still holding Carrie, saying the words to her, to the dog, and to myself. 'We're okay now.'

Carrie peels herself away from my chest, looking up to me. 'I didn't mean to put you in danger. I never would.'

I'm not sure which of us moves first but our lips

meet. Long and steady, in a way that seems to calm us both and the situation. In a way that feels natural. As if there's no question we'd be together through this.

And I have to tell her... 'It's me who should be apologizing. You wouldn't even be here if it wasn't for me.'

'It's just work, Luke. You didn't know we'd get caught up in a hurricane.'

I shake my head. It's not that straightforward. Not since Joe told me the truth.

37

CARRIE

Our voices are raised above the growling wind, the crashing debris, though we're not shouting in anger. The three of us – Luke, Jessie and me – are sitting on the floor with just two candles lighting our bunker. The walls are trembling around us, as if at any moment, they might give in to the relentless battering they're receiving from the outside.

'Joe planned this whole thing? But how?' I ask, not sure I'm following entirely. Not sure if I'm supposed to be shocked or angry or if I'm completing misunderstanding what Luke is trying to tell me.

This might be the worst time ever for Luke to decide to make a confession, but I have to admit, it's a diversion from everything else, at least.

'He only told me earlier when— Well, you saw me leap for him in the basement,' Luke tells me. 'Apparently, Eric really did get stomach flu but Joe knew that you were working at the firm; he'd known for months and not mentioned it to me. Then when Eric got sick and cancelled his trip, Joe spoke to your boss and arranged for you to replace Eric.'

I press my fingers to my temples, eyelids squeezed shut. 'Because...'

Luke nods. 'Because of me. He wanted to bring you over here, where I would be, where we'd be trapped together.'

'But I just... Nothing to do with him wanting me to be his advisor?'

'He thinks you're great,' Luke is quick to say. 'But no. He... I *guess* he thought there was something unfinished between you and me.'

I rub my hands over my face, feeling grit on my fingers and now on my clammy skin, hot and sweaty in the humidity. His words are sinking in, slowly being pieced together by my brain.

'He brought me here for *you*? To be your plaything? A toy? A game?'

'I— Yes. No. I swear I didn't know, Carrie, and for what it's worth, I think he was trying to play matchmaker, not... I don't know.'

'This is mortifying, Luke! Did he tell Rachel his grand design for us? Did he tell my *boss*?'

'I honestly don't know.' Luke watches me from the ground, his knees bent, his wrists resting on them. He looks dirty and tired and defeated. 'I don't know more than I've told you and, if it's any consolation at all, I'm livid about it too.'

'*You* are?' I throw my arms up in frustration. 'Luke, do you know how long and hard I've worked to change the narrative that I'm some kind of whore who tried to sleep her way to the top? Do you?' I'm yelling now and it's nothing to do with the noise of the weather. 'I'm on the cusp of partnership and he, *you*, have made me look like— What the *hell* am I doing here?'

My eyes burn with anger and I have to slam the heels of my hands into them to stop me from crying like some kind of damsel in distress.

Luke's hands are on my shoulders and I move my own to slap his away. 'Don't touch me!'

I walk the entire four steps away from him that I can possibly move in this space. 'It's happening all over again. All *fucking* over again. I fell for you, I slept with you, I'm fucking heartbroken and to top it all off, I look like I've been screwing the firm's biggest client to get my partnership case over the line!'

My eyes are watering uncontrollably and I really wish I could stop them. Trying, I think, takes the last of my energy. This day, this week, the last seven years of hurt and resentment, it's all been too much.

I slump back against the unsteady wall, ironically, for support. 'I really was just a pawn in a game.'

We fall silent, Luke and I facing each other, Jessie coming to sit on my feet. I stare at the man who keeps blowing my mind and messing up my life, and he stares right back. Despite all the madness outside, inside, it feels like I could hear a pin drop.

Unspoken words silently whirl around the air between us, until eventually, Luke says, 'I swear I didn't know, Carrie, and you have *never* been a game to me. *Never.*'

Everything about him is sincere and I believe him. It must be true. Why in the world would he have actually tried to bring me here? He walked away from me once; he'd do it again, I think. It's something even I'm not convinced of anymore. Which is probably a reflection of how much my mind is having to contend with here in supposed paradise.

There's a loud crash of something big and heavy against the steel doors that makes us both flinch like we're dodging bullets, that makes the machine and countertop leaning against the doors shudder, and has Jessie howling.

'Shh, girl, you're okay,' I tell her, trying to convince us both of that truth, running a soothing finger down the crease between her eyes and onto her nose, the way Eddie loves. It seems to work and she calms, leaning into my side when I come to sit next to her on the floor, then draping her head and a front paw across my thighs. I continue stroking that sweet spot and watch the rise and fall of her tummy gradually slow. It's a safer space to keep my focus than on Luke.

'I've no doubt we're going to be fine and that we'll see this storm through,' he says, forcing me to look up to where he's standing on the opposite side of the small space, leaning his shoulders back against the wall, squeezing the peak of his cap between his hands. 'Even so, I don't want to leave things unsaid because I don't know if you'll walk out of here and I'll never see you again.' His lopsided smile is sad. 'I should be well versed in it by now.'

'If I've walked away, it's been for good reason,' I tell him, not snapping; I'm surprisingly composed, though I am having to speak loudly.

He's just watching me, not reacting, completely

unreadable and, oddly, I really want to know what he's thinking. It's also bizarre that we're having this conversation, in this space, with a terrified dog laid across my lap, and I'm thinking Luke looks like strength and home and sexy-as-hell all at once.

'I am sorry that Joe has brought you here if you don't want to be here,' he says. 'Though I don't think it's career-threatening because you've done a great job for him. I've been in awe, listening to the way you've advised Joe, responded to his off-the-cuff questions, and mine. If there's any take away to be fed back to your firm, it will only be positive.'

I clear my throat, which has tightened with his words. I'm not sure if I should thank him. I'm not sure I agree. So I don't respond. Instead, I focus on Jessie.

'Scratch that, I'm irate that he's brought you here and you've gotten stuck in this hurricane. I'd never do anything to put you in harm's way and I want to kick his ass for it.'

I give him my attention now. Without doubt, my presence on this island was a shock to him. Irrationally, it makes me... sad? Disappointed? Maybe I was flattered by that 1 percent of doubt. At the idea that maybe *Luke* wanted me to be here too. Which is stupid, foolish, idiotic, I know.

He inhales deeply, his chest pushing against his damp t-shirt, his eyes piercing mine as he replaces his cap on his head. 'But I'm not going to say I'm sorry about getting to see you again. As much as it killed me to wake up alone this morning, I can't regret last night. Being with you again felt natural, unbelievable. Like I was exactly where I was supposed to be, at last.'

With each of his words, the pressure behind my eyes builds, and I dig my teeth into my lip in an attempt to fight against it, because I didn't expect, I couldn't have expected, him to feel today exactly how I felt. Like we were back where we began, the way things used to be, as if we fit together in a way that could only mean we were intended to be.

But I shake my head. *No.* 'That aside, Luke, what if great sex is all we have, all we've ever had, and if we did this again, made the same mistake again, then when the novelty wears off, you'll go? You'll run off to something you prefer. Something better. Exactly as you did last time.'

He crouches to my level, a little frantic. 'Carrie, are you crazy? Is that honestly what you think I did?'

I shrug, uncertain about what happened in our past for the first time ever, because Luke is so bold and so sure of a different version, even if I still don't know what that is. 'It's what it felt like you did,' I tell him, watching my fingers as I stroke Jessie, glad of her warm weight on my lap.

Luke crouches down in front of me and gently teases my chin until I'm meeting his gaze. He leans his head to one side. 'Then I'm sorry for that too. I'm sorry that that's how you've seen it all this time.'

I don't consciously do it but I seem to have slipped to rest my chin, my cheek, further into his palm. My eyelids close for a moment, just long enough for me to gain some perspective. 'How could I see things any differently? You've never given me an explanation.'

His hand leaves my skin and I open my eyes, feeling the loss of his touch, only to see him coming to sit on the ground opposite me, his knees pulled up and his feet touching mine.

He's going to explain. Finally.

I'm more afraid of this moment than I am of the 285 kph gusts of wind outside.

Do I want to know why he hurt me, ruined me for all other relationships? Do I want to relive it all, right here, right now? Hasn't this week been grueling enough?

'I assumed you knew some or most of this because I've always thought you were the person who opened the first letter I sent to you. I thought you knew but still shut me out.' He takes off his cap and drags a hand back through his hair, giving me the impression this will be as hard for him to say as I know it's going to be for me to hear. Maybe that's why I don't stop him. 'I'll tell you everything; maybe some of it won't be new, I don't know.'

He puffs the air from his lungs. 'The day everything imploded, I found your note on my desk.' His mouth twitches up. So fleetingly, I could have imagined it. 'I was so excited to come to you. I remember the way my heart started thumping and every part of me was running from the office in your direction before my mind could even catch up.'

His words make my heart race in response. I remember that feeling. The giddiness, the heat, the desperation. The insatiable desire. I remember how my fingers trembled with it as I wrote that note.

'As I was leaving the office, my phone buzzed and I thought it must be you. So I took it out and—'

'It wasn't me,' I say, finishing his sentence. I know it wasn't me because I never messaged him. Not at five to twelve, not when he was twenty minutes late, not when he was an hour then two hours late. It was Luke who messaged me, while I was lying on a hotel bed, dressed in new lingerie I had bought for his birthday, a bottle of champagne and two glasses on the bedside table.

He rubs a hand down his face, across his chin and two-day-old stubble. 'I still can't believe Anya told me by text but she did. I pulled out my phone and found out I was going to be a dad. It stopped me dead in my tracks.' He looks from his fingers to me. 'I don't want to give you a sob story but to say I was shocked doesn't cover it. I was— It was a total mind screw.'

I have to know... 'Were you happy?'

I don't realize I'm expecting him to say *no*, maybe hoping he'll say no, until he says, 'Yes. On some level.' He looks back to his fingers, as if he's said something wrong. He hasn't, I suppose, only something I don't want to hear. 'I've always thought I'd have kids. There was a time I thought that would be with Anya. So, I was— I don't know. I guess that's the problem. Only more recently, with the perspective of distance and time, can I see I was happy about the prospect of being a dad but not about being the father of Anya's child. Even now, Carrie, I don't know how bad or evil that sounds, even when I'm saying it to you and it's the thing that messed up everything between us. I couldn't get my head around it in those minutes, not for the six months after that when I was living in Chicago, and not after—'

He leans his head back against the wall, focusing on the roof above us. Trying, maybe, not to look my way, or to hide his expression. For a moment, I'm reminded of the raging storm outside and the reason I'm sitting here sweating, with a dog lying across my thighs. The fact that I'm trapped in here because Luke rescued me and I can't get away from his words.

No matter how much I don't want to hear the story of how and why he left me, it's what I've waited thousands of nights to know.

'There was a baby but it was never mine.'

'What?' I heard his words and saw his mouth speak but... 'I don't understand.'

He gives a short, sad laugh. 'Yep. I left you, I moved to Chicago, I stuck around for six months, decorated a nursery, picked out baby clothes, even tried to convince myself that if I could just fall in love with my son, then I could fall back in love with Anya, despite everything that happened between us. Then he was born and Anya told me she thought we should get a paternity test.'

I feel myself gawping.

'Honestly, I just didn't see it coming. I don't know

if I was blind to signs, but it came completely out of the blue for me.' He shrugs. 'The baby wasn't mine.'

I try to compute that, struggling, maybe feeling a shred of what Luke must have been feeling back then. 'But the timing. I mean, you must have been—'

His eyes widen when the proverbial light switch comes on. 'I swear to you, Carrie, I wasn't still sleeping with her when you and I got together. We had one last senseless night together. Not even a night. A short—' He shakes his head, eyes closed. 'It told me definitively that we were done but it was always a goodbye or for old times' sake, or— *Jesus*, I never considered what you must have been thinking about that. I just assumed you'd know. I guess I've been blind to a few things before this week. Maybe it was easier to blame you because deep down, I know I fucked up something that could have been amazing between us.'

My mouth is dry. We could have been. But we weren't. I feel... deflated.

Though at least he's answered one of the questions that has eaten me up inside for so long. 'The other guy?' I manage coarsely.

'She'd been having an affair. I mean, that wasn't the thing that stung, truthfully. You know that Anya and I were done a long time before we officially ended. The thing that killed me was that she'd let me fall in love with the baby, or at least the idea of him.'

I thought that hearing this would hurt me, but seeing Luke reliving this, seeing his pain, cuts me deeper than his words. 'I'm sorry,' I tell him sincerely.

He smiles a somber smile. 'Don't be. It's how karma works, right?'

I return his sad turn of the lips. 'Maybe.'

He picks up an old piece of string from the ground and starts twisting it between his fingers. 'So, I got her message when I was on my way to you that day and it threw me, blew my mind, but I was still coming, or would have, I'm sure of that. Except, as I was standing in the corridor, wondering what the hell kind of message I'd just received from my ex, Christopher Oakes – the old managing partner of our firm – collared me and asked me to go with him to his office. When I got inside, two other equity partners, Bernie Walton and Bill Lin, were in there, and the HR director too.' He scoffs. 'I knew the second I saw them. They were all wearing the same expression, like a "We gotcha". That was how I knew they'd found out about you and me.'

My breathing quickens, as if I'm back there, in

the thick of the discovery, the immediate aftermath and realization that I was facing it alone, that my career was tanked, that Luke had gone back to his ex-wife and their child. Except, what I thought were truths are seemingly *not*, and while Luke is still talking, I can't process anything more than the facts he's giving me.

'So that's how it happened?' is all I manage.

Luke nods. 'They sat me down in that office, grilling me, making me feel like some kind of predator, like the disgrace of the partnership, for more than an hour. It was as if they were enjoying it.'

If it's possible, my mood dips even lower. I hate imagining that they made him feel that way. That they made him feel as if what we shared was wrong, sordid.

'Luke, it was never controlling and it was *never* one-sided, you know that, right?'

The way he looks at me tells me he doesn't know that at all. Seeing things through his eyes, the fact he *thinks* I ghosted him – I suppose I did – I can understand how I played into that view.

He doesn't answer and it tears through my heart that he maybe regrets us, what happened. Pain fills the space between us and for a while, neither one of us speaks.

'Someone saw us leaving my apartment that morning,' he says eventually. 'Reported it to the partners and in justifying it, I ended up spilling that we were in a relationship, which only made things worse in their eyes, not better.'

I shake my head, furious. 'I hate that. I hate that they would assume I couldn't make a decision about a relationship on my own, that you must have coerced me. I hate that they made you think that.'

'It's the way the old school works, Carrie.' He shrugs. 'They said they wanted me to stay but that I wouldn't make partner and they were going to move you to a different team to separate us.'

'They would have managed me out,' I say as the realization hits me.

Luke nods. 'I thought so too. And I knew how hard you worked and how much your career meant to you. You were still so junior and I had experience under my belt. So, I told them I'd resign, provided they kept you in the position you were in.'

'You did?'

'Yes, Carrie. I did and I'd do it again. I'm not sure when you're going to figure it out but you were bigger than a job to me; you meant more. I was in love with you.'

There's an enormous clatter outside that's so

loud, it makes me duck on reflex. Then it's gone and I've no idea what hit the building, but I can't wait for the wind to start subsiding. I wish I could tell whether it's the storm that's making my ears and my head ring with pain, or if it's my mind trying to deal with everything Luke is hurtling at me.

He was *in love with me?*

After all this time... With all the murky water beneath the bridge between us.

'You surely knew that?' he asks. 'How could you *not* have known that?'

'Because you left me in a hotel room with the only explanation being by message that you were going back to your wife and child!' For some reason, I'm shouting. My confusion emanating as anger or frustration, or both. 'I never knew you gave up partnership for me. All I knew was that you wanted to be back with your ex, as a family. It shattered me into a million goddamn pieces.'

As I vent my anger, I feel pressure in my eyes, I see my vision clouding. I don't *want* to cry, again. I don't *want* to. 'Why? Why her and not me if you're telling me now that you were in love with me?'

'Because I thought I was doing the right thing,' he snaps back. His own frustration silencing mine, unclouding my vision. 'I had no fucking clue what to do for the best. I didn't want to leave you, of course I didn't. But I had a wife in Chicago who was telling me she was having my child and I—' He stands. '*Goddammit*, I didn't know what the *hell* to do.' He thrusts a fist into the countertop that's leaning against the doors and immediately yells, 'Jesus! Christ. *Fuck*.' He's flapping his hand, his face twisted with agony.

I stand, Jessie rising with me, and go to him. 'Let me see,' I say, calmer now. 'Wiggle your fingers.' He does. 'I don't think it's broken.'

I realize I'm holding his hand and I'm painfully close to him when he reaches out to me with his other hand and tucks a loose tendril of hair behind my ear. I can't hold his gaze, looking away. It's all too much. He's too much.

Thankfully, he steps back, and we both move to lean back against the walls, which I notice aren't moving anymore. In fact, the roar outside seems to be slightly less now than minutes ago.

We're facing each other as he tells me, 'My parents separated when I was ten. Old enough to remember and miss my dad, despite the fact he was a dick to my mom. Old enough to understand he'd had an affair and had another family.'

'I didn't know he had another family.'

'It's not something I like to go over. Life without him was tough, awful sometimes. I felt like I was supposed to be the man around the house for my mom and my brother. I was an angry kid, pissed off at the world, even my mom for not— It sounds crazy now that I'm a man, but for not being good enough to hold on to my dad for me.' He shakes his head. 'I couldn't. I *wouldn't* have inflicted that on my own son.'

Finally, I think I'm starting to understand.

'I chose to do right by the baby I thought I was having. I didn't choose Anya over you, Carrie. We were finished. I didn't love her and I truly don't think I'd known how amazing a relationship could be with a woman until you. I've not found it since, either.'

The enormity of his words renders me speechless. He's nailed exactly how I've been feeling, what I've been missing without realizing it for so many years. This is what Callum means when he says there's got to be more to life for me.

'This is the most open you've ever been with me, Luke.' I sigh. 'Maybe the most we've ever talked about how we really feel.' I want to offer him something back, but what I won't allow myself to say is that last night reminded me, too, of everything I feel, or used to, maybe still do feel, for him. Because it's easy to say things, right? It's easy to spin a line but nothing has really changed, has it?

So, instead, I tell him, 'I didn't know all of that about your parents. But I guess it's hard for me to understand that you could feel the way you say you felt for me and walk away. My parents separated when I was a teenager. You know that. But they should have done it a long time before they did. I lived for a long time with arguing and fighting and eventually cheating because my parents stayed together for me.'

His eyes narrow in concentration.

'I suppose what I'm saying is, I don't know if I can believe that there was nothing between you and Anya. That you didn't have options. Something other than leaving me sitting on a hotel bed, watching you walk away to your family. Or at least what you thought was your family. I— I don't know what I'm saying, Luke. This is all a lot.'

'I know.' His voice is as fragile as I've heard it. Maybe he thinks I'm saying no to he and I having anything more. Maybe I am. I'm not sure.

'Has anything changed between us, Luke? Even if there are feelings between us, is that enough? I don't even know *what* I'm feeling and how I'm feeling it. Like, if it's real now or if it's some kind of nostalgia or reflection of something we used to share.'

'Carrie—'

'Please let me *try* to articulate something that makes sense.'

He nods.

'I think that maybe we're only just talking now because things between us have always been about sex. That would explain a lot, wouldn't it? You could walk away from sex. And yes, it was intense and great, but is it enough?'

'Carrie—'

I hold up a hand – *I'm not finished*. 'In any event, Hettich is my client and regardless of whatever games Joe has played here, my firm still sees Hettich as my client. This still reflects on me and my ethics and it isn't a good look. I've worked so hard, Luke.'

Luke sighs, long and slow, his shoulders rising and falling. 'I can't tell you how much weight to place on your career, Carrie. I know how much it means to you and I don't think this has to kibosh it, I really don't. But that's your call. It's a balance for you to make.'

I see the hurt in his eyes – I'm putting my career before him, he thinks. But there isn't an *us*, not now. And *he* put something, some*one* before me once before, when there *was* something real and tangible between us.

'I will say this,' he tells me. 'I don't believe two people can have the connection we had last night, that we've always had when we make love, and not feel something on a much deeper level.' He raises his arms from his sides. 'Maybe we did focus on the sex and not communicate enough. I also think that every relationship where the guy and the girl are freaking head over heels for each other is bound to have a lot of sex. And ours was great. *Is* great. Not just the physical, but...'

I feel my lips rise in agreement. I can't deny it.

'We just didn't have long enough together to get to know everything,' he says. 'I get that it's on me. I didn't, or I didn't want to, accept it before this week, because it was easier for me to put all that pain into a box with your name on it and blame you. I'm so sorry I screwed up, Carrie, and I'll be forever sorry that I hurt you.'

'Me too, Luke. I felt justified in blocking you out of my life and I'm still not sure I completely understand why you left, but I don't believe it was because you were selfish or not thinking about me in it all. So I apologize for misinterpreting everything and not being grown-up enough to speak to you rather than cutting you out.'

Even in the low light of the space, I can see Luke's eyes are glazed, as if we've said things he's been waiting to hear for a long time. A feeling I can understand.

When he speaks again, his first words come with a croak. 'Maybe I don't know everything about your childhood and you don't know everything about mine, but I do know *you*, Carrie. I know what you value, what you're about. I know that if you'll let me in and tell me I have permission to get to know every single thing about you, I will. I want to. And I can handle not making love to you until I know it all.'

I feel my brows rise. *He could?* I guess my lust when I'm around him is stronger, or my willpower significantly weaker.

'It would be painful abstinence. Extremely.' He chuckles and I reciprocate. A welcome relief from the intensity between us. 'But I'd do it. Or at least try really hard.' He rubs the corner of his eye and I wonder if, like mine, his vision is blurred by emotion. 'I've been damaged too, Carrie. You've ruined me for all other women. No one else has had or will have a look in since you. So just consider giving us a chance. *Please.*'

I want to say yes. Because of the man sitting in front of me baring all. Because of the churn in the pit of my stomach, the pounding of my heart when I'm anywhere near him. Because of the honesty and the forgiveness we've finally shared.

But something is holding me back as we stare at each other across the space. Something is stopping me from crossing the space between us, wrapping my arms around his neck and holding my mouth to his.

I just don't know where we go from here.

There's a bang on the steel doors that's less of a sound brought by the hurricane, which has slowly been receding while Luke and I have been lost in our world of torment, and more like a person.

Jessie barks.

'Luke? Carrie? Are you in there?'

Dave.

There's a beat, where I see in Luke's eyes that he isn't ready for us to be found. Then he calls back, 'Yeah, we're in here.'

'Joe! They're in here!'

Just like that, we're back in the real world.

Though I have a sense that something life-altering happened while we were in this concrete shell.

38

LUKE

After hours, or however long we spent, in the dull light of the bunker, though the sky is grey and cloudy and, at my best guess, it's late afternoon, I still squint as Dave and Joe pull open the steel doors and I step outside, Carrie's hand in mine, leading her into the natural air. The wind hasn't completely subsided but it feels more like a standard tropical storm out now, than an unruly beast.

'I've never been so glad to see you, matey,' Joe says, snatching me into an embrace, breaking my contact with Carrie.

'I'm sorry, Joe,' she says from behind me. 'It's my fault. Jessie ran and I instinctively went after her.'

Joe pulls away from me and tugs Carrie into a

similarly rough and compassionate hug. 'No apologies necessary, I'm just glad you're okay.' Jessie barks, jumping at Joe. 'Thank you for rescuing our Jessie.'

'Arguably, she wouldn't have been in danger if I hadn't lingered outside, so—'

'She was a scared dog, Carrie. She ran of her own accord.' Joe's words are firm, leaving no room for discussion, and I'm pleased for them. Carrie doesn't need to add guilt to everything we've felt in the last twenty-four hours.

I feel like I've lived every emotion today already. As if Carrie and I have had a conversation that's been building and that needed to happen for a very long time. I already feel relieved and depleted, burned out.

Still, none of it has prepared me for what I see when I finally look around the island. Charithonia has been devastated. Every tree and plant has been ripped from its roots or snapped and tossed away by the force of the hurricane. Green land replaced by barren dirt. Evidence of the ocean's surge can be seen halfway up the rockface – debris deposited as it has receded, though it still completely consumes the beach and lower rockface. There are branches and tree trunks, coconuts and roof tiles, scattered everywhere.

As we walk up to the main walkway, we have to navigate fallen trees. The main electricity and phone lines have been torn from the cement in the ground and lie across our path. Though the main structures of the house and the pods are intact, the terrace is gone, the infinity pools are covered by trees, corrugated iron, random pieces of furniture that I don't think emanated from this island. One of the large ceiling fans from the terrace has pierced what is left of the roof over Carrie's pod, the arms poking out like a V from the top.

The four of us and Jessie are stilled by the sight. To my side, Carrie brings her hands to her mouth and I fold her under my arm as we stare at the place she could have been sleeping.

'To think most of this is superficial,' Joe says contemplatively. 'It's one of life's greatest injustices that where you're born dictates whether you still have a place to call home today. As soon as we can get across to the other islands to help, we will.'

Of that, we're all in agreement.

'The most important thing is we're all safe and well,' Dave says.

I don't know what it is about their words but something makes me pull Carrie closer and press my lips to her hair. Makes me realize how important it is that I don't let her go again. Not this time.

I'll do whatever it takes to convince her.

* * *

We spend the last hours of relative light rescuing what we can from inside the damaged pods and the staff studios. The main house is remarkably undamaged beyond the superficial and we find everyone who needs to move location a spot to sleep either in a different pod or in the Hettich family home.

Joe makes the call that we'll only use the electricity that's absolutely necessary on account of having two large but not infallible generators and not knowing when the mains power will be fixed and reconnected.

There's no phone signal and no Wi-Fi to get word out to anyone off the island, other than a general note to say we're all accounted for by radio. We have no idea of the extent of the damage elsewhere but, thankfully, it seems there were no deaths across the islands. Amazing, really.

With Troy, as the only qualified chef, taking the lead and the rest of us sitting by candlelight in the main lounge and dining area, helping out as best we can, we all share a meal of pasta and various garlic breads. Nothing extravagant, though Troy somehow manages to make us forget that we aren't eating in a fancy restaurant. It's almost romantic, with the dim lights, medicinal wine, and everyone telling nostalgic tales.

The mood is strange; there's a heaviness in the back of people's minds yet lightness in speech, and laughter. There's a definite sense that we're putting a front on things for the kids, even for one another. Yet we really feel like a family. A community. With a sense of shared experience and appreciation for life. In a bizarre twist, it's one of the happiest meals I've had.

Through it all, Carrie is never far from my side. She's afraid of what is or could be between us. I get it. Hell, me too. But I saw it in her eyes in that concrete shell, and even if she can't articulate it or won't let herself feel it yet, I know she feels something deep for me. Whether it's love, I don't know yet. But the way I feel about her tonight might be strong enough for both of us.

After dinner, Alisha, Ella and Lola leave to take the little humans to bed. By the time they return, Joe has poured the rest of us each a strong drink. The kind that takes the sting out of the day much better than the wine we shared over dinner. But after one more drink with my friends, old and new, the fatigue of the day, the last few days, kicks in. I yawn from my spot on the sofa in the lounge and glance to Carrie. I'll stay up as long as she wants to, then I'll make sure she's set up in her new pod and that she's feeling okay.

I find her already looking my way, her drink barely touched and set on a coffee table next to the chair where her legs are snugly curled beneath her. She looks exhausted.

'Shall we get you set up for bed?' I ask her.

'I'd appreciate that.'

Leaving takes ten minutes, everyone hugging and whispering words of friendship and love. It warms me to the core the way my friends and closest confidantes have welcomed Carrie into our fold. The way they seem to genuinely care about her. It's not as if I've sung her praises over the years. Not that I've slandered her either, but Joe and I have shared some late-night drinks, had some heart-to-hearts in that *Mad Men* kind of way over a single malt or two and I'm sure, on reflection, that I've not always spoken generously about Carrie. How could I have? I didn't know our full story until this week. I had to think of self-preservation.

Yet Joe arranged for her to be here and as mad as I am about that, and that she got caught up in Hurricane Isabel, we're through the storm now, coming out the other side, and part of me wonders what it was that Joe saw or heard to make him bring her here.

I'm not sure why I do it but once I've spoken to everyone, agreed we'll make an early start on repairing what we can tomorrow, and wished them a safe, sound sleep, I hold out my hand for Carrie. She stares at it before slipping her palm into mine, and I lead us out into the night, using a torch as a guide, though unbelievably, the sky is clear enough for the moon to be lighting our way along the now treacherous path.

Rather than being in the pod next door to mine, Carrie's new pod is two away from me. I'm reminded just how lucky we were today as we pass the disaster of her old room. Carrie's fingers tighten around mine, as if she's having the same thought.

It feels right to be walking hand-in-hand. At the same time, strange to let go when we arrive at her new bedroom for the night. We brought down her luggage earlier and set up a couple of candles ready to light inside.

We each light a candle, and on my part, do so

hating the thought of Carrie spending the night alone. It doesn't feel right, and when I turn to tell her, she's already right behind me.

'Carrie, I don't—'

'Luke, would you mind—'

'Sorry, you go.'

'No, you go.'

We share a tight laugh. 'Are you sure you want to stay here, alone?' I ask. 'We could move you up to the main house; I'm sure there's another space. Or—'

'Or?'

Is she suggesting what I'm thinking? If she were, it would stop me from having palpitations over it right now.

'Stay with me,' I blurt, nervously. 'I can take the floor, or the lounge chair. I don't mean— I just don't think you should be on your own tonight. It's been a big day and—'

'I'd like that.' She smiles softly. It's there in her eyes. God, I've missed that look. 'Thank you. I'm sure we're adult enough to share a bed the size of a planet without regressing to teenagers on prom night.'

I chortle. 'Speak for yourself.'

Her laughter bursts from her and after what has

been one of the longest, most draining days of my life, it's such a welcome sound.

We blow out the candles, head back to my pod with Carrie's luggage, clean off using a bucket of water from the tank under the pod, and eventually, shattered, slip under the covers.

Even though she's wearing silk shorts and a cami and looks incredible; despite the fact I'm only wearing boxer briefs; and though we are lying in the same bed, beneath the same white sheet we made love on last night, we're so exhausted that even if my hormones screamed at me to seduce this implausibly beautiful woman, I wouldn't have the energy.

Which is perfect, really, because this is the start of me showing Carrie that we aren't just about sex.

We lie side by side, facing each other, each resting our heads on a hand, a reflection of each other.

'It's been a day,' she whispers.

In so many ways. 'If I promise I'm not making a move and I'm literally going to fall asleep within seconds, could we cuddle?'

One side of her lips turns up. 'Why? Did you forget your favorite teddy bear?'

I smile at her playful obstinance and tuck her hair behind her ear. 'Something like that.'

Her smile disappears but she shuffles my way. I roll onto my back and she lies like she used to, her head on my chest, one leg bent across mine. I blow out the candle on the bedside table and wrap my arm around her. I listen to her breathe. Once, twice, three times...

* * *

We didn't move all night. We crashed, both of us, and the feel of Carrie shuffling on my chest, exactly where she fell asleep hours ago, is the first thing that makes me move.

Sunlight streams through the windows around us, a complete contrast to waking up yesterday in a dark room, alone.

If it wasn't for knowing how busy the coming days will be and that I have no clue where Carrie's head is at when it comes to us, this would be a pretty perfect way to wake in the morning.

Carrie hums against me, cuddling in tighter. Then I watch her eyelids flutter open and see the realization hit her – we're in bed together. I hold my breath, bracing for her reaction, blown away when she rolls onto her front, both hands on my chest, and beams up at me.

The only reason I know my heart hasn't physically exploded is because I feel so alive.

'Good morning,' she whispers, as if she hasn't just made this the best ever start to the day in the history of mankind.

She's looking at me like... like she used to.

I'm too shocked to speak and she plugs the silence by telling me, 'You're a very comfy pillow, Mr Chalmers.'

'Let me see. A room, plus a pillow and designated cuddler for an entire night. I reckon five hundred should cover it,' I tease.

'Dollars?' She comes up to sit. Her leg position means that with a slight nudge to her left, she's straddling my hips. 'You've got to be joking.'

I'm desperate to run my hands along her legs, up to her hips. To pull her down to me, her hair hanging in my face, and kiss her. Since I'm not sure I've been invited to do that, I take my hands behind my head and smirk. 'It's a nice room and my left pec isn't cheap.'

She giggles, playful, youthful, brighter than the rays of sun bursting in through the windows, then moves to strike me. I've seen this move from her before, countless times. It's one of her flirts.

I catch one hand before she can flick my chest,

then catch the other when she tries with the other hand, and somehow, we end up where I wasn't sure we could go, with her on all fours, her hands in mine either side of my head, long tendrils hanging down and teasing my skin. She's exactly where I want her to be and we're locked on each other. I see lust in her dilating pupils that's a match for mine.

In the blink of an eye, something comes over her, taking away the look she was wearing and making her hop off the bed.

'We should get dressed,' she says. 'I'm sure it's going to be a busy day.'

She grabs clothes from her suitcase and scurries into my washroom, closing the door too quickly and too hard behind her.

Tell me you're not into me without telling me you're not into me.

The frustrating thing is, I think she *is* into me, *us*. There are moments I think we'll leave this island, whenever we manage to get off Charithonia, together, as a couple.

And many, many more moments when I fear we'll each leave alone. Me in significantly worse shape than I was when I arrived because Pandora's box has been opened.

Carrie takes only minutes getting dressed,

though enough time for me to pull on a pair of shorts. When she steps back into the room, she stares at my bare chest, embarrassed all of a sudden, her cheeks flush, despite spending the night lying on this same part of my body.

'You didn't need to go in the bathroom, Carrie.' I pull my t-shirt on over my head. 'I've seen you naked once or twice before.'

She gives a tight laugh. 'I know. But it's different now.' She fusses with her luggage, then stands, pulling her hair into a tie as I tug on socks and sneakers. 'Luke, as far as everyone else is concerned, please can we just say I slept in my own pod. I mean, if it even comes up.'

Her words cut like a dagger.

'Sure.'

She folds her arms across her chest. 'It's just I wouldn't want anyone to think—'

'That we're two consenting adults who spent the night in the same bed, comforting each other after a really long and disastrous day?'

She sighs.

'It's fine, Carrie. Our dirty secret won't be disclosed by me.'

'Thank you.' She shifts her tone to something breezier as she points to her black t-shirt with the

Charithonia staff logo on the breast pocket. 'I'm technically staff now, and I don't want to be seen as fraternizing with my guests.'

Unfortunately, I'm not feeling quite so breezy. Not when her joke has nailed the exact reason she doesn't want anyone to think there's something going on between us.

Because... 'I get it. Work means that much to you.'

'Luke.'

Her words land on my back as I make to leave the room and head outside to wait for her, before she can see DISAPPOINTMENT spelled out on my face. 'It's a shame Hettich doesn't have the same work–life boundaries you do, huh?'

My own words cut me to say, because the implication is, it would have been better if she hadn't come here at all.

There's not even a cell in my body that believes that.

39

CARRIE

'Morning, girlie,' Alisha sings, surprisingly bubbly given the circumstances. She's fluttering around the dining table in the main house with Sanza on her hip and using her free hand to help Monique lay out plates of pastries, cold cuts and cheese. 'The uniform looks good on you.'

'In which case, let me help you.' I take two jugs of juice from a side table that's loaded with food from the kitchen and set them into the middle of the table. 'You really didn't have to do this, especially today.'

'Nonsense,' Alisha says, waving her now free arm after setting down a tray she was carrying. 'We all have to eat, and it's not as if we won't be working for it today. How did you sleep?'

Only now do I really glance around the room and amongst the faces we started the day with yesterday. It's surreal the way everyone is working, sitting around the table drinking coffee or eating, normally, as if there wasn't a hurricane outside. Luke and Joe are standing together in the wall of windows overlooking what, just a day ago, was a plush terrace.

As if he senses me watching them, Luke turns, the same stern look on his face he gave me before he left his pod. I turn my lips up gently, tentatively, and mouth, *I'm sorry*. He held me all night and didn't try anything else. He was there for me when I needed him and, while the sentiment remains – I just can't be fraternizing with my client's CFO in front of my client's CEO, who happens to own the Hettich empire – waking up in Luke's arms this morning was idyllic.

I panicked, again. I was afraid, *am* afraid, and that's not a position from which to put everything on the line. But I really don't want us to be bitter. Worse, to not be speaking. I don't want to see him hurt. I also don't want to give away that something, though God knows what, is happening between us. Something I'm terrified of. Something reckless. And something I absolutely need to confront said CEO about.

So when Luke dips his head and gives me just the slightest smile in return, it dials down my inner mayhem by a notch.

I take a seat at the table between Jenny and Ella, who is plating up fruit and pancakes for Toby.

'I see the lovebirds kissed and made up, then,' Ella says, giving a flick of her head in the direction of Luke and Joe.

'More like Luke has decided it wasn't such a bad plan after all,' Jenny says, smirking in my direction.

'You knew?' I ask, aghast.

'Most of us knew, honey,' Ella says. 'Henry is usually shy and he was all over you, playing the flirting game because Joe told him to, until Joe saw how serious his game had become and stepped Henry down.'

I literally gasp. 'That's— This is, like, some kind of violation of some kind of rights I have, surely? And Henry was basically employed to flirt with me? That's... mortifying. And wrong. *So* wrong. And... can I really only get a hot guy to flirt with me if they're being *paid* to do it?'

Jenny laughs. 'I don't think Henry needed much convincing, Carrie, believe me. And if all of this had gone badly, I think there'd have been a lawsuit or three you could have brought, but, alas, all's well that ends well, right?'

I feel my eyebrows shoot so high, they might have temporarily abdicated my face. 'For the record, nothing has ended well and, client or not, Joe has some major explaining to do.'

Jenny and Ella exchange a look that says something akin to *yikes*.

I need pastries. Comfort pastries. For so, *so* many reasons today. There's one of my absolute favorites, a pain au raisin, left on the tray that has my name written all over—

An arm reaches across me and grabs my beloved pastry. I know that arm, I know the cologne in the air around me, and sure enough, when I spin around in my seat, I see Luke looking smug-as-hell because he *knows* pains aux raisins are my favorite. Given I had one nearly every day we shared an office together for more than a year, I think the evidence is unequivocal.

'You wouldn't,' I say, scowling as he pauses, his lips almost touching my pastry.

'Rock, paper, scissors?'

I stand and face him. 'Three, two, one.' I hold out my hand, as does he, and I take great pleasure in banging my rock against his scissors, then snatching my pastry back from him and moaning theatrically as my teeth sink into it.

Luke leans forward and I fear for my pastry, but he bypasses it and brings his mouth to my ear instead, whispering, 'I've heard that sound before. I was well behaved last night but don't tease me, Carrie.'

I'd be amazed if the people on the next island over couldn't hear the depth of my swallow. I had better not tease him because if he pulls that move again, my own resolve will be seriously tested.

I'm not. Can*not*. Under any circumstances, go there. *Again.*

I watch him move as he walks around the table, choosing the seat directly opposite mine to sit. I resume my place at the table, not daring to look at either Jenny or Ella.

* * *

The lightness of the morning among the group fades, though people are surprisingly upbeat as we work as a unit to clear pathways, chop down trees, tarpaulin holes in roofs, clear away sandbags and mop floors.

More than once, I wonder how bad the other islands must be if this hurricane-proof island has come out of the storm so badly. Joe's right, it's a mess, and it will take months, longer even, to regrow and to fix, but he can financially afford to put it right. The main structures are in one piece. His family has a home. There'll be many families for whom the reality is very different.

That's probably the version of events that will wind up on the news, so I keep checking for phone signal throughout the day. I need to get in touch with my mom, my dad and Callum, my boss too, but there's nothing.

I'm trying again, standing on the pathway looking out at the dirty sea from the highest point of the island. Like someone out of a comedy sketch, I'm holding my phone as high as I can in the air, still not receiving any signal.

'We've managed to make radio contact off island.' Joe appears next to me. I've been so lost in wiggling my phone at the clouds that I didn't hear him coming. 'I've let them know who's here and they'll spread the word. They have your mom's number to let her know you're safe.'

In true Joe style, he's wearing an outrageous sky-blue shirt that's decorated with eye-wateringly bright flamingoes all over it. It hasn't stopped him pulling his weight today, though. Joe is atypical in many respects. His lack of pretentiousness for a man so wealthy is probably the number one thing I like about him. Or liked, before he dragged me here under false pretenses, got me stuck here with my ex who broke my heart and for whom I am catching all the forbidden feelings again; oh yeah, and had me endure the fun of a category five hurricane.

Nevertheless, what he's done is kind. 'Thank you, I appreciate it. My mom has a fairly nervous disposition at the best of times. She'll be worried sick about me.'

He nods. 'Just so you know, I'm working on getting a chopper here for you. As soon as the airport is open on Tortola, we'll get you home.'

'Thank you.'

He pouts and wiggles his lips, tucking his hands into his pockets. The space around us feels awkward all of a sudden.

'Do you have a minute?' he asks, as if anyone ever says no to him.

But I do feel like saying no. Particularly because I suspect I know what the topic of this minute will be and I haven't really put my mind to how I want to handle this whole false-imprisonment thing.

He walks to the edge of the pathway, the sun slowly beginning its descent in front of us, and when I follow, he asks, 'Shall we take a load off?' He comes to sit on the ground. 'It's been another long old day.'

'It has,' I agree, sitting next to him and crossing my legs in a way that looks like I'm meditating. It would be a good spot for it.

'Thank you for all your help, before, during and after the storm. We all really appreciate it,' Joe tells me. 'You're a massive hit with my family.'

I smile. 'Well, they're great. You have a truly beautiful family. While I'm here, I'm glad I can help. I want to. I'm sorry this hurricane happened to anyone.'

'Let's get to it, Carrie. Luke told you about my grand plan. I want to say, for the record, it was all well-intentioned but, as my wife told me before this week even began, I overstepped, and I'm sorry.'

'Wow. I'm not sure I was expecting you to tackle it so directly and issue an apology right out of the traps.'

Joe snorts. Genuinely snorts. 'I may be rich, Carrie, but I'm not a dick. *Mostly.*'

If someone had told me that a week ago, I probably would have said something like, *Yeah, sure.* But after getting to know Joe, I actually do believe him. He's a good human.

I could let this whole thing slide. I probably should let his faux pas go. He's one of the world's wealthiest men and my firm's biggest client. But I'd be letting myself down if I did.

'Why did you do it, Joe? *How* did you do it? Does my firm know about Luke and me, our history? Is Rachel in on it?'

The sinking feeling of dread comes back to me as I imagine the fallout from all of this that's awaiting me in New York.

'*How* is easy, so let's start there,' Joe says, picking up a stick and making marks in the ground as he speaks, the way a naughty child might do while being told off. 'I've been a client of your firm for years and I like to know who is coming and going; it's one of my arrangements with Rachel. When you joined eighteen months ago on the partnership track, I was told. I knew your name and job from Luke and I vaguely knew your face because I've seen pictures of you, so it wasn't at all difficult to put two and two together.'

'Did Luke know?'

'I decided not to tell him, for reasons that will become clear.'

When Joe frowns, I feel his expression reflected on my own face.

'Eric was supposed to come here this week and he really did get stomach flu.'

I nod. 'You could have rescheduled. None of what we've discussed this week has been drastically urgent.'

'I could have. But I saw the opportunity and told Rachel I wanted you to come in Eric's place.'

'She didn't question it or encourage you to re-arrange?'

He looks at me now and grins. 'Very few service providers question me, Carrie.'

I give a short laugh. 'I'm sure.'

'Rachel was curious as to why, after years of dealing with Eric, I would request you in his stead.' He looks at me directly now. 'You've been fantastic, by the way. More than capable of filling Eric's shoes.'

I clear my throat, thrown by the compliment. 'Thank you.'

'Alas, I told her you had a personal connection to my CFO and that I'd like you to come. She asked what the connection was, I fobbed her off with you two working together previously, she asked if there was any conflict of interest, I assured her there wasn't, blah, blah, blah.'

Oh God. This is *awful.* She asked if I was conflicted? *Yes!* A huge, big, fat, massive *yes.* Ethically, morally, *yes.* I had an affair, or legitimate relationship that turned out to be an affair, with the CFO of my client.

I don't realize my head is in my hands until Joe says, 'This is my doing, Carrie, and I'll happily explain the full extent of my manipulation to Rachel.'

At this stage, maybe Joe should just *not* explain anything to anyone.

I puff out my next breath and look at him. 'Why?'

He leans his head to one side then the other, as if he's bouncing to a beat. 'Hmm, that's the part I hoped you and Luke would figure out for yourselves. But since you don't seem to have got quite that far, I'll tell you this: I've known Luke longer than any man could care to.'

Despite myself, I laugh.

'He used to be the life and soul of everything, everywhere. Then after you two were involved and split, and, admittedly, Anya was an absolute dick to him, he was dark. Bleak. I've never seen him that down. It took him a long time to get happy again.'

My throat tightens as my chest swells. In a weird way, I wish I could have been there for him.

Joe's eyebrows rise. 'He never got ecstatically

happy again. He'll probably rugby tackle me for saying this, but he has sabotaged every relationship he's been in since. They never last and usually it's of his own doing. Imagining things that aren't there, faking this love of his job that means he can't invest time in a relationship, all the stereotypical moves of a man whose heart isn't whole.'

This is like listening to Callum talk about me. Which makes it easy for me to say, 'I get it.' The words roll off my tongue before my mind tells them not to. I'm not speaking with an agony aunt but my client.

'I brought you here to see if you two couldn't close things off once and for all, one way or the other.'

Tension seems to flow out of my body with his confession.

'Thank you for being honest with me.'

'At last.'

I smile. 'At last. It's not okay, Joe. You've meddled in my life and with my career and you didn't have that right.'

'It's fair to say that sometimes I get ideas above my station,' he concedes.

He stands, dusts down the back of his shorts and offers a hand to me. I take it, standing up.

'I suppose I can see why you've done it. As a friend to Luke.'

He holds his arms out wide. 'Can we hug it out or am I overstepping again? Feel free to tell me it's too much. I know I can be.'

Shaking my head in amusement, I give him a hug, which ends with mutual awkward back pats.

'You know, I'm still hoping the ending is a happily ever after, though,' he says when we separate.

'Joe,' I say, my voice low, ominous.

He laughs as he walks away and I watch him head toward the main house.

'Are you okay?'

Luke's voice is like a warm blanket folding around me after a very long day.

I turn to face him, to tell him, yes, I'm fine, but when I do, all I can think is, this is the man whose heart isn't whole, asking a girl, whose heart hasn't been whole since him, if she's okay.

Without knowing what I'm trying to express, I step into his chest and welcome his arms closing around me, the feel of his lips on my hair.

'I'm fine,' I mumble against his body. 'Thank you for asking.'

We end up sitting where Joe and I just were, side-by-side, watching the setting of the sun. I feel uncommonly calm. At peace even. Which, given the circumstances, speaks volumes about how stressful my real life is. I don't think I've noticed the level of stress I operate at, or considered the things I could be doing and the places I could be seeing if I wasn't always working and trying to squeeze in snippets of non-office life around the edges.

Callum is right. There's got to be something more than that. But it's taken me being here, in the wildness of this island, the scariness of the storm, and the craziness of the eclectic mix of people I'm surrounded by, to actually *hear* his words.

I suppose that's why, after a group dinner (which ended with an all-parties dance-off to Disney tunes), when we're walking back to our pods, Luke asks me, 'Would you come back with me? As friends, no funny business.'

'Friends? No touching, no flirting?'

'Friends. Just two people who enjoy each other's company, hanging out.'

I blush, glancing to my feet. 'Sure, Chalmers. I'll hang out with you.'

Even by the moon's light, when I look up, I see his eyes widen and dance in a way that makes me think being *just* friends with Luke will be tricky. But better than nothing, and all that I'm willing to offer.

40

LUKE

We fell asleep facing each other, our heads on pillows, the thin covers over us. Carrie closed her eyes as she talked about taking a trip around Italy and as she spoke, her pauses for breath between words grew longer, her voice became quieter, until eventually, with her hand still tucked under her cheek, she'd fallen asleep.

I watched her – serene, beautiful – and willed myself to stay awake, to take her in, because I knew that today we might get power back, the airport might reopen, and she might head back to New York without me. *Then what?* I have no idea. I don't know if she found being friends last night, getting to know new things about each other from the last seven years, speaking of dreams and aspirations we've not spoken of before, as amazing as I did. Simultaneously excruciating because I kept forgetting, in our proximity, in our shared smiles and laughter, in the gazes we held for a beat too long, that I promised her no funny business. No touching, no holding, and definitely no *other stuff*.

If today does turn out to be our last day together, then I don't want to spend the entirety of it with other people. We'll be with others long enough when we boat across to Virgin Gorda to see what help we can provide. So this morning, I slipped quietly out of the room, hoping she wouldn't wake and find me missing, while I went to the main house to grab coffees and a tray of breakfast for two.

Now, I set down my tray on the deck outside my pod, tease the door open, then pick up the tray and move inside.

The sun is up, casting shadows across Carrie's soft skin, highlighting her eyes that start to flicker. A few of the others are up already and sitting around the dining area in the main house. No one questioned why I was stacking a tray to leave. Either it was obvious, or the obsession with Carrie and me has faded.

Bringing the tray to the bed, I slip off my footwear and sit onto my side, back against the wall, coffee in hand. I wait for that moment when Carrie will open her eyes. When she does, she finds the coffee, the food, then me, and it's me who gets her biggest grin. That small fact makes me feel ten feet tall.

I'm trying my best not to come on too strong. I'm forcing myself to be a friend if that's all she's willing to give me. But my soaring heartrate has nothing to do with caffeine.

'You brought me breakfast in bed?' she asks sleepily. Adorably so.

'Yoghurts, fruit, boiled eggs and bread. You get first dibs because you know I'll eat anything.'

'Not true!' She comes up to sit, her back against the wall in my t-shirt, the bedsheet across her otherwise bare legs. She reaches for her coffee with one hand and points to me with the other. 'You refused to eat jellied eel in that sushi place we went to for a meeting in Midtown that time.'

'Oh, come on! Jellied eel? That's not food.'

'In your nitpicky opinion.'

'Said by a woman who refuses to try olives.'

She slurps her drink then swallows. 'Actually, also not true. I have tried black olives on pizza and

Callum made me try one of those big green ones in a dirty martini.'

'And?'

'Awful. Disgusting. Wouldn't feed them to Eddie.'

I laugh so loudly, I think I startle her, because she pauses – dragon fruit mid-air – then lowers her head shyly. 'I like that I can still do that,' she says. She must register my perplexity because she adds, 'Make you laugh like that.'

I'm staring at her, and she's staring at me, and all I can think is how badly I want to reach over and kiss her lips. How badly I'd like every weekend morning to start like this. Us in bed together, laughing, joking, eating, with no place to go, no one to please. How I'd touch her and she'd touch me and eventually the bedsheet would go, then our clothes would—

I jump, literally jump, from the bed and head to the bathroom. 'That coffee's a strong antidiuretic,' I say, running off to hide and chill out before I blow this whole friendship thing.

* * *

We're loading a boat with water and other aid – Carrie, Roy, Henry, Jenny, Monique, Dave, Glen and me – ready to head to Virgin Gorda to see what help we can be over there. Not knowing what state the island will be in when we arrive. We're all set when Joe jogs down to the dock of the boat house.

'We've got service and Wi-Fi back up and running,' he says, one foot on the dock, the other on the boat.

He seeks out Carrie and the way my internal organs seem to fall through the boat, to the bottom of the ocean, and continue going, tells me I know what's coming.

'The airport in Tortola hasn't reopened yet, Carrie, but I can get you on a helicopter this afternoon from here to Puerto Rico, then a flight back to New York tonight.'

'You can?' Carrie's response is relieved, excited even, and, though it shouldn't, it kills me to hear it.

She has to leave at some point. On Monday, when she arrived, I'd have been ready to dance on the runway behind her plane as she left. But things changed. Something beyond my control. Now, the idea of her leaving is gutting.

She glances my way and, though she's wearing shades, I wonder what she's looking for.

'I— That's... great, thanks so much, Joe. I— Ah,

really appreciate it.' I hear it in her voice. She's conflicted.

It's a small win; maybe I'm just wanting to hear something, but it still gives me hope. I think, through my disappointment, I smile at her. Reassure her it's a good thing. Or try, at least.

'It's the least I can do,' Joe says. 'If anyone else wants to go, there'll be three spare seats.' He looks at me. 'Luke?'

I could go with her. Back to New York. *Then what?* There's no guarantee of something between us. Besides that, Joe and his family need me here and they've been there for me when I've really needed them. So, while I'm conflicted, too – heavily so – I shake my head. 'I'll stay a few more days and help out as much as I can.'

'I'm happy to stay, too, of course,' Carrie says.

'I wasn't suggesting you should, Carrie,' I tell her. 'My work, my friends, half my life is here. You need to get home to see your friends and family. To see Eddie. To work. You—' My voice breaks, forcing me to cough. 'You should go.'

Joe shifts his focus back and forth between the two of us. 'Settled then. Yes?'

Carrie gives him a nod with little conviction. But it's affirmative.

She's going.

Back to her life where I don't exist to her.

'I'd still like to come to the island with you all and help for as long as I can today,' Carrie says. 'Is that feasible?'

'Absolutely,' Joe says, hopping onto the boat. 'We'll come back in time for the chopper.'

I check my watch. I might have four or five hours left to convince her that...

What? That I can be a friend with no funny business? That she should want my companionship in her life?

That I'm the guy for her. I've changed. I've learnt. I see my mistakes and I know that if I don't make her mine, I'll spend every day for the rest of my life regretting it.

Probably die a lonely, old, celibate man, because she's reminded me this week that no one compares to her. Nothing compares to the way I feel when we're together.

There's no going back.

Henry kicks the boat into gear and we drive across the, paradoxically, tranquil water to Virgin Gorda.

* * *

It doesn't matter that the sound of the boat skating along the water is too loud to hold a normal conversation because my thoughts are loud enough to drown everything else out in any event.

The balance is this: on the one hand, I can be miserable and act like I'm doomed, as if Carrie and I have no chance. Or, on the other hand, I can make the most of the next few hours. This is what I decide to do.

I hop off the boat when we dock at a very different looking harbor to the one we arrived into three days ago. It's hard to comprehend this is the same place. Boats have been flipped and crashed into one another by the storm. The surrounding buildings are in various states of destruction. No roofs. Cars picked up by the wind and dropped into buildings. A laundry machine sticks out of the shell of what used to be a small, family run restaurant.

As we drive deeper into the island – aiming mostly for the same places as three days ago – the mess is unconceivable. While before, the locals were still remarkably upbeat during our last visit, jovial, perhaps even disbelieving that a storm would transpire, today, there is laughter, there are jokes, but there's a subdued undertone.

Though I want to spend time with Carrie, our

hours on the island seem to disappear; time seems to have sped up exactly when I want it to slow down. We hand out water and provisions and help out in any way we can. Some of the stops we made on Thursday are unreachable, due to fallen trees and landslips, so we support the clearing of roads as best we can.

Between efforts, I watch Carrie working alongside us, when she really doesn't have to. She shouldn't even be here. I watch her chat with islanders as if she's part of their community. Through it all, she exudes warmth and empathy. She listens, she offers words of support, and she displays a confidence and ease in her own skin that she's developed over the years we've been apart.

I can imagine her as a partner in her firm. An incredible one. One who works hard, but deals with others with compassion. One who can win over colleagues and clients with authenticity and kindness.

Against the backdrop of destruction, she is the cliché of a breath of fresh air.

This whole experience is giving me a sense of perspective. An explicit guide as to what I need to do. I've tried not to come on too strong, but screw that. This is my chance and I might not get another one.

When we get back to Charithonia, I'm going to lay it out for her. Exactly how I feel about her and what I want. Then, I guess the ball will be in her court.

* * *

We pull into the boat house on Charithonia and I hold out a hand to help Carrie off the boat. Just the simple feel of her hand in mine gives me even more conviction that I'm going to do the right thing. What feels natural and essential.

Only, Ella is waiting on the dock. 'The helicopter is inbound, Joe,' she says. Carrie and I turn to look at her. 'Twenty minutes. I tried to get in touch with you but either your phone was switched off or you lost signal.'

'It's still patchy,' Joe replies. Then he looks to me apologetically, as if he's been reading my inner turmoil all day, then to Carrie. 'Can you be ready in twenty, Carrie?'

'Ah, yes. Sure.' She drops my hand and I feel... burned. Bereft. 'I'll run up to get my luggage now. I'd like to say goodbye to everyone. Where will you all be?'

I feel lost, as if I'm still at sea, without a boat or

even a paddle. I thought I had time when we got back to speak with her. Now... Maybe this was never meant to be. Maybe the universe is trying to show me this is a bad idea. Accept a friendship, if it's on the table. Take nothing, if not, as punishment for screwing up so badly in the past.

'We'll meet you at the helipad,' Joe says. 'You've seen it, up on the hill?'

She nods, twists her lips into a smile I sense she doesn't feel, then looks at her feet. 'Great. Great. Perfect. I'll run now to clean up and get my things. Ah, thank you, both.'

She glances up at me so fleetingly that I don't get a sense of what she's feeling and I wish I had, because perhaps it would give me a clue as to what to do next. As it is, I watch her jog from the dock and when I step out of the boat house, see her still jogging up the hill.

I feel a hand come down on my shoulder and I know it's Joe, though I'm not able to look at him or speak to him.

* * *

She hugs everyone in turn – Alisha, Ella, the kids (who are fairly distracted by looking far into the distance for a speck they think is a helicopter coming our way), Lola, Dionne, Monique.

When it's Henry's turn, Carrie jibes, 'Are you getting paid to hug me goodbye?' But the way one of her eyebrows is raised tells me she's toying with him.

I hear him apologize to her and I feel my hackles rise when he adds, 'For the record, if it wasn't for the whole Luke thing, and my job, there'd have been no holding me back.'

Carrie rolls her eyes, smiling. 'That self-assuredness will get you in trouble, Henry.' I suppose it was a nice thing for him to say. But I *am* here. There *is* a whole Luke thing.

Next comes small talk with Dave, Thom, Kevin and Jenny.

It feels like a never-ending procession because I'm desperate to hold her, to see what she has to say to me, and, I think, building up the courage to say the things I've been thinking about all day. Or a very abbreviated version of them, because that speck in the sky actually was the inbound chopper.

I start to shift my body weight, ready to move in next, but Joe steps forward.

He tugs Carrie into an embrace so hard that she thuds against his chest, chuckling as she lands. 'Thanks for hosting me, Joe. It's been... honestly, life changing. Wholly unexpected but, for lots of reasons, a trip I'll never forget.'

'Are we good, Carrie? I promise, if I'm ever going to try to get you and Luke in the same place again, I'll be upfront about it.'

She briefly looks at me, where I'm standing a little way in front of the group now, having wandered with my hands in my pockets, kicking up dirt with my toes, because I feel like a petulant child so I'm acting like one. A child whose favorite soft toy has been taken away and can't imagine ever sleeping without it.

'We're good,' she tells Joe. 'And I'll bring Eric up to speed with everything when I get back. He'll be in touch.'

'For the record,' Joe says, 'Eric has been our point of contact at the firm for a long time but you never missed a step, Carrie. I know I had an ulterior motive for bringing you here but your advice was great and I'll feed that back to Rachel.'

'Thank you.'

They hug again, then the sound of the chopper is drawing closer. 'Well, goodbye, everyone, and good luck with everything. If I can support from New York, you must let me know, okay?'

Finally, she's walking toward me, as the chopper

comes firmly into view across my shoulder, getting louder and louder on its approach.

We face each other, a little way from the group, her luggage like an unwanted interruption on the floor by her feet. Suddenly, all my rehearsed words and sensible thoughts from today have gone.

41

CARRIE

I can barely hear Luke above the sound of the helicopter that's now so close, it's bringing down something like a hurricane of wind, dirt blowing up from the ground around us, as if we haven't had enough of late.

'I can't hear you!' I shout to Luke, despite being less than a yard away from him.

I don't know what I was expecting but I didn't expect this week to end like this. Rushed. Too quick. Unplanned. It's not like I knew what I would say to him at the end of this week. What I would have said at the beginning of the week versus now are probably quite different, yet neither would be fully correct or true to how I'm feeling.

Because I'm feeling like I *am* glad that Joe manipulated me into being here.

Like I don't hate Luke anymore. Quite the opposite.

Like I miss him already and I'm standing right in front of him.

But also... like it can't count as serendipity if Joe arranged our meeting after all these years. It wasn't the universe sending us a message, or even chance.

And I don't know how I'll feel when I get back to New York. What I'll say to Rachel, how I'll explain this. What Callum and my mom will think if, after all the hours I've spent down about Luke leaving me previously, I tell them I want him back.

Closure. That's what Callum told me after I slept with Luke.

It was just closure.

I've worked hard to set the record straight and get my life and career to where they were just a week ago.

But when Joe just whispered in my ear that the one thing money can't buy is true love, my mind went straight to Luke.

Luke yells his words again, leaning closer to me as the helicopter descends to the helipad. 'I said, can I bee too en I get pack to New York?'

I glance to the fast-whirring propellers, to the door that's opening and the pilot who's giving a thumbs-up signal to Joe.

'I can't hear you!' I virtually scream in order to be heard.

Then Luke is looking at my mouth, and I'm staring at his, and I'm willing him to kiss me but I'm also reticent because Joe Hettich is right across my shoulder. So I thrust my arms around him and he squeezes me tightly against him.

Then we part and all I can think is, *That's it. That's how this ends. It's how it has to end because... because... because of my job.*

I'm running to the chopper with one bag as Luke jogs with my suitcase and hoists it inside. *My job? Is that it now? Is that all that stands between Luke and me and potential happiness?*

At some point, I've climbed inside the helicopter and someone has put earmuffs on me and strapped me in and I'm staring out of the window as the helicopter starts to rise. I don't need to wipe my cheek to know that a silent tear is rolling down it.

We've explained the past away. We've apologized to each other for our mistakes.

Luke holds up a hand from where he stands in

front of the others down below. I press my fingertips to the window, wishing I could touch him.

Now, he's running back toward Joe and taking something from him and there's a voice in my headphones saying, 'Carrie, Luke is on the radio for you.'

Then...

'Carrie? Can you hear me?' It's Luke's voice and I'm being handed a radio from someone in a seat opposite me, who's demonstrating for me to hold down a button on the side as I speak.

'Luke?'

'Carrie, I've thought about what I was going to say as you left all day and I— Damnit, when it came to it, I just froze.'

I exhale, my words breaking. 'Me too.'

'We could have died this week. I could have seen my last sunsets here with you.'

The thought of that makes my tears fall harder.

'As if seeing you wasn't enough, the disaster we've been through this week has shown me that life's too short to not at least try to be happy.' The image of him is blurring now, shrinking to the size of an ant as my ride moves away from Charithonia. 'I don't know how many sunsets I have left, Carrie, but I know that I want to spend as many as I can with you.'

His words catch on my next breath. I know exactly what he means because I've had the same thought this week, more than once. I squeeze my eyes shut, willing myself to be rational, not emotional. To remember what's real, off this paradise island, away from Hurricane Isabel. 'I know, Luke.' I sniff. 'But you're my client. I've worked so hard—'

'No, Joe is your client. Hettich is your client.' His words are urgent. I wish I could see him but he's gone. All I see is the island and tropical waters surrounding it. 'I'm just some guy who works for them, Carrie. Some guy who is crazy in love with their tax advisor.'

In love? My eyes shoot open, landing on the woman opposite me, the one who strapped me into my seat and handed me a radio. The one who is smiling at me as she hears every word of my conversation.

'I wish that were true, Luke, but we've been here before. I've been here before. We risked everything and it went badly.'

The woman's smile fades.

'Not this time, Carrie. Because my head is straight this time. I know exactly what I want. What I've wanted for the last seven years. Longer. Before I even knew it.'

'Luke—'

'That's you. Only you. I loved you from the moment I was born; I just hadn't met you yet. So if you tell me the only way for us to be together is for me to walk away from Hettich, then, Joe, I quit.'

I hear Joe in the background, clearly now with no sound of propellers around them. 'Didn't like working with you anyway,' he shouts, making me giggle.

'I'll do whatever it takes to make this work,' Luke says, and I can hear the sincerity in his voice.

'Including having no money?'

'I don't need money. I'm in love with a woman who earns plenty of it.'

I laugh this time. 'Couldn't you have told me this before I took to the skies?' I tease, unable to keep the smile from my voice.

I hear Luke's amusement. 'Tell me I can see you when I get back to New York and I promise to tell you to your face. I promise to tell you every day for the rest of my life how much I love you.'

'Okay.'

'All right now.'

I'm giggling and smiling so wide, my face aches. 'So I'll see you in New York next week?'

'It's going to be the longest week of my life.'

42

CARRIE

Rachel insisted I take the week off when I eventually landed back into JFK on Joe's private jet in the early hours of Monday morning. Though I reluctantly accepted – I could actually use a break to process the madness of everything that happened in the British Virgin Islands – she agreed we could meet this afternoon, Friday, to talk.

I've barely spoken to Luke since leaving Charithonia. Quick calls here and there because the power on the island is still coming from the generators and his signal has been intermittent.

Still, I know I'm doing the right thing by going to see Rachel today. I knew before I spoke to my mom over breakfast in my apartment yesterday, when she told me, 'At this point, my counsel for or against Luke won't make a difference.'

We were sitting at the small table in my open-plan kitchen-diner, eating French toast that Callum made, Eddie drooling at my feet.

'You're too far gone,' she said, blatantly trying to be stern but with the slightest curve at the corners of her mouth betraying her. 'Let me just say this: he had better treat you right this time because if I see those lonely eyes of yours again, he'll have me to answer to.'

'And me,' Callum called from my stove, waving a spatula.

Mom placed her hand over mine and though she shook her head, her expression was tender. 'You're already on a moving train, darling. To jump off now will hurt anyway, so you might as well close your eyes and lean into the ride.'

I made a sarcastic comment about her swallowing a psychology textbook, but she was right; I *am* too far gone.

I alight the subway and head for my firm's high-rise. I drop my tote and laptop at my desk and go straight to Rachel's office, right on time, primed to tell her that I want to be with Luke. That, yes, he is the CFO of the Hettich group but I won't work on any Hettich files, I won't share any confidential information one way or the other, and once I've handed recent matters back to Eric, I'll have nothing to do with Joe or his business.

If she sees me being with Luke as a blocker to partnership, then... I'll be sorry. I'll hate it. But some things, I've finally realized, are more important than work.

I knock on the door of her significant office space and when she calls, 'Come in, Carrie,' I step inside.

Rachel is behind her desk, as I'd expect. Only I don't expect to see Joe Hettich sitting in one of two chairs in front of her.

'Joe?' I ask, as if my eyes have deceived me.

He chuckles. 'Hey, Carrie.'

'What are you doing here?'

He gestures to Rachel. 'Rachel and I were just having a chat about a few things. I was explaining to her the extent of my, ah, misdemeanors, shall we say? And she agreed to let me stay here to witness you sign those.' He points to the desk in front of Rachel.

Rachel picks up a short stack of papers in front of her. 'Your partnership contract,' she says, grinning.

'My what now?' I ask, aware I must look gorm-less with my mouth wide open.

She laughs. 'You want to be a partner, don't you?'

I move closer to her desk. 'Yes, of course, but I—' My synapses abruptly start firing again and I re-member why I requested this meeting. 'But, Rachel, I need to tell you something first.'

She leans her head to one side. 'If it's that the Chief Financial Officer of one of our biggest clients has fallen in love with you—'

'Again,' Joe adds.

'Again,' Rachel repeats. 'Then, I already know that. I also know that Joe here played the role of cre-ator in that relationship, so I'm taking that as his waiver of any conflict, even if there was one.'

'Waived,' Joe says, making me chuckle, again. This time, I think with disbelief, or giddiness, or just something that's making my stomach jiggle like it's full of yo-yos.

'So, would you like to come on over here and re-view your partnership contract?' Rachel asks.

'Yes.' I press a hand to my tummy to steady it. 'One hundred percent, yes.'

* * *

I'm typing a message to Luke as I walk back to my office, having signed my partnership contract and shown Joe to the elevator. I can't believe that from the first of next month, I'll be a partner. I've waited and worked hard for so long for this.

Yet, more than my new role, I'm ecstatic that Luke and I are in the clear. We can be together, at last, and I can't wait.

I had no idea he was back in New York; he's kept it secret. But now that I—

I stop dead in my tracks when I open the door to my office and here, in the flesh, dressed in a dark-blue suit and a crisp powder-blue shirt, looking exactly like the man I fell in love with seven years ago, is Luke.

He's giving me a lopsided smile, casually perched on the edge of my desk, his hands in his pockets, a box of flowers to one side of him and a bottle of champagne and two full glasses on the other.

I bite my lip, trying my best not to run to him before my door has even closed behind me.

'What are we celebrating?' I ask.

He leans his head to one side. 'Your well-deserved partnership, of course.'

I cross the space between us, unwilling to take

my eyes from his, my lips turning up. I step between his thighs, my breath hitching when his hands take hold of my hips.

I reach for the two glasses of fizz and hand one to him. 'How about, to trying to get it right this time?'

His eyes narrow, and his pupils dilate. He clinks his glass against mine. We each sip, then set down our glasses. As he replaces his hands on my hips, I take mine into his hair, twisting the longer strands against the top of his neck between my fingers.

'I love you, Luke Chalmers,' I whisper.

His eyes close and his half smile turns into a full-blown beam. 'I love you so much, Carrie.'

Our lips meet. For the first time, there's nothing taboo about our kiss, and it's brighter than any flowers, it fizzes more than any champagne, and it's sweeter, so much sweeter, than any promotion I could have gotten at work.

43

LUKE

Six Months Later

I light the final candle in the hotel room, too nervous to sit on the bed that's covered in rose petals, too weak at the knees to pace the floor.

I check my watch, again; it's eleven fifty-nine in the morning, though the room is lit only by candles, the blackout curtains drawn across the windows. A playlist of songs we've created together during the evenings we've spent on the sofa in my apartment or Carrie's over the last six months is playing through my docked phone.

I hope today will be the beginning of the end of our separate living.

In one minute, she should be here, because that's the time I wrote on the note I left her:

*MEET ME AT OUR HOTEL. ROOM 252 –
12 p.m.*
      HAPPY BIRTHDAY! x

In fact, it wasn't my note but hers. The note she wrote me more than seven years ago on *my* birthday, asking me to meet her in our hotel room. The only time I never turned up for her. The note I kept all this time, I think subconsciously as a reminder of how much I messed up. I won't make that mistake again, ever.

As I hear footsteps in the corridor outside, my heart that has been racing starts pounding to be released from my chest. My stomach that has been jiggling is spinning like a laundromat. I pat the pocket of my suit jacket to check the ring box is still there, despite knowing it is.

Then I hear the keycard she's collected from Reception being slid into the door lock and slowly, excruciatingly slowly, the door begins to open.

I can't breathe. Genuinely, can't draw breath. She steps into the room wearing a black dress that fits every curve of her perfect body. She's styled her long red hair just the way I like it, though, frankly, I like her just as much when she wakes in the mornings, when she's cold in the evenings and wearing her thickest winter pajamas, when she's fresh out of the shower, no make-up, wet hair, wearing nothing but a towel. Those are the times when it feels most intimate. The versions of her I know are truly special and hidden behind closed doors, just for me – and Eddie.

But hot-damn, she looks mesmerizing right now, and when her green eyes widen as she takes in the room, she near knocks me dead.

Between tracks on our playlist, the door clicks shut and though I had every intention of playing this cool, of pouring her a glass of champagne, maybe even making love to her among the rose petals first, I just can't wait.

Finally coming back into my body, I draw the ring box from my pocket and bend to one knee, lifting the lid to display the sparkling diamond and emerald ring that I've had made for her because it reminds me of the most beautiful irises I have ever seen in my life. The eyes I hope my children will have one day too.

Carrie gasps, slowly moving toward me. Though

my throat constricts and my eyes burn with emotion, I'm going to get through this.

'I got my note,' she says, while I'm gathering myself. 'You kept it all this time and you waited for my birthday to give it back to me?'

I nod. 'I finally showed up to correct the biggest mistake of my life,' I tell her, trying to push the weakness from my voice. 'That note was a reminder of everything I regretted walking away from, Carrie.'

She steps so close, I'm looking directly up at her, feeling small against the power she has over me, my heart. 'It feels like I've waited forever to ask you something I knew I wanted to ask a very long time ago. Something I've regretted walking away from ever since. Carrie, you are the smartest, funniest, kindest, most beautiful woman I have ever met, or will ever meet. I don't want to change anything about you, or the way you are, the things you do. All I am asking is if you can find space in your life for me.'

She sighs. 'Of course I can, Luke.'

The sight of her eyes filling finally makes mine crack too. I need to get this out. I exhale heavily and finally ask her: 'Carrie, will you make me the happiest man in the world, for the rest of our lives, and marry me?'

She laughs and cries and nods all at once and when I stand, she throws her arms around my neck, pressing her mouth to mine.

'Yes, Luke. A hundred, thousand, million times, yes!'

I slip the ring on her finger and lift her from the ground, twirling my wife-to-be in my arms. 'I love you, Carrie. I love you so fucking much.'

She giggles. 'I love you too.'

ACKNOWLEDGEMENTS

My husband and I were living in the British Virgin Islands in 2017, when Hurricane Irma struck. It has been seven years since the events of that enormous storm and there have been many life events since, each one a ripple effect. I don't know that I set out to write about those experiences. Like every other book, my characters came to me first. Their back-story, their shared history, their personalities. They spoke to me so loudly that I asked my editor if I could change the schedule for my upcoming books because I *had* to write Carrie and Luke's story.

Things kept falling into place with these two characters. I knew theirs would be a second chance romance. I knew it would be haters to lovers. And when the idea of forced proximity popped into my head, I knew there was nowhere better to get these two feisty former lovers stuck than in the paradise of the Caribbean. As I plotted out their second shot at love, a different sort of storm appeared in my notes.

Perhaps it has been lingering in my subconscious, a story untold, waiting for the perfect opportunity for catharsis.

Hurricane Irma was devastating for many people, homes and families. *But* I am also a romcom writer. I hope I have woven the storm into this story with the respect it deserves, with tenderness and sincerity, whilst making it as light and escapist to read as possible. After all, out of catastrophes, love is born, right?

To any geographers and meteorologists who read this book, please excuse any small inaccuracies. They're all mine. Sometimes fiction needs to tweak facts for a good story.

Now, I really did spend Hurricane Irma squished into a tiny concrete utility store with my husband and a dog. Our own *gorgeous* fur baby. And as I said in the dedication to this book, there's no one I would rather weather a storm with. So, my first thank you is to my husband, for keeping me safe. You're protection. I'm administration. I love you, forever.

To every wonderfully generous person who helped us or helped a neighbor, through that storm and any of life's storms, I'm incredibly grateful. You know who you are, as do we. Kindness is a person's greatest gift.

I remember relaying this story idea over lunch in a very giddy, monologuing kind of way, early in the first draft, to both my fantastic agent and wonderful editor. They both asked me questions that they probably didn't realize at the time were pivotal to how this book unfolded. Thank you Tanera and Emily for those questions, for your endless support and hard work, and for allowing me to reschedule the order of things to write this story next. And I really hope I did succeed in making tax sexy, Tanera.

As I always say, I am but a wheel in a cog and it takes an army of people to bring a book to market. Massive gratitude to all the people whose names don't appear on the front of the book but who have an enormous impact on how it looks, feels, reads, sounds and sells. Laura, your help and cheering is top. Rachel, your covers melt me. Emily R, you spot the unspottable, every time. Jenna and Nia, your marketing and sales prowess is second to none. Ben, your organization is slick. And this is a great juncture to shout out to the fantastic narrators of the audio book, Kate Handford and Craig Van Ness, and Ulverscroft for pulling the audios together. At the risk of adding to printing costs, thank you, of course, to Amanda, Marcela, Claire, Issy and Jennifer. If I have missed anyone from the fabulous Boldwood team, I didn't mean to!

Dear, dear, beautiful, mind-blowingly generous reader, I have to pinch myself sometimes. I get to write books as a job. Like, this is a *thing!* And it's all because of you.

I hope you love *Stuck in Paradise with You*. It's only words on a page, until you believe. *Thank you.*

ABOUT THE AUTHOR

Laura Carter is the bestselling author of several rom-coms including the series *Brits in Manhattan* which she is relaunching and expanding with Boldwood. She lives in Jersey.

Sign up to Laura Carter's mailing list for news, competitions and updates on future books.

Visit Laura's website: www.lauracarterauthor.com

Follow Laura on social media:

instagram.com/lauracarterauthor

x.com/LCarterAuthor

facebook.com/LauraCarterAuthor

ALSO BY LAURA CARTER

The Law of Attraction

Two to Tango

Friends With Benefits

Always the Bridesmaid

Fake It 'til You Make It

Stuck in Paradise With You

LOVE NOTES

LOVE IN EVERY CHAPTER

WHERE ALL YOUR ROMANCE
DREAMS COME TRUE!

THE HOME OF BESTSELLING
ROMANCE AND WOMEN'S
FICTION

WARNING:
MAY CONTAIN SPICE

SIGN UP TO OUR
NEWSLETTER

https://bit.ly/Lovenotesnews

Boldwood

Boldwood Books is an award-winning fiction publishing company seeking out the best stories from around the world.

Find out more at www.boldwoodbooks.com

Join our reader community for brilliant books, competitions and offers!

Follow us
@BoldwoodBooks
@TheBoldBookClub

Sign up to our weekly deals newsletter

https://bit.ly/BoldwoodBNewsletter

www.ingramcontent.com/pod-product-compliance
Lightning Source LLC
Chambersburg PA
CBHW01065810726
47900CB00010B/2704